P9-CAP-944

Praise for *Good Peoples*

"A cast of supporting characters whose determination to tell the truth is often hilarious and sometimes outrageous, and Major's wise commentary on the modern black family contribute to the quick pace of this entertaining narrative."
—*Publishers Weekly*

"Major, with a gift for dialogue, creates an amiable work."—*Kirkus Reviews*

"Dynamic . . . a look at the other side of the love game—the thin line males must cross when making a commitment."—*City News* (Newark, NJ)

"Humorous yet serious, and witty, yet filled with street talk . . . Marcus Major shows much talent as he provides an entertaining relationship drama that *Good Peoples* everywhere will enjoy."
—*Midwest Book Review*

"Rollicking."—*Book Page*

"Vibrant . . . offering a fresh take on the age-old problem of love.
—*Heart & Soul*

good peoples

Marcus Major

AN ONYX BOOK

ONYX
Published by New American Library, a division of
Penguin Putnam Inc., 375 Hudson Street,
New York, New York 10014, U.S.A.
Penguin Books Ltd, 27 Wrights Lane,
London W8 5TZ, England
Penguin Books Australia Ltd, Ringwood,
Victoria, Australia
Penguin Books Canada Ltd, 10 Alcorn Avenue,
Toronto, Ontario, Canada M4V 3B2
Penguin Books (N.Z.) Ltd, 182–190 Wairau Road,
Auckland 10, New Zealand

Penguin Books Ltd, Registered Offices:
Harmondsworth, Middlesex, England

Published by Onyx, an imprint of New American Library,
a division of Penguin Putnam Inc.
Previously published in a Dutton edition.

First Onyx Printing, March 2001
10 9 8 7 6 5 4 3 2 1

 REGISTERED TRADEMARK—MARCA REGISTRADA

Printed in the United States of America

PUBLISHER'S NOTE
This is a work of fiction. Names, characters, places, and incidents either
are the product of the author's imagination or are used fictitiously,
and any resemblance to actual persons, living or dead, business
establishments, events, or locales is entirely coincidental.

BOOKS ARE AVAILABLE AT QUANTITY DISCOUNTS WHEN USED TO PROMOTE
PRODUCTS OR SERVICES. FOR INFORMATION PLEASE WRITE TO PREMIUM
MARKETING DIVISION, PENGUIN PUTNAM INC., 375 HUDSON STREET, NEW YORK,
NEW YORK 10014.

For my mother,
Carmen Major

ACKNOWLEDGMENTS

I have been blessed through the years to have met many wonderful people who have encouraged me to write and to whom I am deeply indebted, some of whom I would like to take the opportunity to thank. My parents, Ronald and Carmen Major, who never let their children believe that anything was beyond their reach. Thanks for the gift of life and the years of hardship putting up with your pain-in-the-neck son. My brothers, Ron and Ryan (I apologize for all the beatings you guys got because of me). My sister-in-law, Tamika, and my nephew, Amir. My great-grandmother Ruth Mitchell and my grandparents Mimi and Caroll Curley, and all my aunts, uncles, and cousins living in Alabama, Maryland, Michigan, Minnesota, and New York. Victor Sherwood-Saul, Carol Lewis, and their newborn daughter, Ananda (Congratulations!). Dwayne Carruth and family. Dhanie Scott—thanks for reading it chapter by chapter when it was in its infancy and not laughing at me. Mike Poindexter, Janeth Cuenca, Karl Johnson, Sylvia Nazario, Mike Menefee, Tim Gilbert, Danielle

Hunt, Paul Burnett, Chris Craft, Greg Langella, Kirk Hartman, Larry and Danielle Gray, Randy Holland, Marlene Lindsey, Erika Herrera, Kathy Rivera, Sue Fletcher, Jay Keesler, Steve Townsend, Stephanie Jones, Cheryl Jackson, Cory Cooke, and Kim Garlic. Though I've lost touch with some of you, you're still in my thoughts. Thanks for the years of friendship. The Parker family. My agent, Harry Costello, and his family.

Much respect is due to the many wonderful faculty and staff I had encourage me at Richard Stockton College: Tony Bethel, Ruben Britt, Stephon Davis, Pam Kennedy, Frank Smith, Shawn Donaldson, Adele Beverly, Gene Robinson, Larry James, Jean-Andree Nelson, and Tom Kinsella. Go Ospreys! The juggernaut of the NJAC.

Nykita Thompson, Edith Battle, Esther Elliott, Denise Williams, Carlos Lopez, Ivan Holmes, Eva Chambers, Donna Arrowood, and the rest of the faculty, staff, and students at Peshine Avenue and Hawthorne Avenue schools in Newark, New Jersey, as well as those of Woodrow Wilson High School of Camden, New Jersey, and Haddon Heights High School.

Much gratitude to my editor, Audrey LaFehr. Thanks for making the book ten times better than when you first received it. John Paine, Genny Ostertag, and Fred Huber at Penguin Putnam, thank you all for all efforts. Terry McMillan, Eric Jerome Dickey, and to all of the other many talented authors of contemporary African-American fiction, thanks for paving the way.

Thank you for reading *Good Peoples*. Post a review on Amazon.com and let me know what you think. If you would like to chat, e-mail me at marcusmajor@aol.com or visit the Web site at marcusmajor.com.

♊ One

"Geh up, Un-kel Myles, Geh up!"

Some people are awakened by the first rays of the sun gently kissing their foreheads to signal the dawning of a new day. Others are awakened by the soft coos of a lover nuzzling them on the nape of their neck. Still others have their noses tickled with aromatic scents cooked by a lover whose world was *rocked* the previous night. But they are all fools, Myles thought, for they do not know true morning joy unless they are stirred out of their slumber by the fingers of a pair of three-year-olds, digging into their eyes and telling them, quite loudly, to "geh up!"

They were not exactly the female companionship he had in mind, but there were worse sights to behold first thing in the morning than his twin nieces, Deja and Jade. Their hair was braided and beaded, and they were looking cute in their bright (a little too bright first thing in the morning) yellow matching jumpers. He couldn't resist the opportunity to play the "mix-up game."

"Good morning, Jade," he said to Deja.

"Nnnnoooo," they replied in gleeful unison.

"I'm(she's . . .) . . . Jade/Deja . . . she's(I'm . . .) Deja/Jade."

"Ooohhh," he replied, "now I understand. Hello, Deja," he said to Jade.

"Nnnnooo," they answered.

As the twins squealed with laughter, accompanied by his bulldog Winston's yelps of bewilderment, Myles's brother decided that he'd had enough of this foolishness.

"Myles, I know Deja and Jade are probably the first females that you have had in your bedroom in months, but could you get a move on, please? I'm ready to play some basketball, and I'm feeling kinda right today."

His brother, Amir, always ready with the snide comment.

"Girls, go in the living room so Uncle Myles can get ready. Winston wants to play with you."

The dog glared at him as if to say, "Yeah, right." Then he headed off to the living room with the little girls hot on his trail.

Myles went to the bathroom to brush his teeth. As he looked up from rinsing his mouth out, he saw Amir's reflection in the mirror. His brother was looking over his shoulder, admiring himself while pretending not to.

Amir was the type of man that sisters swooned over. He was a regal, tall, muscular man with smooth chocolate skin, thick eyelashes, and a curly crop of "good hair." Further adding to his ego was that his eyes were a shade or two lighter than the average brother's and would sparkle when hit by light. Being the younger brother by two years, Myles had considered him the bane of his very existence when they were children. Amir was personable, a natural athlete, while Myles was the pudgy, contemplative, intellectual child. One guess as to which one was the star in their neighborhood. Even aunts, uncles, and grandparents, when they weren't poking Myles in his stomach to see if he said, "poppin' fresh dough," focused the majority of their praise and attention on Amir.

"You know," Amir said, taking a break from looking at himself, "I don't understand this monk lifestyle of yours. You're not a bad-looking guy."

"But, I'm no 'you,' right?"

"Hey, don't set the bar so high. If you try to reach that ideal, of course you're doomed to fail."

Even Myles had to laugh.

"As I was saying, you're a good-looking guy. You seem to have got that weight situation under control, you're smart, available, professional . . . what's the problem?"

"Just because I haven't turned my apartment into a sanctum of skankdom does not mean there is a problem, Amir. Lord knows, before you got married you had enough women for the both of us, Mr. Seventeen-hoes-in-his-freshman-year-alone."

"Hey, hoes can be good people."

"I'm sure they can be," Myles said as he brushed past him to go back to the bedroom. He peeked into the living room and saw that the girls were engrossed with some cartoon on the TV, much to Winston's relief. "But if I try for something more than empty one-night stands, should I be faulted for holding myself to a higher standard than 'skank-'em and thank-'em'?"

As Myles put on a pair of sweats and laced up his sneakers, Amir answered in an affected, hat-in-his-hands, southern drawl, "I reckon us common Negroes can't wait for true, undying love because we just like the feeling of a pair of titties in our back at night."

"As do I," he replied, ignoring Amir's sarcasm. Myles opted for a T-shirt rather than the tank top he had on because that showed the top of his surgical scar from childhood heart surgery. Another source of insecurity was that he had been born with a heart murmur. "But I don't know . . . I'm just tired of meaningless encounters with women."

He regretted saying that as soon as he said it. Had he forgotten who he was talking to?

Amir gave him a look of incredulity and cracked up. "You ain't had enough pussy in your life to say what you *tired of*. You have zero credibility about what you're *tired of* until you staaaa-rrrrrt fuckin'. "

Myles glanced into the living room. "Damn, you're ignorant. Don't say anything when one of your daughters comes in here to ask you what 'fucking' means."

"True that, which would be funny because this is the *last* place they would actually see anybody doing any."

"All right, all right, your point is made. You ready to go?"

"I'm waiting on you, remember?"

The ride to the basketball courts took about ten minutes. After they strapped the twins into the back of Amir's Pathfinder, Myles turned on WPRS. They were playing "It Only Takes a Minute" by Tavares, which had been one of his and Amir's favorite songs when they were kids. They alternated lead vocal duties and still remembered the words after all these years.

When they stopped at a red light next to a car driven by a pretty woman, Amir could not resist the opportunity. He pulled up alongside her car on the left. He then tapped the horn lightly while at the same time rolling down the passenger's-side window from the master control panel. The horn tap got the woman's attention. She looked directly at Myles, giving him a "what the hell do you want?" look.

Now, having been the victim of this before, Myles knew there were a couple of ways he could play it. One way was to duck your head down, act like you dropped some change on the floor. It sounded good in theory, but then Amir would yell something along the lines of: "You reach across my car, honk my horn, bothering this attractive young lady and now you gonna duck your head down like some scared little punk?"

The better option, Myles had learned, was to feign indifference when Amir tapped the horn and rolled down the window. The key was to look straight ahead and hold it. This worked best because Amir ended up looking like the fool. Myles looked like the indifferent, intriguing dude who could care less.

But with this particular Latina in question, he got caught looking, and Amir moved in for the kill.

"Excuse me *chula*, *mi hermano* has not been out

with a *mujer* in *muchos años*. He has no *cojones*. *Por favor*, help him."

The woman and Amir were still laughing at Myles as the Gods of Mercy changed the light to green and they took off.

"Amir," Myles said, pissed for letting himself get embarrassed, "must you always be the jackass?"

Amir put his hand on Myles's shoulder, looked him straight in the eye, and said, "Yes, I must." He then started to laugh again.

"It must be nice to be able to crack yourself up, Amir." Myles turned around to face the twins. "Deja and Jade, your daddy is a funny guy. Can you say 'simpleton'?"

"Thimbleton."

"Shimpledon."

"Look at you trying to turn my daughters against me. Talk about ungrateful. This is the thanks I get for trying to help you out?"

Myles looked out the window. That woman in the car had had a pretty smile and catching laugh, even if it was at his expense. It would be nice to have a woman like that laughing because of him and not at him. He leaned back in his seat and closed his eyes. Myles pictured them window shopping down some quaint little street, strolling arm in arm. She would toss her head coyly and say cute things like "Oh, Myles, you're something else." Since it would be cold outside, a picturesque winter day, she would be bundled up from head to toe, which would draw even more attention to her sweet, gentle face. As they continued their stroll they would reach a jewelry store, where she would slow down to give him the not so subtle hint that she wanted him for a long-term commitment. Because he was too good a thing to let go of. Subconsciously, as she looked at the rings, she would be squeezing his arm tighter, hoping that he felt the same way about her.

The smile that spread across Myles's face quickly turned to agitation as he felt a sharp elbow in his side. He opened his eyes and glared at his brother.

"There will be no daydreaming on my shift. You should've said something to her when you had your chance."

ℛ Two

Marisa looked through the huge glass window of the restaurant. She had asked for a table in the front because she was dining alone, and figured that she could occupy herself by looking at the passersby. It was nearing noon, and the tony Georgetown street was starting to bustle with activity. Nannies pushing strollers, groups of old ladies, and college students all vied for sidewalk space with the influx of businesspeople and government workers looking for a place to eat.

She was admiring the cute summer outfits of two young Latinas who walked by when she saw a shiny black Jaguar approach and then stop in front of them, beeping its horn to get their attention. The passenger's-side door opened, and a girl just as pretty as the other two stepped out and walked around to the driver's side to engage in some serious lip lock with the driver. As she leaned in as far as she could, her short skirt rode up. She was dangerously close to showing her ass to the world, a problem which she was apparently oblivious to because she took her sweet time before she finished. She finally pulled her head out of the car, blew the driver one last kiss, and giddily bounced up on the sidewalk to join her friends.

The Jaguar pulled away down the block and toward the restaurant where Marisa was sitting. It stopped in front, where Marisa had parked. She knew that the driver had spotted her car, so she waved at the Jaguar's tinted window. It was a simple, quick "yes, I do see your sorry ass" wave, which could not have possibly been interpreted as "why don't you come inside and join me?"

Nevertheless, ten minutes later, while she was enjoying her spicy chicken wings, Ruben walked in and sat down next to her. He leaned over and gave her a kiss on the cheek, smelling and looking as good as he always did. He glanced at her plate.

"That looks good."

"It is, but you can't have any."

"Any what?" he said softly, leaning toward her. Someone once must have told him that it was sexy when he whispered.

"Any of that, either," Marisa said, irritated.

He took his sunglasses off, leaned back, and laughed. "That's okay, I don't eat chicken anyway."

"Yeah, you just eat *chicas*."

Ruben wasn't sure what she meant by that remark. Before he could answer, the waitress came over and gave him a menu and refilled Marisa's water. He put his sunglasses back on and pretended to look over the menu. Really he was studying Marisa's face for what she meant, even though he knew it was a waste of time. In the short time that he had known her, she had never revealed anything. He ordered a slice of cheesecake and a cup of coffee and handed the waitress back the menu.

"I've never had any complaints," he said as he stuck out his tongue in a lapping motion.

Marisa recoiled in disgust. If these wings weren't so damn good, this asshole was almost enough to make her lose her appetite.

"I wasn't talking about your bedroom habits, Ruben. I'm referring to your need to corrupt and devour as many women as you can."

"Damn, where did that come from? I got out of the car for this? Do you know how hard it was for me to find a parking space?"

"Oh, and here I thought you were just circling the block waiting for your young girlfriend to turn the corner."

The waitress put Ruben's cheesecake down in front of him. He had been hoping that Marisa hadn't seen him until he pulled up alongside her car. His look of chagrin at being busted was shortlived, however, and was soon replaced by a self-satisfied expression. When Marisa saw it, she knew that he had misinterpreted her level of interest.

"You jealous?" he asked.

"Actually, I am. I should have had the cheesecake, too."

"That wasn't anything, Marisa. Her sorority invited me to speak at her college. To give a lecture on entrepreneurship, you know, successful minorities in the business world." He took a forkful of cheesecake.

"Oh? And what was your lecture titled? Pimping

in the New Millennium: How to Get More Bucks for Your Bangs?''

Ruben put down his fork and started laughing, enjoying Marisa's comment far more than she thought he should have. His dumb ass was probably taking it as a backhanded compliment. He leaned back in his chair and looked at her.

''Funny and pretty, that's what I like about you, *morena*. Nah, seriously, my construction business has been doing well. A lot of houses have been going up. Speaking of which, how is it going selling your aunt's place?''

''I close tomorrow.''

He stopped his fork in midair, hesitated, then put the food in his mouth.

''So you decided not to have those repairs done I suggested? That's too bad, Marisa, 'cause you could have got more for the house.''

''I had them done,'' Marisa said, checking her watch.

''What!'' he said, too loudly. He put his fork down for good this time. ''I told you I would have done them for free.''

''And I told you at the time I appreciated the offer,'' Marisa said as she looked at the bill and reached for her purse.

''Then why didn't you let me do it?''

Marisa closed her purse and looked at Ruben, sitting there with a stupefied look on his face, and decided that there was nothing wrong with him other than his ego being bruised. He was handsome and rich and simply not accustomed to women not going along with his program. They had been introduced a while back by a mutual friend, but Marisa wouldn't allow herself to take him seriously and she knew she had done the right thing. Hell, he had been pursuing her for a couple of months now and had no shame about getting caught tonguing some co-ed in front of her. He was the last man that she wanted to have thinking that she owed him something. Besides, she had asked around, and Ruben's company had a reputation for doing shitty work.

"It wasn't meant as a slight, Ruben. How about you let me pay for your cake and we call it even?" she said, getting up, and putting the strap of her purse on her shoulder.

"Hey—hey now, where you going?" he asked, tugging at her sleeve.

"I have to get back to the office," she said, adjusting her purse so that she could free her arm diplomatically.

He wrapped his arms around her waist. "Let's do something this weekend."

This was the second time that he had put his hands on her to prevent her from leaving.

"Look, Ruben," she said, taking his hands into hers to get them from around her. "We just don't have a lot in common, and we aren't what each other wants right now." She gave his hands back to him.

"What do you want? What do you want that I can't give you?" he asked, trying his damnedest to look earnest.

She wanted to laugh at him, but hell, she was game. She looked him straight in the eye with an equally dramatic look on her face.

"Devotion. Unconditional, till-hell-freezes-over devotion."

Ruben sucked his teeth and turned back to the table. The waitress came over, and Marisa gave her the money for the bill and tip. She then said goodbye to Ruben and headed for the door.

"Unconditional devotion, huh? Hell, Marisa, I think what you need is a dog," Ruben called out.

"Well, if I do decide to get one, I know where to go, Mr.—" She then imitated the lapping-tongue motion he had done earlier, opened the door, and left.

As she stepped out onto the sidewalk and headed for her car, she heard a tapping sound. She turned around and saw Ruben holding his fist near his ear, thumb and pinkie extended, miming that he would call her. She could tell he was turned on by her sticking out her tongue. She already knew that Ruben had her pegged as a freak who just needed some dick. She put her sunglasses on and walked to her car.

As she opened the door and got in, she looked back at the restaurant. Ruben was still leering at her. She shut the door, turned the ignition, and began to pull away.

"You may be right, Ruben, but it won't be your worthless dick."

☃ Three

When Amir and Myles arrived at the courts, the usual suspects were already there. Under one basket Vince Lewis and Jamal Bey were stretching their hamstrings and talking animatedly. David Adkins and Gerald Dungee were sitting in David's jeep listening to some new CD Myles didn't recognize, and shooting lay-ups at the far end of the court were Carlos Roque and Brian Boyd. They were both colleagues of his at Lawndale Elementary School where Myles taught fifth grade. Carlos was a guidance counselor, and Brian taught seventh- and eighth-graders math.

Lawndale itself was a town of approximately three thousand people on the Jersey side of the Delaware River about fifteen miles from Philadelphia. It had been incorporated in 1922 and had mainly come into being because the affluent white communities surrounding it needed a place closer than Philadelphia for their black servants to live. It prided itself on being a close-knit, working- to middle-class enclave where black people could live peacefully. The original inhabitants of Lawndale strove to see that their children were better educated than they had been. Indeed, the town motto was, "Each generation to stand on the shoulders of the previous generation to elevate them to greater heights." The racial composition of Lawndale today is about seventy-thirty black to Latino, and it is still a decent, clean, safe place to raise a family.

Though Carlos and Brian both worked with Myles, his feelings toward the two couldn't be more different. Carlos had lived in Lawndale for a relatively short time, but he was probably Myles's best friend. They had many of the same interests—African history, acid jazz, Pedro Almodovar movies—and shared a passion for baseball, particularly the New York Yankees. Ever since their initial introduction by their principal, Mrs. Still, they had just clicked. At the opposite end of the spectrum was Brian Boyd, his sworn nemesis.

He and Brian had known each other since the third grade, and Myles could not remember a time when they weren't competing for the same thing. They always liked the same girl, or wanted the same part in the school play, competed for the better grades or the most expensive sneakers. They often fought as children, either because Brian crossed the line (by making one fatboy crack too many, dammit) or Myles hit a sore spot (Brian had a speech impediment and stuttered when he got excited). As adults, they still often competed, most recently for the attention of a cute but dim-witted substitute teacher who chose to go out with Brian's equally simple ass.

Adjacent to the basketball courts was a playground

where David's wife, Shanta, and Vince's wife, Hope, sat on a bench talking. Playing on the slide were David Jr., who was called D.J. by everyone, and the other children.

Amir walked the twins to the playground, where he would leave them under the charge of Hope and Shanta while he was playing basketball. It was a pretty smooth setup they had. On alternate weekends, Hope and Shanta would switch off with Kenya, Amir's wife, and Gerald's fiancée, Lisa. Ostensibly, this was done so that the mothers could sleep in every other Saturday and get a break from the kids. The real reason was that Kenya didn't particularly care for Hope. As far as Myles could tell, the reason was that Amir had had a brief fling with Hope while he and Kenya were dating. Myles thought Kenya was being a little unfair. Not that Hope wasn't guilty, mind you, he just thought she was being singled out. Hell, Amir had fondled half the women on the eastern seaboard before he and Kenya were married, including Shanta. Like Amir once told him, "Whenever you're trying to figure out how many previous men your girl done skanked it up with, always add one. Because there is *always* a man you don't know about. I am. . . . that man."

"Well, glad to see the Moore brothers could join us," Brian said as Myles approached. "I was beginning to think that you weren't going to show up, Myles," he added as he passed him the ball. Myles caught the ball and lined up an eighteen-footer.

"Actually, Brian, I had to make a stop," Myles said as he clanked a shot off the front of the rim. "I stopped by St. Mary's on the way here to ask Father

Louis if there was some act of penance I could perform for the action I was about to undertake. Father
Louis told me, 'Son, that depends on the seriousness
of the transgression you are about to commit.' When
I told him that I was going to play Brian Boyd in
basketball, he punched me in the neck and told me
to get my God-forsaken ass the hell out of his church!
On my way out, he yelled at me, 'You can't perform
enough acts of charity to excuse humiliating that hardluck nigger's ass again!' "

Carlos started laughing as the other fellas made
their way over.

"What's so funny?" David asked.

"Myles is making with the jokes again," Brian said.

The teams were as usual. On one team were Carlos, Amir, Vince, and Myles. On the other side were
Gerald, Brian, Jamal, and David. The teams usually
fell like this because they were evenly matched.
Myles made a free throw to win first possession of
the ball, and Brian, naturally, decided he wanted to
cover him. Gerald was on Carlos, David on Vince,
and Jamal was matched with Amir. Jamal and Amir
were the two best players and liked to duel each
other.

Myles inbounded the ball to Vince to signal the
beginning of the transformation. Every Saturday morning the group of them would change from decent, rea-
son-minded adults to bickering children with delusions
of athletic grandeur. Some of them took their basketball so seriously, you would think their audience
were NBA scouts offering multimillion-dollar con-
tracts instead of five indifferent children and two ap-
athetic women. But no matter how silly they acted,

Myles dared not laugh at them. He had made that mistake once and got cursed out so bad his ears hurt for a week. Since then he made sure he maintained his "game face."

This particular game was nip and tuck. Brian was hot and was kicking his ass early and often. He peppered his play with insults: "Goddammit, Myles, are you gonna play some defense?" and "Jesus Christ! Go get D.J. off the teeter-totter. He can do better than this motherfucker!" But despite his poor play, Myles's team held a 14–13 lead after Amir banked in a difficult turnaround jump shot. If they scored the next point they would win. Myles inbounded the ball to Carlos and made eye contact with him. He then drifted nonchalantly off to the right of the key while Amir called for the ball at the dotted line. When Carlos faked a pass to Amir inside, Brian took a step toward the paint to collapse on him. Myles seized that moment to break for the basket. After giving Brian an illicit shove in the back to get him off balance, he caught Carlos's perfectly thrown ball and dropped in the game-winning lay-up a split second before Brian and Jamal could swat his shot into the next county. A textbook "give and go" perfectly executed, just like it's diagrammed in Basketball 101. Ballgame.

Now came the ritual that is as indigenous to black men as woolly hair and broad noses. It's practiced all over the globe wherever groups of men of African descent choose to congregate, but has reached its highest form in barbershops and on basketball courts. Yes, friends, it was time for the trash talking to commence.

Myles considered himself something of a word-smith and didn't take his trash talking lightly. The ability to orally ridicule—play the dozens, crack, hike, bust-on—one's fellow man to the point of utter humiliation and societal ostracization was a talent that was as much a part of him as the blood that coursed through his veins. It had been passed down from one generation of Moores to the next like a priceless family heirloom.

He decided to delve into his English Lit back-ground and whip out a little 𝔈𝔩𝔦𝔷𝔞𝔟𝔢𝔱𝔥𝔞𝔫 𝔈𝔫𝔤𝔩𝔦𝔰𝔥 on them:

"Vanquished! Thou art vanquished, I say! Thou were worthy opponents indeed: stout, hale men full of vigor and ale. Alas, thou must now take a hearty swig from the poisonous flask of defeat no matter how bitter the taste, for thou hast come up against finer warriors who givest no quarter, but dolest out pain and suffering. With all Godspeed, thou shouldst take thyself to a basketball camp to brush up on thy fundamentals. I smite and rebuke thee, and doom thee to spend eternity in the torment of suffering dogs."

Maybe it was because of the slight nudge Myles had given him to free himself to score the winning basket, or maybe it was because he was talking way too much for somebody who had done so little, but Myles noticed that Brian looked pissed. Any intelli-gent adult would have ignored him—David and Amir had walked to the playground to play with the kids—or just brushed it off like Gerald and Jamal, who were sitting in the shade laughing at his act.

But when the criterion was "intelligent adult," Brian was one component short.

"Y-Yo, Shaquille O'Value Meal, you sure running your m-mouth a lot. Must be all that extra energy you got. Oh, yeah, Tracy says hi. I admit she sapped some of my energy last night. B-by the way, have you gotten any ass recently?"

Gerald and Jamal hooted from the sideline. Vince stopped in mid-shot from where he and Carlos were shooting around, fell out and started laughing. Even Carlos allowed a sly smile to tug at the corners of his mouth.

Before Myles could come back with a clever retort, a Geo Tracker pulled up. The female driver beckoned Brian to come over.

"Speak of the devil," Carlos said.

Brian started over to the lot where Tracy was parked. While she waited for him to get there, she waved at Carlos and Myles. They both waved back.

After a brief conversation, punctuated by two long kisses, which Myles was certain were for his benefit, Brian returned to the court.

"I gotta go, fellas," he said, picking up his keys.

Amir, who had come back from checking on his daughters, hadn't near satisfied his basketball fix and wasn't trying to hear that.

"What? You leaving after one game? Yo, man, I haven't even broken a sweat yet."

"Sorry," Brian said, zipping up his warm-up jacket. "I made a commitment that I forgot about."

"You can't get out of it? At least for a little while longer?" Vince asked.

"Naw, I'm already running late."

"Damn!" Amir said with disgust. "I didn't know she had you in check like that!"

Brian waited for the laughter to subside before answering.

"It's not about being in check, Amir," Brian said. speaking like he was an authority. "Y'all know how it is when you're dealing with your woman. It's about compromise. One hand washes the other." He started across the court, but stopped before he reached the sideline and turned back around.

"Well, those of you that have a woman know what I'm talking about. Myles, for you it'd be like alternating between your right and left hand, so one doesn't get too jealous."

Myles seethed. Brian had said that last remark loud enough for Shanta and Hope to hear it. Dammit, he had crossed the line. If Shakespeare was right, and revenge is truly a dish best served cold, then Brian had better wear his long johns from here on in.

Carlos sidled up to Myles.

"Don't even sweat that fool."

"I'm not," Myles said, lying.

"Besides, I have a feeling something will be breaking your way soon."

Myles was uncomfortable with the sorry state of his love life being the topic of conversation.

"Who are you supposed to be now?" Myles asked derisively. "That Latino psychic I see on TV?"

"Who?"

"You know who I'm talking about, 'Los," Myles said. "The one that comes on Univision. Dresses like Liberace."

"Oh, the *effiminado*. Walter Mercado." Carlos laughed.

"Yeah, Walter." Myles laughed.

Carlos rested his elbow on Myles's shoulder. "Naw, Bro, Walter sees into your destiny by reading the stars." He looked skyward for effect. Myles looked up too, for which he immediately felt stupid when he realized what he was doing. Carlos looked back at him. "All I need is basic arithmetic."

"How do you mean?"

"I mean, damn. I just figure the law of averages gotta catch up with your ass sooner or later."

☙ Four

Marisa turned the key and stepped inside the home of her childhood for what she knew would be the last time. She had felt the house pulling her to it today, and now she could feel her aunt's presence. She sat down on the stairs of the deserted house and soaked it all in: the faint scents of the almost dry paint, newly waxed floors and freshly cut lawn; the last rays of the setting sun that cut a wide swath through the shadeless living room windows, and the conflicting emotions that she felt tugging at her.

Though it was a relief that she had finally sold the house, she couldn't help feeling that there was a betrayal in her doing so. The floors that had been kept so painstakingly clean by her Aunt Esther would now be trod upon by strangers. Strangers who might have—heaven forbid—pets, which had always been denied to Marisa when she was a child. "I don't want beasts wandering through my house like it's the Serengeti," her aunt once snapped. A wandering niece was something she didn't want either, and for a long time Marisa was forbidden to go beyond the fence that encircled the house.

Marisa stood up and walked into the dining room. The big oak table that had dominated it for so long had been removed some months back when the charity where she donated most of the furniture came and took it. The faded beige wallpaper with the gold candelabra design that her aunt refused to get rid of was gone as well. Marisa had found the pattern so creepy as a child that she had taken joy in watching it come down, getting rid of it before any prospective buyers had even seen the house.

Couldn't wait to start destroying my home. Could you?

"Leave me alone, old lady," Marisa said aloud as she went through the kitchen and stood looking out the back door. If her aunt hadn't been so stubborn, she would have sold the house years ago. Marisa couldn't remember how many times in the last couple of years that she had asked her aunt to take a cruise, or travel abroad, offering to foot the bill, only to be politely refused. The only time Esther would venture far from the house would be for the occasional trips to Atlantic City she took with the old ladies from her church. But as far as any of the exotic locations that Marisa suggested, she would simply not be moved. It was as if she was scared this old house wouldn't be here when she got back. Marisa chuckled. That wasn't too far from the truth. Her aunt probably thought Marisa would torch it if given the chance.

When Marisa bought her own house, she asked her aunt to come live with her, but Esther steadfastly refused. Part of Marisa was angry with her aunt for her stubbornness, but she had to admit that she didn't exactly relish the idea of living with Esther again, even as an adult, though she had felt obliged to make the offer. After all, her Aunt Esther and Uncle Eli (who were actually her great-aunt and great-uncle) had taken her in, right off the boat from Cuba, when she was ten, newly orphaned and unable to speak a lick of English.

Esther had become the dominating influence in Marisa's life. She was a retired schoolteacher and a stern taskmaster. She had met and married Marisa's great-uncle when they were both in their forties, and they had decided not to have children of their own. When the responsibility of Marisa was handed to them, Esther finally had a chance to raise a child and she was determined to do it properly.

Esther made sure that Marisa attended the best private schools, and had all the same advantages that her affluent *gringo* classmates were afforded. School for Marisa did not end with the dismissal bell, however. She did homework for three hours, broke for dinner, then worked on her English *and* Spanish with Esther (who, as a former Spanish teacher, spoke it fluently) until bedtime. TV was banned. The weekends offered some respite, but it was during these times that Esther taught her how to cook, clean, eat, dress, sit, walk, speak and conduct herself like a well-heeled lady. Esther was African-American, not Cuban, and she made sure that Marisa was well versed in African, Latin, and world history. The old lady could take anything she came across and find a lesson to be gleaned from it.

After her uncle had passed, her aunt had used her

life savings to pay for Marisa to attend college and law school. "To attend" was correctly stated too, for her aunt paid for classes and books, that's it. Since she and Eli had bought Marisa a reliable used car, she didn't see why she couldn't commute from their Randallstown home to College Park. Marisa sensed that the only reason Esther had agreed to get Marisa a car was so she would be able to live at home.

Marisa was itching for freedom, though. Her first two years of college were an epic battle of wills, particularly since Eli was no longer there to act as a peacemaker. Each side refused to yield. Rather than live at home, Marisa worked two jobs in the summer and full-time during the school year to be able to afford to pay her share of rent, food, and expenses in the campus apartment she shared with a roommate. Knowing her aunt would use a slip in her grades as an excuse to try to force her back home, she never let working affect her grades, maintaining a 3.85 G.P.A.

During the September of her junior year, Marisa was shocked to find in her mailbox a letter from her aunt. When she opened it, she found checks for her tuition, books, *and* her share of the semester's rent and living expenses, which her aunt had somehow correctly estimated almost down to the exact dollar. Marisa still remembered the exhilaration she had felt that day, not at the relief that the money would provide, but that she had outlasted her aunt in a test of wills.

I was just trying to keep you busy. If you weren't going to be here where I could keep an eye on you, I didn't want you to have any time for foolishness.

"Unfortunately, Aunt Esther, I still found time for

that," Marisa whispered as she opened the back door and sat down on the three steps that led to the backyard. Her aunt had been right. Marisa found that her problems dealing with men became even worse when she had more free time, which was probably the reason why to this day she kept herself so busy with work.

Marisa heard a faint ringing in her head which she soon realized wasn't her aunt's voice but a phone. She rushed back into the house and pulled her cellular out of her purse.

"Hello?"

"Hello, is this Ms. Marrero?"

"Yes, it is."

"*Buenos noches*, Ms. Marrero. This is David Rios, station manager at WLAT. Am I catching you at a bad time?"

"No, not at all, Mr. Rios, but please call me Marisa."

"Only if you promise to call me David."

"You got yourself a deal."

"Good. Yes, well, I'm calling to welcome you to the WLAT family."

"Thank you, I'm very excited."

"Believe me, we're thrilled to have you. As a matter of fact, I know you still have some time before you start, but I would like to know when you will be in the area so I can officially welcome you, show you around the building, and have you meet the staff."

"I'll be in Philly tomorrow, David. I have an appointment with a realtor in the morning, and an engagement in the evening, but I'm free in the afternoon."

"Tomorrow afternoon? That'll be fine. How does two o'clock sound?"

"Two o'clock sounds good."

"Great. Oh, and if you have trouble finding a place to live, let me know. I know this city like the back of my hand."

"I appreciate that. I'll let you know."

"Please do. So, I'll see you tomorrow."

"Looking forward to it."

"Okay then, good night, Marisa."

"Good night, David."

Marisa closed her phone and looked out the window. Damn, it *was* almost night. She had been there far longer than she realized.

He seemed nice enough, Marisa thought as she went to lock the back door. She hadn't met anybody at the radio station yet, because she had been hired directly by the owner of the broadcasting company, John Lopes. He had seen Marisa as a guest panelist on a local D.C. morning show at his station and had offered her a contract almost on the spot. Lopes had recently purchased a radio station in Philadelphia, and thought Marisa would be perfect in the drive-time slot, as well as the host of a local TV show his company produced called *Conexion Latina*.

After thinking it over for a few days, Marisa decided to take him up on his offer. She wasn't happy at the law firm she was at anyway, and was looking to move. The only downside was that she would have to relocate, but the deal she signed was so lucrative, she could hardly complain.

She chuckled softly. If her aunt wasn't already dead, this career move of Marisa's most certainly would have killed her. She had raised a lawyer, by God, not Oprah Winfrey.

Marisa picked up her purse and took a deep breath. The past was over. She opened the front door and walked out into the encroaching darkness.

🦮 Five

"Who is it?" Myles asked.

"It's 'Los, cockmeat, let me up."

Myles buzzed him in and went into the bedroom to get his wallet. When he came back into the living room, Carlos was just coming through the front door. Winston approached him and started to sniff his leg.

"Myles, call off your mutt."

"Mutt? I'll have you know that you're being sniffed by a hundred percent purebred English bulldog. Don't worry. As soon as he gets a good whiff of that potent combination of stale beer and cheap cologne, he'll leave you alone."

"Ha-ha. Yo, I noticed that they're painting the apartment down the hall. What happened to that lady that used to live there?"

"Grace? I guess she moved out."

"See, Myles, another opportunity wasted. You had a single woman, readily available, only a couple of doors down, and now she's gone. You blew it, kid."

"Why are you acting stupid? She was eighty years old. I think her kids put her in a rest home."

"Still, old girl had a nice tight ass—"

"Are you ready to go? I'll drive."

"Yeah, but if the game runs long, do you mind if we leave after the seventh inning? I told Jackie I'd be back by five o'clock."

"Damn, 'Los, I didn't know your wife had you under those kinds of constraints," Myles said as they stepped out into the hallway. "Next thing you know, you'll be wearing a beeper. You most certainly blow the stereotype that Latin men have their women in check. What happened to you when they were passing out the machismo?"

"First of all, I will never be one of those fools with one of those electronic leashes. Second of all, I'm oozing with ma-chis-mo. And finally, the reason I agreed to it is that Jackie and I have somewhere to go tonight. She told me to ask you if you wanted to come, but I told her you wouldn't be interested."

"How dare you be so presumptuous as to speak for me? Just because Jackie has got you in check, don't try to assert your manhood over here. Now, where exactly are you guys going?"

"Just over to Jackie's aunt's house in Camden. She's having a party."

"Oh, yeah? What's the occasion?" Myles asked as they exited the building.

"Why does there have to be an occasion? We're a festive people. Anyway, there's gonna be a lot of single women there."

"Oh, so that's the reason Jackie wants me to come. She's always trying to set me up with somebody." Myles unlocked the car and they slid in. "I think I'll pass."

"Myles, Jackie has given up on you. She halfway has you pegged as a *maricon*. But it's too bad you're not coming. Jackie's mom will be disappointed. She's cooking, ya know." Carlos tried to fight the sly grin that formed on his face.

Whoa now, Myles thought, that's a whole different story. Jackie's mom was an excellent cook. And if she was cooking, that meant all types of delicacies would be in abundance, including his favorite, homemade *empanadas*. Carlos knew how to hit a brother where he lived.

"Well," Myles said as he wheeled the car out into traffic, "maybe I'll stop by."

"I thought you might."

"Yo, Jackie doesn't really think I'm gay, does she?"

"Nah, but she thinks you're too particular. Bro, she takes her shit seriously and you're the first blemish on her record. You know she's trying to get voted into the matchmaker hall of fame."

They did have to leave the game early, but Myles didn't mind in the least. The Mets were pimp-slapping the Phillies 9–0 by the time the seventh inning rolled around. He and Carlos swore a solemn oath not to pay money to see those sorry bastards again. Whenever they wanted to see a game, they'd just have to go up the turnpike to see the Yankees.

"Isn't that right, Winston? You got to go to the Bronx to see real baseball." Winston turned around and looked at him quizzically, haughtily turned his ass back to him, and resumed walking. They usually spent a couple of hours outside every Saturday, but Myles had blown him off to go to the game instead.

When he returned, Winston was looking at him balefully, so he decided to take him for a walk.

"I know you don't have a 'tude, Winston. Maybe you want to go over to Amir's house. They have a big backyard for you to romp around in, and I'm sure that the twins would enjoy playing with you for a couple of hours."

The dog stiffened his back slightly and never broke stride. They made their way back to the three-story building that they called home. Each floor had four apartments, and they lived on the top. As they made their way up the stairs, they were met by the strong odor of wet paint and by the building's super, Bernard.

"So Mrs. Grace is gone, huh?" Myles asked as Bernard locked her apartment door.

"Yeah, she moved in with her daughter's family in Marlton. I guess I'll have to put an ad in the *Courier-Dispatch*. So how's your summer going? Do you miss the kids?"

"Oh, yeah, more than they'll ever know," Myles answered wryly. "I don't know how I'm ever gonna make it through August without seeing them." Truth be known, he did often find himself thinking of his students, worrying if they were letting their brains turn to mush.

"How about you? How's the baby, dad?"

Bernard puffed out his chest slightly. "He's fine, getting big, looks just like me. When you gonna have one?"

"When I meet a good woman like yours to be the mother. You know how hard that is. It's getting to

the point were I'm about to lower my standards from 'good' to 'decent' to 'not that scandalous.' "

"Man, you don't have to tell me. Serita might have her ways. . . ."

"But she's respectful of herself. You don't have to worry about her going somewhere with your son and men saying, 'Cute kid, now let me tell you what I used to do to his mother.' "

"Ya know."

"Or even worse, your son hits about ten years old and comes running up to you with tears in his eyes. You ask your son what's wrong with him and he tells you, 'Daddy, w-why did you have to choose a skank to be my mother?' I can't have that, Bernard."

The super was still laughing as they parted company. Myles went into his apartment and undid Winston's leash. He walked over to his CD collection to put on some music as he got ready to go over to Camden.

He let his eyes scan the rows and rows of CDs until he found one to fit his mood. He owned somewhere in the neighborhood of eight hundred CDs, which caused his father no small amount of consternation every time he came over.

"Damn, Myles, all that money wasted. Do you know what you could've done with that money?"

"Yeah, Pop. I could've snorted it up my nose." That was his subtle way of telling him to mind his business. His father was a simple hardworking man whose idea of nirvana was sitting in his drawers with a cold brew, chicken wings, and a championship fight on the television. He couldn't fathom how he had produced a son who spent so much money on music, clothes, books, art, and movies. And don't even get him started on his particular taste in any of these areas, Myles thought. He was just thankful that his mother had imbued in him some appreciation for the finer things of life.

He decided to put on his favorite Lenny Kravitz disc while he got ready. He left the bathroom door open while he was in the shower so that he could hear the stereo. As he lathered up, he sang along with Lenny about being ready for love. Lenny's the man, he thought as he turned off the faucets and exited the shower. Myles could feel his pain.

As he toweled off, he decided to call Jackie. It would be a nice gesture if he brought something to the party. It was the least he could do considering how much of her mother's food he always ate.

He went into the bedroom and hit the speed-dial button for Carlos's house. He hoped they hadn't left yet. After three rings Jackie picked up.

"Hello?"

"Hey, Mrs. Roque, how ya doing?"

"Hi, Myles. Don't tell me you're calling to tell us you aren't coming."

"No," he said, surprised by the concern in her voice, "I just wanted to ask if there was anything I could bring."

"Oh," she said, sounding relieved. "No, just come over. You know where my aunt lives, right? Do you want to ride with us?"

"No, thanks. I'll drive myself over. I want to be able to leave there at a decent hour. I know you and 'Los. Once the *cerveza* starts flowing, you guys will be

dancing until the rooster crows. Are you sure there is
nothing I can bring, like flan or something?"

"Oh, yeah, Myles, run over to the Pathmark and
pick up some flan, so I can watch my mother and
aunt take turns smacking you around for dishon-
oring their table with some store-made *ca-ca*."

"I was just asking. I don't feel right coming empty-
handed."

"Don't even start that bullshit. Next thing out of
your mouth will be 'I'm not going' and your antisocial ass will be spending another Saturday night with
your head in a book and that dog's head in your lap.
Just make sure you come, okay? I already told my
mom you were coming. You know how much she
likes you."

"All right, I'll see you guys over there."

"You sure you know how to get there?"

"Yeah, yeah, bye."

"Bye," she said sweetly, and hung up.

And I'm not antisocial, Myles thought. He just considered himself to be good company. He liked being
with other people, but he didn't need them all the
time. If Jackie had truly given up on trying to set
him up with somebody, it must be because she ran
out of girlfriends. He'd probably be bumping into a
couple of them tonight.

He looked at the different colognes on his dresser.
He decided to go with the Paul Sebastian that Kenya
got him last Christmas. At first he hadn't liked the
scent, which was why he still had three-fourths of a
bottle left, but it was starting to grow on him. He
went to the closet and picked out a pair of beige
linen slacks and a white linen shirt and removed

them from the dry-cleaning bag. He got almost everything dry-cleaned because he hated ironing. Now the final accoutrements: brown belt, brown Fossil watch, beige socks with flecks of brown in them, and two-toned brown and beige hush puppies. He decided not to go with a necklace he had bought from a street vendor in Philly, though it matched his ensemble. Someone was sure to ask him what its cultural significance was, and he couldn't remember, though he thought it was Yoruba. If he didn't know for sure, he didn't need to be wearing it.

After applying some African Royale to his hair, strictly for the sheen because his hair was cut so low during the summer he didn't even bother with a brush, he went over to the full-length mirror for one last look. Pleats sharp, check; shoes scuff-free, check; cologne applied, check; idiot-expending-far-too-much-effort-to-be-going-to-a-Rivera-family-houseparty, check. A resounding check. Geesh, where did he think he was going? Who did he think was going to be there? The best scenario he could hope for was that the *empanadas* were plentiful and that the music was bumping.

He scooped up his car keys and headed for the door. "Yo, Winston, your food and water are in the dish. Don't play the radio too loud, don't stay up too late, and don't be running no bitches up in here while I'm gone. Get wit' ya."

"It's about time. I've been calling your house," Jackie said pointedly as she opened the door for Myles, her face glistening slightly from dancing.

"I got tied up," he replied as he stepped from the porch into the house. He was too embarrassed to tell her that he had been driving around for the past hour trying to remember where her aunt's house was. He could've sworn it was in South Camden, but that must have been another one of her many aunts or cousins or friends that he had encountered. He then remembered that she had an aunt here in East Camden, and he just drove through the neighborhood until he found a block lined with cars, and spotted her Camry.

"Carlos has been telling everybody that the *pendejo stupido* is probably driving around lost."

"Oh, has he now? You know, Jackie, you should really make Carlos get a beeper. Then I could've contacted you guys to tell you I was running late. Plus, it would be nice for you to be able to reach him if you needed to."

"Ya know, that's a good idea. I think I will pick him up one." She turned and briskly walked away toward the back of the house before he could tell her where she could find one cheap and in designer colors.

That'll fix his ass. Myles hoped that he enjoyed his electronic leash. He surveyed the room. The living room was empty save for an old lady sitting on the sofa holding a toddler and two children watching Univision, apparently oblivious to the music that was thumping from the backyard. It sounded like Luis Enrique, but he wasn't positive. The D.J. (Damn, they got a D.J.? They *are* a festive people) was speaking into the mike, saying something in Spanish, probably asking the partygoers to dance. Myles hoped that he would play "No Morira" by Dark Latin Groove; that was his shit.

He realized Jackie was leaving it up to him to navigate his way to the backyard. He said hello to the lady on the sofa and walked through the foyer, stopping there momentarily to gaze into a large mirror to take one last accounting of himself. The kitchen was bustling with activity. Latin women, none of whom he recognized, scurried to and fro carrying various platters of food and beverages. They were speaking in Spanish, and the chatter was far too fast for him to make sense of. Jackie was still nowhere to be found, which aggravated him slightly. Where had she been in such a hurry to get to that she had to leave him walking through her aunt's house by himself? God forbid she miss the opportunity to shake her ass to every single song that played. He was trying to negotiate his way through the crowd without having food spilled on him when he felt a sharp nudge in his kidney. "Oh, I'm sorry," a voice said from behind.

Happy to hear words in a language he comprehended, he turned around to accept the apology. Instead he very nearly pissed himself.

Before him stood the most stunning woman he had ever laid eyes on in his twenty-eight years on this planet. He seized up and temporarily lost voluntary muscle control. It was almost like a religious experience, the feeling people get when a preacher's sermon touches them deeply and they're moved by the spirit. His cheeks flushed, his ears became warm, and his heart's thumping started to compete with the bass in the speakers as it slammed against his chest.

She spoke again, but the combination of the clatter around him and his flustered state kept him from understanding what she said. He thought she had asked him if she'd hurt him.

"Umm, no," he offered lamely.

Two soft, lush, lashy, doelike eyes looked up at him. "So you *don't* accept my apology?"

Uh-oh, he had misunderstood. "Oh, no, I thought you said . . . I mean, yes."

"Well, which is it, yes or no?"

"Yes."

"You mean, 'Yes, affirmative, I don't accept your apology'?" she asked.

"No-no, what I mean is . . . " Idiot, Myles thought, she's playing with you. Show some composure and pull yourself together. "What I mean is, I don't accept your apology, because I was at fault. One should never block an angel's flight path."

"But your back was turned."

"I should have heard your wings fluttering when you approached."

She smiled. "Aren't you a clever one?"

"I'm sorry, did you say something else? I can't hear you over the music." He looked up at the ceiling. "I think . . . it's a harp playing."

She rolled her eyes playfully, his blatant compliments wearing her down. She folded her arms across her chest and looked Myles directly in the eye, as if wondering what to make of him. While she was deciding, he had an opportunity to soak her in.

She was *negra*, about his complexion but with a reddish undertone like there was an ember glowing under her skin. Though her eyes were her most prominent feature, she had an inviting mouth, especially with her lips slightly puckered and moist as they were now. Her hair was jet black and lustrous. She was wearing it straight to a little past her shoulders. She looked about five-five. He didn't look at her breasts because he didn't want her to catch him drooling any more than he already had. Besides, her arms were obstructing his view of them.

It was a little disconcerting to Myles how she was studying him. Finally, she motioned for him to follow her and turned, not even making sure he was coming. She seemed to know that he would have followed her to the very gates of hell to give Lucifer an enema with holy water if she asked him to.

She looked as good going as she did coming. She was wearing a light blue and cream summer dress that partially exposed her back. His eyes followed a path down the spinal cord of her lithe body until they rested on their intended target, her ass. She sported a tremendous, highly "cuppable" ass; meaning if he ran his hands down her back to massage her behind, his hands would be cupped in the shape of the letter C. He sighed with appreciation as her supple, shimmying ass bounced against the fabric of her dress with each step she took.

They reached the foyer before he finally pried his eyes off her backside. When he looked up, she was looking dead at him in the same big mirror that he had used when he came into the house. His face turned so hot with embarrassment that it felt like it was on fire. In fact, he wished there was a fire, so he could've stopped, dropped, and rolled his ass right out of that house.

Damn. Caught leering. Not glancing, mind you,

but leering, with the saliva practically dripping down his chin. What could he possibly say for himself?

Before she could say anything, he heard Jackie's familiar voice.

"Marisa?"

They both turned toward Jackie, who hadn't gone back outside at all but was coming out of one of the bedrooms at the end of the hallway.

"Hey, Jacqueline." Marisa held out her arms to receive Jackie's embrace.

"When did you get in town?" Jackie asked.

"Just this morning. When your cousin called me last weekend, she told me that you guys were having a get-together today. Since I had to come to Philadelphia on some work-related business this weekend, I decided to stop by."

Thank God for Jackie, Myles thought. First of all, by the time Jackie got done running her mouth, maybe his staring would be forgotten. Second, he was learning information. He knew her name was Marisa, she didn't live in the area, was here on business, and so far nothing about a man. Good. Keep talking, Jackie, keep talking . . .

"So, is Myles behaving himself?" she asked, nodding in his direction.

Shut up, Jackie . . . shut up, Jackie . . .

"Myles? So that's the name that goes with this gentleman. Well, actually I am a little concerned for him. I think he may have misplaced something, because he seems a little distracted. Did you have a contact lens pop out, Myles?" Marisa asked innocently.

"No, I thought I misplaced my keys," he offered weakly, "but I have them."

"So, you're sure, everything is in its proper place then, as far as you can tell?"

"Spectacularly so," he replied, understanding her innuendo.

"Spectacularly so? And yet you had nothing pop out?"

"Well, momentarily, but it's back in its proper place now."

"Bueno."

Jackie was looking at them, clueless as to the subtext of their conversation.

"Well, Marisa, it's nice seeing you, I'm going back outside. I'm sure Carlos is looking for me." Jackie hugged her again. "We'll talk later."

Jackie went toward the kitchen, leaving Myles and Marisa standing in the foyer.

"So, Myles, would you like to join me on the porch?"

"Sure."

She took a step toward the door and stopped. "After you," she said, extending her arm.

"No problem," he said, laughing. He led her outside and leaned against a rail. She sat down in a chair facing him.

"So, do you have a last name, Myles?"

"It's Moore. And you're Marisa . . ."

"Marrero," she answered, rolling the r's in her last name with a sexy flick of her tongue.

"Double 'm' initials, too."

"It would appear so. What do you do for a living, Myles Moore?"

"I'm a schoolteacher. What do you do?"

"A little of this, a little of that."

"I heard you tell Jackie that you were in town on business. Where do you live?" he asked.

"Outside Washington, D.C., in Silver Spring for now."

"For now?"

"I'm transferring to Philadelphia. That's partly the business I had to check on, going with a realtor to look at some places. So, how do you like teaching?"

She was being evasive about her job. He hoped she wasn't an exotic dancer.

"I enjoy it a great deal. It's an opportunity to mold young minds and be a positive example for minority children."

"Is that what you told the people when you interviewed for the job?"

"Yep."

She laughed. She had a wonderful, ebullient laugh that made him smile when he heard it.

"That's where I met Carlos, Jackie's husband. We work at the same school together."

"Yeah? So you and Carlos are good friends?"

"Best of. I'm close to Jackie, too. They're good peoples. Do you know them well?"

"Not well, but I'm good peoples, too. We stick together."

He looked at her and slowly shook his head. "I'm sorry, you can't get that," he said gravely.

"What? Can't get what?"

"Marisa, you can't just arbitrarily call yourself 'good peoples.' That title has to be earned. It has to be bestowed on you, preferably by other 'good peoples.' "

"Of which you are one, I assume."

"I've been a member of the Benevolent Society of Good Peoples since 1994," he said proudly.

"Yeah?" she said, showing that wonderful laugh again. "What if I decide to just call myself 'good peoples' without being inducted into the club?"

"You can do that. Just like I can go around calling myself the 'Most Royal Lord of Poppycock' or the 'Grand Duke of Balderdash.' "

"Your insinuation being it would just be an empty title with no real meaning?" she asked.

"Exactly."

"Well, since you're a member of the club, you can get me in, right?"

Myles took a deep breath and let it out slowly, as if his decision would have an immeasurable impact on the future of mankind.

"I'll see what I can do, Marisa. However, be fore-warned, it's a long and exhaustive process. It will require spending a great deal of time in each other's company. If you have a pen, I'll give you my phone number."

Marisa smirked. "Nice segue."

"Hey, I'm trying to help you out," Myles said defensively. "If you want to go through life not being known as good peoples . . . "

"Don't misunderstand me, I appreciate it. I'm just wondering what I've done to deserve this great show of altruism."

"You had the good fortune to run into me, literally."

"But how could I possibly pay you back? I wouldn't want to be indebted. Do you have any ideas?"

"Hmmm, nothing immediately comes to mind, but

you're a bright lady. Maybe if you thought long and hard, things might just pop up in your head."

"Now see, that never happens to me. Long and hard, things . . . just popping up. Does that happen to you often, Myles?" She winked and stood up. "Will you excuse me? I'll be right back." She opened the door and went into the house.

Alone on the porch, Myles almost swooned, like one of those old white matriarchs on a soap opera. The ones that stagger back and clutch their pearl necklaces before they faint dramatically onto the couch. He didn't know what Marisa was serving, but he was already in a state of intoxication. He couldn't believe how at ease he felt around her. Usually with a woman that beautiful, it was all he could do to form complete sentences.

It sounded like the party was going full throttle in the backyard. Mimi Ibarra was singing "Duele." Funny, though, he hadn't even noticed how loud the music was when he was talking to Marisa. When she got back, he'd ask her if she wanted to dance. He'd bet she was an excellent dancer.

But when she opened the door and came out, she had her purse and car keys in hand. A cream-colored shawl was wrapped around her slender shoulders.

"Will you walk me to my car?"

"You're leaving?" He was incredulous.

"Yes, I decided to drive back home tonight. I want to be on the road before I get sleepy. I've had a long day, and I have some things to take care of tomorrow."

He stood there mystified, unable to move. He had heard that love can be fleeting, but damn.

"Come on," she said, and started down the steps. He caught up to her at the sidewalk, and they walked to her car.

"Marisa, the night is so young."

"True, but it's already been fruitful." She looked over at him and put her hand on his forearm. "Do you think it's been fruitful, Myles?"

He looked down at her hand and realized that it was their first physical contact, except for the inadvertent elbow she had given him in the kitchen. He also looked for a ring, which would explain her vagueness, and why she was leaving now, but her fingers were bare.

"Yes, Marisa, I do."

She looked at him and smiled. Jesus, those eyes made him want to melt. It was all he could do not to scoop her up, throw her over his shoulder, and abscond with her.

"This is my car," she said as she disengaged the alarm and opened the door.

This was her car. A cream-colored Mercedes convertible. Two thoughts came to Myles's mind: One, cream was definitely her color, and second, he still didn't know what she did for a living. He just hoped it wasn't something shady, like being some kind of courier for a major East Coast cartel.

She slid in and opened the glove compartment, taking out a pen and a notepad.

"Write down your phone number, Myles."

He wrote his name and number, and handed it back to her. He never asked for a female's number because of something Amir once told him. You not only make it seem as if you have something so good to offer that it would behoove her to call you; you also don't come across as one of those brothers who are desperate for pussy.

"There's more paper in that pad," she said.

"Meaning?"

"Meaning, I'll give you my phone number if you . . ."

"If I what?"

"If you tell me I'm good peoples." She batted her eyes in an exaggerated coquettish manner.

Myles smelled a test. She wanted to see how much he wanted her phone number. In effect, she was trying to punk him, because there was no guarantee that she was going to call him.

"I'm sorry, but I have to stand on my principles. Marisa, I've told you what you have to do."

"Okay," she sighed, feigning dismay, but he could tell she approved. He would have appeared desperate, and underfoot. And she struck him as the type who might dig her heel into a brother's spine once she had him underfoot.

She turned on the ignition. "Well, Mr. Moore, maybe I'll be calling."

"Well, Ms. Marrero, maybe I'll be waiting." Which was a pretty sophisticated thing to say considering what he really wanted to do was drop to his knees and plead with her to take him with her. He stepped back onto the curb.

"Bye," she said.

"Good night, and drive safely, you're carrying precious cargo."

"What's that?"

"My heart," he said, sincere as all hell.

She smiled and pulled off. According to Amir, the thing to do now would be to wave once and to walk back to the house, to not let her see him standing there like some lovestruck puppy. Yet Myles just stood there, long after her car had turned the corner and was out of sight.

ℛ Six

A week had passed since the night of the party, but Myles was still thinking of Marisa. She hadn't called, and he was definitely stressing. He had been trying to keep himself busy, but inevitably, without fail, she would regain her position of dominance in his thoughts.

He had been waking up every morning at six o'clock to go to the gym with Amir. He didn't say anything to him about Marisa, mainly because there wasn't anything to tell. He thought she had taken to him, but maybe she was just a genial person by nature. As for her flirtation and sexual innuendoes, maybe she really was an adult entertainer and it came naturally to her around men. Maybe she was some high-priced call girl and had some appointment to get to. That would certainly explain her leaving so abruptly. Now that he thought about it, her interest had probably waned when she found out he was a schoolteacher. She knew he couldn't "afford" her right there. Yep, he bet that she was a hooker. The skank!

He laughed at his stupidity. He was ready to con-

demn her as a whore rather than admit that he probably just wasn't that interesting to her. Maybe he had
misinterpreted her level of interest.

He was over at Carlos's house Saturday night when
Jackie came in. He asked her, as casually as possible,
about Marisa, and she told him that she didn't know
too much about her. She said that she only knew Marisa through one of her cousins. She offered to "help,"
and got that excited matchmaking gleam in her eyes,
but Myles declined her services. He figured, what
was the point? Marisa knew how to contact him, not
vice-versa. If she didn't want to, she didn't want to.
So he said good-bye to Carlos and Jackie and headed
out to meet Amir.

Shortly after he left them, their phone rang. Jackie
picked it up.

"Hello?"

"Hey, Jackie, it's me."

Jackie broke out in laughter. "Well, you just missed
Myles. I wish you could've seen his hardluck, pitiful
ass. He's acting like he lost that ugly ass dog of his."

"He asked about me?"

"Did he. And he tried to do it in such a nonchalant
way. 'Jackie, what do you know about that girl I saw
at your aunt's house? I think her name was, um,
Marisa.' What a fraud! It was all I could do not to
laugh in his face."

Marisa laughed. "You're becoming quite the ac-
tress, *nina.* Your performance last weekend should
have earned you an award."

"Me? What about you? When you 'accidentally'
elbowed him, did you see that look on his face when
he turned around? I about near died. I know why

you took him out of the kitchen. You didn't want anybody tripping over his tongue."

Marisa giggled along with Jackie. "Stop picking on him."

"That's right, Marisa, defend your man."

"Whoa, now. He's not near my man. However, he's my type. Just the way I like them. Big, strong, cute and . . ."

"Dumb?" Jackie supplied. She and Marisa started laughing again.

"No," Marisa said, calming down, "not dumb, but malleable. Easily controlled, docile. Just the way I like them."

"Yeah, wrapped around your finger. You're something else, girl."

"Hey, somebody's got to be in charge. It may as well be me."

"In charge is one thing, Marisa, but you've brought more men to their knees than the Catholic Church."

They both had to laugh again.

"It's not my fault if some men don't know how to handle a strong, independent woman."

"I hear you. So, when are you gonna call Myles" I'm starting to feel sorry for him."

"Tomorrow. I had to make him suffer a little for not taking my phone number, for acting like he had some *cojones* around me."

"You're twisted. And if he had taken the phone number?" Jackie asked.

"He would've been finished, done, written off as a *cabron*." Marisa chuckled.

"Tomorrow's good. He said he was going somewhere with Amir tonight," Jackie said.

"Who is Amir?" Marisa asked.

"His brother."

"Oh. So what was Myles like after I left the party?"

"He was of no use to anyone. He sat down at a table in the backyard, didn't dance, didn't drink. He even turned down my mama's *empanadas*!"

"He's too cute. Loss of appetite is one of the first symptoms of 'Marisa-itis.' "

"You're sick, girl, sick."

"Me? You're the one that set him up, and you're supposed to be his friend."

"Hey, it's for his own good. If he knew I was setting him up with somebody, he wouldn't have come, with his fault-finding, picky ass. You're about the only one of my friends he hasn't dated. Besides, Ms. I-don't-do-blind-dates, you wanted to see what he looked like."

Marisa remembered that she had been in the bedroom on the phone with one of her clients when Jackie came in to tell her that Myles had finally made it to the party. When she saw him standing in the kitchen, she was more than pleased with Jackie's selection for her.

"Well, you're right about one thing. He is my type."

"Yeah? So call him already, please?"

"All right, all right. I said I'll call him tomorrow."

"Well, I'll let you go, Carlos is making dinner."

"Speaking of Carlos, how did you convince him not to tell Myles about our deviousness?"

"Convinced him? Please. He's convinced that he doesn't want me to kick his ass."

"And you have the nerve to call me sick! All right, I'll talk to you later."

"Call him."

"Bye, Jackie."

"Bye."

Marisa hung up the phone. She didn't want Jackie's meddlesome ass to know it, but she'd wanted to call Myles earlier in the week but had fought off the urge to do so. He was articulate and quick-thinking, and he was funny, which she liked. He also struck her as a decent person. She liked the bumbling way he couldn't hide his attraction to her. A straight-up dog would have been more adept at concealing it. She remembered how cute he looked when she drove off, like some oversized little boy whose best friend was moving away. Humph, snap out of it, girl, she thought to herself, you're just horny. He's probably about as innocent as that embezzler you got off on a technicality last week.

Yeah, she thought as she sat at her desk in her office to review some briefs. It had been a while since she'd been with a man, and as far as fulfilling that particular need, he'd do just fine.

Myles and Amir took one of the little round tables in Club Zanzibar near the front, where the stand-up comedians would be performing. Myles recognized some of the ones scheduled to appear, and knew this was going to be a raunchy show, which probably was the reason Kenya didn't want to go.

Neither Myles nor Amir really drank, but they ordered some beers just to cover the club's minimum drink policy. They still had some time before the show started, so Amir got up to go talk shit to some of the pretty women he spotted. Myles thought Amir was weird to do that. It was as if he had to be reminded that he could still pull women at will, but *chose* not to because now he was married.

Amir never took it past the flirting stage as far as Myles knew. Nevertheless, Kenya wouldn't have let him go out to a club in Philadelphia unless he took Myles with him. That was their unspoken deal. Amir could do whatever he wanted as long as Myles came along. Other than that, his ass better be home before dusk.

Myles just hoped Amir didn't take it upon himself to bring any women over for him to meet. He was good for doing that. Myles sometimes thought that Amir obsessed more about his love life than he did.

Despite his brother's thoughts to the contrary, Myles had had his fair share of no-strings coochie. Like any man, he liked the feeling of a lady in his arms, maybe more than most men because, if anything, he tended to overromanticize and idealize, which got him into trouble. But last year he'd had an experience that forced a change in his outlook.

While he was in his last year of college, he met this girl named Katrina. She wasn't a student but was on campus to visit a cousin he knew. They were as different as night and day. Katrina was from one of the roughest neighborhoods of North Philadelphia while he was from the safe environs of Lawndale. Katrina was flashy, loud, and brutally honest, and would curse you out without thinking twice, whereas he tended to be more restrained and polite. She was the most overtly sexy woman he had ever met. In fact, the only reason he had the courage to talk to her initially was because she approached him first.

When school let out that summer, he and Katrina started to see each other. He would go across the bridge to Philly to pick her up, and they'd go to baseball games, Baltimore's inner harbor, clubs, movies, or sometimes just walk along South Street. That in itself was an adventure, Myles remembered. Men would gawk at her when they saw her approaching. Katrina dressed provocatively but tastefully. She knew she was fine and didn't mind letting you know that she knew. Apparently she was too fine to succumb to Myles, because she forestalled every attempt he made to sleep with her.

Myles figured that Katrina had tagged him with the most dreaded of all labels, a "nice guy." Like his brother always said, when a sister calls a man nice, it is equivalent to the kiss of death.

Nice. Women want their children to play nice. They want other women to look at their living room furniture and say, "Girrrl, this is n-ice." When they go shopping they want the salespeople to *be* nice. The last place they want to see niceness is in their men. For, in a woman's mind, "Mr. Nice" lives a little too close to "Mr. Weak" who lives next door to that most dreaded of neighbors, "Mr. Punk." So, whenever Myles got the impression that a woman thought he was "nice" or just a "friend," he knew that his chances of getting laid were minimal. That was okay if all he wanted was friendship, but if he wanted sex, he would sever ties. He had difficulty being around a girl in the capacity of just friendship if he was attracted to her, particularly if he had made a play and she knew that he wanted her. Once a man lets a woman know how he feels about her and she says no, every time she looks at him he'll see a smug, self-satisfied, condescending, "you-can't-help-wanting-me" expression on her face even when he no longer does.

At least that was Myles's theory. While he knew he hardly qualified as an authority on women, there was one thing he was certain of: Women choose men, never vice versa. Some are simply clever enough to let the man think that he has chosen her.

So, after Katrina let it be known that he simply wasn't getting any, his visits became less and less frequent until he stopped visiting at all. After a while she gave up on his returning her phone calls as well. They didn't see each other for five years until last summer, when he bumped into her at the mall.

She was eating lunch with one of her co-workers in the food court and looked just as fine as when he had last laid eyes on her. She called Myles over, and they had one of those casual "catching-up" conversations. She was working at one of the women's clothing stores in the Gallery. If there was any animosity on her part toward him, she didn't let it be known. In fact, she gave Myles her number and told him to call her.

He called her that night, and they made plans to go out that weekend. During the phone call he kept waiting for her to ask him why he had ended their friendship. He figured that she hadn't wanted to get into it in front of her co-worker at the mall, but she never brought it up. Maybe she was waiting to ask him in person.

When Myles picked her up from her job, they decided to go to dinner at Lamberti's, and then for a walk along Penn's Landing. The meal was uneventful except for the puzzling fact that Katrina never brought up their past involvement. After a while he figured that Katrina probably had so many other guys at the time and in the interim that she simply forgot.

When Myles asked her what she wanted to do next, she said she wanted to go across the bridge to his apartment. He'd had to quell the canine instincts in him. "Ooh, ooh, we's gettin' sum top o' the hog booty tonight!"

They had just driven off the Ben Franklin Bridge when Katrina asked him in a soft voice, "Do you think I have nice breasts?" Myles looked over at her. In the darkness she had opened up her blouse and unfastened her bra. Though it was dark, he had no doubt that before him was the most perfectly round, beautiful set of breasts in the western hemisphere. The nipples looked like two moist, partially melted Hershey Kisses. His mouth started to water, and Mr. Happy asserted himself in his pants.

"They're nice," Myles said, as matter-of-factly as he could, and turned his attention back to the road, trying his best to appear nonchalant. He didn't know where she was coming from yet, and was wary because this was a girl who would barely even kiss him before.

"Myles, would you like to suck them?" she asked in a voice even softer than before. She lightly brushed her left nipple with her thumb and forefinger. Her voice was so damn sexy.

He didn't need to be asked twice. He practically

dove over the gear shift to get at her. His Honda followed suit and swerved into the right lane. His head was buried in her bosom while Katrina grabbed the wheel. He was hungrily tasting and caressing her, but even with her help he was driving a little too erratically. She made him stop. He sat back up and drove to his apartment as fast as possible.

When they got inside, he made no pretense of foreplay but instead urged her down on the bed, took her clothes off, and commenced to have his way before she could change her mind. Katrina seemed to be more interested in doing a lot of sustained, open-mouth kissing, which he endured in order to get back to what he really wanted to do to her. She spent the majority of the night with her face in a pillow or up against a wall as he sank to new lows of debauchery. They would take a break, she'd pull his face toward hers so he could kiss her, something else would come to him, and she would resume her role of contortionist. Myles often thought that if the citizenry of Sodom and Gomorrah could've caught his act that night, they would've been appalled. He could almost imagine them saying, "Now, *that* freaky bastard deserves hellfire."

Sometime after he had exhausted himself, Katrina got out of the bed. For a long time there was no rustling, no sound of any kind. He couldn't even hear her breathing. He turned to face her and heard a quiet voice speak to him from the direction of the chair.

"Myles, I don't—I just don't do that . . . you know, sleep around . . ." Her voice trailed off.

Oh boy, he thought, here it comes. That speech

women give when they feel ashamed of themselves for skanking it up, though he wasn't expecting it from someone as free-spirited as Katrina. It's a truly awkward moment for the man, because it makes him the skanker, the brutish perpetrator. But hey, it wasn't his fault if Katrina didn't think of the long-term ramifications going in; she definitely wasn't thinking about them when she whipped her titties out in the car. Just once, for every man who has had to endure it, Myles would've liked to interrupt the speech by saying, "Imagine how I feel, cheapening myself by sleeping with your trick ass," but he didn't have the balls.

Myles let his eyes focus on her in the darkness and gave her his attention.

"When was the last time you think I did this?"

He told her he didn't know.

"I haven't done this in . . . the last time I slept with anybody was two years ago," she said in a barely audible voice. "Myles, I just want to feel pampered, I mean . . . you know, be valued."

His eyes were becoming accustomed to the darkness, and for the first time he could see Katrina clearly. Myles could see the weariness etched on her face and hear the hurt in her voice. He realized then that he had never seen Katrina as a human being but rather as an object to be had and ultimately discarded. He had never been her friend. He had plotted on her from day one and when she failed to acquiesce to his demands, he had abandoned her. He had "befriended" her, won her trust, and dropped her because she hadn't put out. He felt a sick, wrenching pain in his chest.

He knew she had slept with him in hopes of keeping him around this time, for this was the lesson men like Myles had taught her. Her value was in that she had a cute ass, nice tits, and a pretty face.

And now, five years later, how many times had Katrina thought of him as the decent one that got away? In the last five years, how many men had she not refused? Had her thoughts turned to him during those encounters as a positive oasis of manhood? If they had, he was ten times worse than the sorriest of them. For at least with men like Amir, there was no pretense. With Myles, he had insinuated his way into her heart with pretensions of decency when in reality he was a fraud.

"Maybe, this time we could . . . I don't know," Katrina was saying.

Myles didn't even think she was speaking to him specifically at this point. In her voice he heard a sorrow and desolation that was in sharp contrast to the cheerful lilt and excitability that he had remembered. She seemed distant, perhaps thinking of a place away from her depressing neighborhood and the equally depressing men she knew. It was a long night for Myles, a long night of soul searching and, he hoped, growing up.

When they arrived at her house in North Philadelphia the next morning, she hesitated before getting out of the car. Finally she said, "Are you gonna call me?"

Myles reached over and softly kissed her on the cheek. "Of course, Katrina." He said this as if her question was preposterous, almost insulting. He lightly brushed the back of his hand against her smooth face.

She appeared relieved. She allowed a faint smile and got out of the car. He waited for her to disappear into the house before he pulled off.

As he drove away, Myles was certain of two things: that he wouldn't shop at the Gallery anymore and that he wouldn't call Katrina.

He tried to delude himself into thinking that it was the "conquest" of Katrina that prevented him from calling her, but he knew better. He knew that he was too cowardly to face her, because he was ashamed of himself for treating her with such callousness.

Katrina's only mistake was giving him the benefit of the doubt. He knew it was wrong, but he couldn't face her again.

So it was then that Myles decided that until God saw fit to send him a woman, he'd just have to endure. If Malcolm X could go seven years without while in prison, and Mandela twenty-seven, he could survive for a while.

"Yo, man, I said there are some bad bitches up in here," Amir repeated. He sat down at the table just as the lights began to dim. "What's wrong with you?"

"Nothing," Myles said, "I was just thinking of something."

"You oughta be thinking about getting with one of these women."

The first comedian came out and began his act. He started a bit on anal sex, and how since his wife denied it to him, it only made him want it more.

Amir howled. When he asked the men in the audience if they agreed with him, Amir was ready.

"I feel you, dog! Ain't nothing wrong with a little ass play!" he called out.

Myles looked over at his brother and laughed. Amir looked as happy as a pig in slop, which, the more Myles thought about it, was a pretty accurate analogy.

❧ Seven

Myles was just getting in from walking Winston when the phone rang. He had made Winston a nervous wreck all week by running to the phone each time it rang, in the hope that it was Marisa. But he had decided that he was going to stop acting like one of his students afflicted with their first case of puppy love, so he made himself take his time before answering it. He picked it up on the fourth ring.

"Hello?"

"Hello, may I speak with Myles?"

He recognized the slightly accented voice immediately. His heart started to race with excitement. Now, according to Amir, the thing *not* to do was let a female know you recognize her voice. You never want a woman you're just getting to know to think that she has no competition.

Despite Amir's advice, Myles was too enthused to follow it.

"Hello? Hello?" he said, louder this time.

"Hello? Myles?" she said, speaking a little louder herself.

"Hello? I'm sorry, all I can hear are harps playing, birds singing, and organ music. Could you please call back lat—wait a second, this must be Marisa!"

"You are a silly one. Though I am impressed you recognized my voice. How did you pick it out from all those other women since I've spoken to you?"

He didn't respond.

"Well, Myles?"

"I'm sorry, I didn't mean to ignore your question. It's just that you lost me with 'other women.' I think that was once a part of my vocabulary, but since last Saturday, I—I . . . just don't know what it means anymore."

Marisa laughed. It was the sweetest sound his ears had ever heard.

"You'd better not start down that road, Myles. I just might be conceited enough to believe I'm worthy of such compliments."

He smiled. Would another woman make an admission like that, or just her?

"So, how was your week?" he asked.

"Hectic, been tying up some loose ends, you know, getting ready to relocate."

"You found a place up here? Do you need help moving?" he volunteered, a little too eagerly. Calm down, he told himself.

"No to both of those questions. I'm going to leave all my things here. I decided to just move into the Mendham Suites in Center City."

Mendham Suites were those furnished places where professionals lived when they relocated to a place short-term. They were very nice and very expensive. Damn, what did she do for a living?

All of a sudden a flash of brilliance came to him. "Marisa, you don't want to live in the Mendham Suites. They're so impersonal, so cold, you'll feel like you're in a hotel room. And you most certainly don't want to live in the city, come on, now."

"You have a better suggestion?"

"As a matter of fact I do. I happen to know of a cheery, roomy apartment available in a historic, quaint little town located fifteen minutes from Philadelphia and forty-five minutes from Atlantic City. This particular apartment is in a secured building, has huge rooms, walk-in closets, plenty of light, all the modern amenities, and fantastic, friendly, helpful neighbors."

"Wow, what is the town?"

"Lawndale."

"Hmm. Now, how can you personally vouch for the kindness of the neighbors?"

"It just so happens that I am one of them."

"Ohhh, okay, a place in your building. Hmm, how convenient—"

"Whoa, now, Marisa. I think I detect a little cynicism in your voice, as if you think I have some kind of hidden agenda. I'm just trying to help you out."

"You didn't let me finish. What I was going to say was that it would be convenient for me to have you nearby. You know, to help me in my quest to become good peoples."

"Ex-actly."

"I would never call your intentions into question, Myles. For I know that you are true in spirit and pure of heart."

"Now see, I knew you were a bright lady."

She chuckled. "So, when can I see this apartment?"

"Anytime you want."

"What about tomorrow?"

"Umm, sure, no problem." Damn, that meant he had to clean *his* apartment tonight. And he had better get the key to the vacant apartment from Bernard tonight, because tomorrow was Sunday and he and Serita sometimes spent all day in church.

"And since you're coming by, why don't you let me cook dinner for you?"

"Wow, a man offering to cook for me. I'm touched. You know, Myles, you're just so generous and giving."

"That's good peoples lesson number one, Marisa, to be giving."

"Ooh, let me write this down. 'Be . . . giving.' "

"That's right, remember to be giving, be giv-iiiiing."

There was a pause before she replied.

"Oh, I've been known to be very giving with certain men."

His ears perked up. "Yeah?"

"Oh, yeah, giving them stress-induced ulcers, or just giving them the boot. Oh, I can be quite giving, Myles, when the need arises."

I'll bet you can, he thought. He deserved that. He was being a little too familiar with his "giving" reference, especially considering he just invited her to his apartment for the first time. A strategic retreat was in order.

"You know, Marisa, I got a little mixed up. I meant to say that giving comes much, much later, near the very end of the 'good peoples' program, in fact."

"You know, Myles, you have quite a way with

words. Does it come honestly, or is it from years of telling women what you think they want to hear?"

"Marisa, I decided long ago that I'm not clever enough to figure out what a woman wants to hear. I speak from my heart and let the chips fall where they may."

"That's a novel approach."

"Marisa, do you need directions to get to Lawndale?" He couldn't wait to see her.

"No, I remember passing the exit when I went to Camden. What's the address of your apartment building?"

"It's at the corner of Heaney and Warwick. When you get off the interstate at the Lawndale exit, Warwick is the street you'll be on. You'll pass two lights, and Heaney will be the next street on your right, you'll see the building. Ring the buzzer, I'm in apartment 3-B."

"That's easy enough. Can I bring anything?"

"What do you mean?"

"For dinner, a bottle of wine or something?"

"Just your lovely self and winning smile is all that I require from you."

"I told you to watch the flattery. Believe me, I'm already a handful."

What a nice thought, handfuls of Marisa.

"I know, I wouldn't expect anything less."

They said good night, and he knew he would be devoting a great deal of time to prepping for Marisa's visit, so he decided he'd better call Amir. One of the twins answered the phone.

"Hel-lo?"

"Hello, is this my Deja-boo?"

"Yes."

"I'll bet you don't know who this is."

"Yeah, I do, it's Un-kel My-els."

"Wow. Deja-boo! You're so smart. I thought I could fool you!"

Outsmarting her uncle brought Deja a great deal of joy. She was still full of glee when her mother took the receiver from her.

"Hello, Myles?"

"Hey, Kenya, what are you guys doing?"

"Amir went to the video store to get a movie. I just got done giving the girls their bath—wait a minute, Jade, I'm talking on the phone."

"Do me a favor and tell Amir I won't be able to make it to the gym tomorrow morning."

"Okay."

"Oh, Kenya, before I forget to ask you, I want to take the twins to the zoo before the summer is over." The Philadelphia Zoo had rare white lions on loan from another zoo, and Myles wanted to go see them himself.

"You gonna try to handle these two by yourself? I know you're a teacher and used to dealing with kids, but these two worrisome-behind children, I don't know," Kenya said, laughing. "Hold on, Myles—Jade, I said, wait!" Kenya said a little more sternly than before.

"Worrisome? Don't talk about my two perfect nieces like that. Besides, I'll probably take Carlos with me."

"Oh, that's a source of comfort," Kenya said sarcastically. "No problem, just let me know when."

"What movie is Amir getting?"

"I don't know, I told him to choose. But if he comes back with some stupid Son of Superfly meets Dolemite shit, he's taking his ass right back to that store. Why, you coming over?"

"Nah, I gotta get ready for . . ." Oops.

"Excuse me? Get ready for what? You got someone coming over there tonight? Out with it, who is she?" Kenya teased.

"All right, just don't tell Amir. I don't need him on my back until I at least see if it's going somewhere. Her name is Marisa, I met her at a party, and she's not coming until tomorrow."

"And you're getting ready tonight? Awwww, ain't that sweet."

"Just give Amir my message about the gym, please. Will you do that, Ms. Funny Lady?"

"Sure. Speaking of funny, you ought to see how Jade is looking at me with her lip all poked out."

"What's the matter with her?" Myles asked.

"She wants to talk to you. You got time?"

"I always got time for one of my baby girls, put her on."

"All right, I'll talk to you later, hold on."

"Hel-lo?"

"Is this my fairy-tale princess named Jade?"

"Yes."

"I bet you don't know who this is . . ."

Five seconds after Marisa hung up the phone, it rang. She chuckled to herself because she thought it was Myles star-sixty-nining her, to just make sure she said two o'clock, or to ask what she'd like to eat, or using some other lame excuse to call her, since he had now procured her number.

"Yes?" she said as she picked up the phone.

"Hey, baby, it's Ruben."

Ugh, she thought. "*Hola*, Ruben. But I think you're mistaken. I haven't been anybody's infant in twenty-eight years."

"Yeah, but I'm not just anybody. You're my baby," Ruben said, his voice barely above a whisper.

Uh-oh, he was starting to put on his phone-sex voice. She was going to have to nip this in the bud. "Is there something you want?"

"Can I come over?"

"No."

"Well . . . ah, let's just talk then."

"And I'm not going to talk dirty to you just so you can diddle yourself."

"What the hell is your fucking problem, Marisa? Damn! You on your period, or something?"

Had it come to this? Had it really come to this? Marisa almost had to laugh at her fate, being cursed at by this dumbkoff. He was of Cuban descent, like her, and admittedly very good-looking, but he was about as simple-minded as they came. Whatever slim chance he might have had ended when she caught his act in front of that restaurant.

"You're right, Ruben. I'm so evil, I don't blame you for not wanting to deal with my moods. You can have so many other women, as *mozo* as you are."

"Uh, yeah, I could. So—"

"So I understand you not wanting to put up with a bitch like me anymore. And, Ruben?"

"Huh?"

"Thanks for letting me down easy." She hung up.

You're about five years too late, Ruben, she thought to herself. There was a time where she would have turned gooey inside over a dog like him. But those days were over. When she reflected on her past relationships, she could honestly say that she was still waiting for a real love. A love the way she saw, heard, and read other women describe when they were in love. It would *not* be that degrading, low-self-esteem, pins-and-needles bullshit too many women were afflicted with, either. Those days were over for her.

She supposed that some of her hardheaded, hard-hearted attitude was formed by past experiences, but she knew that she was primarily a product of Esther's handiwork. Marisa remembered a time when she was having a particularly hard time dealing with a breakup. The man she had been dating was a professor who was nearly twenty years her senior. Marisa didn't have the type of relationship with her aunt where she felt she could talk to her about men. But this time Marisa was in such a state that Esther knew something was wrong with her.

The next time Marisa came to visit her, Esther wasn't home. There was a note addressed to Marisa sitting on her aunt's desk.

Marisa,

Emotion is the worst betrayer of a woman and the heart the abettor of its treason. Reason is a woman's greatest ally and the brain its facilitator. Use your brain when you make your life choices. Use your heart to pump blood throughout your body.

For Marisa, there was a comfort zone in dealing with transparent, one-dimensional men like Ruben. They didn't require too much emotional investment, and without feelings to cloud her judgment, she could call the shots clearly.

But weren't women supposed to be equipped with the capacity to pick themselves up and love over and over again?

She feared she had more of Esther in her than she cared to admit. That clown Ruben notwithstanding, men often told her she was too cold. She was rapidly approaching thirty, and was indifferent to the thought of children. The tick of her biological clock didn't bother her in the least.

That night as Marisa lay in bed, her thoughts turned to Myles. He sure wasn't the type to be able to play it cool. She was accustomed to dealing with men who were more careful about not revealing themselves. Who didn't tip their hand so openly, especially if their motives were purely lust driven. But Myles sounded like he would've pulled her through the phone line if he could have. She could hear the eagerness and excitement in his voice as he spoke to her.

Suggesting an apartment in his building seemed a bit forward. But then again, if her initial impression about him was correct, then it fit. If a man is a dog, he doesn't want any of the women he's screwing up under him, because they might prevent him from running other women. Secrecy is a dog's best friend. Myles didn't seem worried about it, though. Apparently he had nothing to hide.

🕭 Eight

Myles was up until two-thirty in the morning cleaning his apartment. He scrubbed and disinfected the kitchen and bathroom, including the floors, washed the windows, polished, dusted, and vacuumed every square inch. Such meticulousness really wasn't necessary because he never allowed the place to get too dirty. But he was too excited to sleep, so he decided to put all that energy to good use.

Winston didn't escape his wrath, either. The next morning after he came back from buying the food he was going to cook for dinner, Myles took him outside and gave him a bath. "A malodorous dog around Marisa simply will not do," he told him as he scrubbed. Amir and Carlos thought he was crazy for talking to his dog, but he swore Winston communicated with him. "And, Winston, any acts of flatulence you may feel inclined to perform, I would appreciate it if you would wait until after she leaves." Winston looked at Myles and yawned. Myles knew what he was thinking. If he had female company over more often, he wouldn't be in such a panic.

After he finished with Winston, he took a shower.

Afterward, he went into the bedroom to choose something to wear. This decision required a lot of thought. He didn't want to be too dressy, as if he was some yokel unaccustomed to having a pretty woman in his place, and he damn sure didn't want to be too casual, and risk giving her the impression that she warranted nothing better. It was unseasonably cool but still August, so he wanted to wear something that wasn't too heavy. Hmm, or maybe he should just stand in front of his closet like a jackass and wait for her to get here and let her choose something for him to wear. Get a hold of yourself, son. It's not like he was proposing to her, it was just Sunday dinner at home. He pulled out a pair of gray slacks and a white rayon shortsleeve shirt he had bought at Structure earlier that summer. He added a burgundy belt and loafers and went into the kitchen.

He had decided to make curried shrimp over rice. It was one of those dishes that looks like it takes a lot of painstaking effort, but in actuality takes about twenty minutes. One of the secretaries at school had given him the recipe, and whenever he made it, people raved. He had bought one of those salad mixes at the supermarket, which he opened, tossed into a bowl, and put into the refrigerator.

Though he seldom drank, he always kept liquor for company. He checked his supply. He had a six-pack of coolers, five beers, one bottle of dark rum, two bottles of wine, and stuff to make white Russians with, which Jackie had left from the last time she was over with Carlos. He didn't know which wine was appropriate for the dish, so he decided to put the red out and take the chilled white from the refrigerator. If she wanted dessert, they would just have to go out for it.

He checked the time: 11:50. Damn. What the hell was he going to do for the next two hours?

As Marisa was driving on the interstate, her thoughts again turned to the previous night's conversation with Myles. She did need to find a place to live quickly and was free today, but she knew that she also wanted to see him, and that is why she asked to see the apartment. He had pissed her off with his "be giv-iiing" bullshit, but she let him wriggle out of it. She had *wanted* to let him off the hook, which surprised her. Still, he'd better check himself. She would decide if and when she was going to give him some.

When Marisa reached the Lawndale exit, she checked the time. It was one-fifty. She didn't have time to stop by Jackie's house. She had told Jackie that she was going to Myles's today and that she would stop by. Oh well, she would go by there afterward, before she headed home.

Myles practically leaped off the couch when he heard the buzzer. He went to the call box.

"Yes."

"Hello, Myles, it's Marisa."

"Marisa? Marisa who?"

"Marisa about-to-turn-her-ass-right-around-and-drive-away, that's who."

"Oh, Marisa Marrero, now I remember you. Come on up." Don't take that ass anywhere, he thought. He went into the hallway to wait for her. "All right, gird yourself. You know she's beautiful, so don't make a big deal about her looks. You think you'd be the first man to tell her she was gorgeous? Hell, no. So compliment her on anything besides her looks. Don't stare and don't say anything stupid. Be yourself. Check that, be better than yourself. Be someone else."

Marisa opened the stairwell door and emerged.

His heart started to pound. Jesus Christ, this shit didn't make any sense. She was actually *prettier* than he remembered. She smiled when she saw him. As she walked from the end of the hallway toward him, he realized she was carrying flowers.

"*Hola*, these are for you," she said, holding out the roses.

"Thank you, Marisa," he said, taking the flowers. Damn, he never had a woman give him flowers before. "Please, come in. I'll find a vase for these."

She stepped inside and looked around the living room.

"Hey now, this is niiiice," she said as she walked around. "I'll take it. So, where do you live, Myles?"

He came out of the kitchen with the flowers in a vase and set it on the coffee table. "The vacant apartment looks just like this one, with the skylight and everything. I have the key, so we can look at it whenever you're ready. Can I get you something to drink?"

"Do you have ginger ale?"

"No, how about a Sprite?"

"That'll be fine."

As he headed to the kitchen, Winston walked out of the bedroom into the living room.

"Aww, look at the cute little bulldog," Marisa said when she spotted him. "What's his name?"

"Winston."

"Oh. You're named after Churchill, aren't you, puppy? With your jowls and your stubby little body."

Impressive, he thought. She was the first person to know why he named his English bulldog Winston without his first having to explain it. He turned off the pot that he had simmering on the stove, and went to the freezer to get some ice.

"Something smells good," Marisa said from the living room.

"It's curried shrimp. I hope you like it."

"Please, I'm from the Caribbean. If I opened a vein, I'd bleed curry. And who doesn't like shrimp?"

"My thoughts exactly. Carlos isn't big on curry, though. I think there is something wrong with him."

"You know, where I'm from, we would have shunned him. Speaking of being big on something, your boy Winston is getting amorous out here, Myles."

He walked in from the kitchen with her Sprite and a glass of ice in either hand. Winston was trying clumsily to mount Marisa's shin and hump it. He set her soda and glass on the coffee table and scooped Winston up.

"I apologize, Marisa," Myles said as he hurriedly walked toward the bedroom with Winston under his arm. "He usually doesn't do that."

He put Winston down on the bedroom floor and glared at him. He swore Winston was smiling.

Myles closed the bedroom door behind him and

walked back into the living room. Marisa was standing up, looking at his CD collection. She was holding one in her hand.

"Sorry about that."

"No need to be. Young dogs want to mount everything that they're drawn to," she said. "I'm just wondering what oversexed big dog he learned the behavior from."

She was looking at him inquiringly with those huge, luscious, dreamy eyes of hers.

"Me too, Marisa. I'm going to stop letting him watch *Wild Kingdom* on TV."

"Yeah, right. Typical. Blame the television for the ills of your home. Myles, can I borrow this CD?"

"Sure, take whatever you want."

"If you say so." She grabbed a couple more.

He didn't mind in the least. It guaranteed another visit for her to return them. "Marisa, if you're hungry now, we can eat, or if you want, we could look at the apartment now."

"I'm hungry, so let's eat. Where can I wash my hands?"

"Down the hall on the right."

He watched her go. She was wearing blue jeans, a Gap T-shirt, and black boots. The way she looked, she didn't have to obsess too much about what she was wearing. She made anything look good. His eyes involuntarily went to her butt when her back was safely turned. It was as if God himself went to Africa, dipped His hands into the most fertile mud possible, and sculpted the most breathtaking ass the world had ever seen. It was glorious, spectacular, and life-affirming.

"What are you thinking about?"

While he was in his daydream, Marisa had finished in the bathroom and come back into the living room.

"*Nada,*" he said. "Let me fix you a plate."

She followed him into the kitchen. "Two bottles of wine, Myles? If I didn't know better, I would think you were trying to get me drunk."

"No, I . . ." He decided to just tell her the truth. "I wasn't sure which would be appropriate for this dish."

She laughed. "Oh, worried about the appropriate wine to serve, are you? My, my, I didn't know I was going to be dining with royalty."

Myles laughed too. It did seem silly in retrospect.

"Well, I figured white for shrimp, but didn't know if the curry made it fall into a different category," he said.

"Shoot, just give me a plate of chicken wings and a glass of Kool-Aid and I'm happy," Marisa said.

"Aahh, but what flavor Kool-Aid goes with poultry, the grape or the pink swimmingo? There's the rub."

Marisa leaned her head back and laughed, then looked at him and shook her head, biting her bottom lip.

"That's good that you can laugh so easily, Marisa. A prerequisite to becoming 'good peoples' is having a sense of humor," he said as he handed her a plate.

"Thank you," she said. "Do you mind if I turn on the TV while we eat?"

"Marisa, *me casa es su casa.*"

"*Gracias.*" She grabbed a placemat and set it on the coffee table. "Hernandez is pitching today."

"Do you mean Orlando, the Yankee pitcher? You're a baseball fan?" Myles asked incredulously.

"You act like you're shocked. *Beisbol* is a religion in Cuba. When I was a little tomboy growing up, I played it every day. 'El Duque' is one of the best pitchers that Cuba has ever produced."

"I didn't know you were Cuban, Marisa." He had assumed she was Puerto Rican.

She looked over at him and put her fork and plate down. "Well, go ahead," she said expectantly.

He swallowed a forkful of the curried shrimp. Too much curry, he thought. Damn.

"Go ahead?"

"You know."

"I know I don't have a clue as to what you're talking about," he said.

"I'm waiting for the obligatory, supposedly witty remark about Cubans. Like 'Can you score me some cigars?' or 'Do you know Fidel?' "

"I'm appalled that you would think so little of me." Myles put down his plate as if he was disgusted and hurt. "You truly wound me, Marisa."

"I'm sorry if I offended you, Myles," Marisa said, smiling. She then turned deadly serious. She leaned toward him, leaned her face about a foot from his and casually put her hand on his thigh. He could practically taste the sweetness of her breath. Her eyes traveled to his mouth and then back to his eyes.

"Maybe you'll let me make it up to you . . . " She slid her hand down his leg and squeezed his knee.

Hummina, hummina, hummina.

" . . . by letting me, um, letting me . . . cook for you one day," she said contentedly as she picked up her plate and resumed eating. "Myles, I think I will try some of that chardonnay. Can you pour me a glass, please?"

No fair, Myles thought. She's not right and she knows it. Toying with a man like that, it simply isn't right. What's more, he had the sneaking suspicion that she knew he was in no position to stand up and get anything—without revealing the state of arousal that her hand on his leg had caused.

"And another plate of this curried shrimp, it's delicious." She handed her almost empty plate to him. "If you don't mind," she added innocently.

A little too *innocently* for his taste. So he played dumb, too. "Well, actually I do mind, Marisa. I told you to make yourself at home. *Me casa es su casa*, remember?" he said as he attempted to hand her plate back to her.

"Ah, but I'm just so relaxed here. Will you please get it for me, Myles?" she asked, looking at him from under her long, gorgeous lashes.

She's good, he'd give her that. But if she thought he was getting up so that she could see his pup tent impersonation, she must be crazy.

"Well, once you're rested, the wineglasses are in the third cabinet from the refrigerator, the corkscrew is in the drawer directly adjacent to the—"

"You won't get it for me? I thought you were a gentleman. Oh well, the very least you can do is stand up and . . . *point* me in the right direction." No longer able to contain it, she burst out laughing. Myles waited for her to calm down before he attempted to speak.

"So you take pleasure in ridiculing others, huh, Marisa? In making sport of the infirm?"

"I don't know what you're talking about," she said, wiping away a tear.

"I think you do."

"I know I don't."

Cute. Using his words against him. By now his erection had begun to subside, so he picked up her plate and stood up. He thought he saw her sneak a peek at his groin, but she was too sly to let him catch her.

"Marisa, would you like some salad, too?" he called from the kitchen.

"Sure." She walked into the kitchen. "Where is your salad dressing?"

"There should be some in the refrigerator door."

She brushed past him, close enough for him to get a whiff of her hair. Whatever she put in, it wasn't something he was familiar with. But it sure smelled good.

They took their plates and glasses of wine back to the living room so they could watch the game. The Yankees were in Chicago playing the White Sox.

Marisa wasn't lying, she knew her baseball. During the game she commented on different plays, subtleties of strategy that only a knowledgeable fan would appreciate. She was a passionate fan as well. As they were watching, she took off her boots, stretched out on the couch (he did say his house was her house), and became so engrossed that she barely spoke to Myles.

The combination of his lack of sleep, the meal, the wine, and her silence started to catch up with him.

He felt himself becoming drowsy around the fifth inning. He fought it off until the seventh inning, when he finally succumbed.

"Myles . . . Myles."

He was rousted out of dreamland. Marisa was standing over him and gently shaking his shoulder.

"I dozed off? I'm sorry . . . what's the score?"

"The game is over. The Yanks won 4–2. Bernie Williams doubled in the go-ahead runs in the eighth inning."

"Bernie-*beisbol*, baby. That's my boy." He could've killed himself for falling asleep.

"Mmm-hmm, he's one of my favorites as well. However, I have to admit that my feelings are a little hurt that you fell asleep on me. Maybe we should just go see the apartment now, and then I'll be on my way."

Myles couldn't tell whether she was serious. She couldn't possibly be, could she?

"But I was dreaming of you, Marisa," he said sweetly.

"Oh, yeah? Why don't you tell me about your dream, I would love to hear it."

Myles scrambled to think of something.

Just then the phone rang. He looked at Marisa and smiled.

"Saved by the bell," she said.

He picked up the phone. It was Jackie.

"What's up?"

"I just called to see if Carlos was over there."

"Nope, he's not here."

"Shoot, I wonder where he got off to."

"I don't know. Hey, why don't you beep him?"

"Oh, yeah. I forgot that he has a beeper now. So what are you doing with your Sunday? Did you go to church?"

Damn, Jackie wanted to chat. How could he get off the phone without arousing suspicion? He didn't want to lie to her in front of Marisa, because he didn't want her to think that it was easy for him to lie to women. And he didn't want Jackie to know he had company over, particularly Marisa, because her nosy ass might want to meddle.

"Actually, I'm kinda busy. I promised the super that I would show the vacant apartment on my floor to a prospective tenant." Marisa winced when she heard him say that. "So, I gotta go."

"Oh, the person's there? What's she like?"

"Who said it was a 'she'?"

"Oh . . . well, what's he like?"

"Why?"

"Okay, okay, no need to get testy," Jackie said. "I'll talk to you later."

"Bye."

"Bye."

"Sorry about that," Myles said.

"It just gets worse," Marisa said. "I've gone from being an angel to someone you find so boring you fall asleep. Now I'm just a 'prospective tenant.' "

Now he knew she was kidding.

"Marisa, the only reason I didn't tell Jackie that you were over here is out of respect for your privacy. If it was up to me, I would have commissioned a plane to sky-write your arrival."

"I don't know . . . I need more convincing. Tell me about your dream."

He thought she had forgotten about that. No problem, he had had time to prepare.

"Well, I was returning from a long pilgrimage with about a dozen or so other men—"

"Wait," Marisa said. She stretched out on the couch. "I just want to be comfortable when I hear this dream of yours. Proceed."

"Are you sure you're comfortable?"

"Yes, go ahead."

"I mean, I can go in the bedroom and get you another pillow."

"Are you stalling?"

"No, no, of course not. Well, as I was saying, I was returning from a long pilgrimage with about a dozen or so other men. I'm not sure where we were coming from, but we were war-weary and worn out. In our possession we had spoils of war, enough riches to last each of us a thousand lifetimes. We were making the long trek home, wherever that was."

Marisa closed her eyes. Myles started getting into it.

"Along the way, we came upon a brothel teeming with beautiful women. A couple of the men decided to stop there. The rest of us pressed on. Farther along we came upon a glittering, flashy resort casino full of games of chance and opportunity for wealthy young men. The rest of the men decided to stay there except for me and two others. We pressed on. We then came upon a clearing with a huge monastery. One of the two remaining men with me decided to stay there and devote his life to doing good works. That just left me and one companion. We pressed on.

The lone other man with me explained that he was a newlywed and that he wished to get home to his wife, for she had borne him a child that he had not seen yet.

"Well, after many more miles he and I reached a river. The only way to get across the river was to pay an outrageous fee to an old man who had a boat. The man with me refused to pay and said he would wait and see if he could find another way. I handed all my wealth over to the old man without hesitation, and he ferried me across.

"After I came ashore, I walked for another couple of miles and discovered a lone house. I tapped on a window and the most beautiful woman I'd ever seen opened it. How lovely she looked on that clear night. The moonlight bathed her skin in its soft glow. My heart skipped a beat when she extended her delicate hand to me and afforded me the privilege of kissing each of her fingertips. As I tasted their sweet nectar, I knew I had made the right decision. For I knew I was a thousand times more smitten than the most satiated of my comrades; I was a thousand times more fortunate than the luckiest of them, and a thousand times more blessed than the most sanctified of them. For I had found Marisa." Myles paused for dramatic effect. "That's when you woke me up."

Marisa opened her eyes and stared at him with wonder. "That is so amazing. You just made that up, right on the spot?"

"Marisa, all I did was recount the details of my dream."

"Well, let's test its validity."

She got up and came over to his chair and sat on

its arm. She lifted her hand and traced her index finger slowly along Myles's mouth. When she touched where his lips met, he opened his mouth slightly to take in her fingertip and softly kissed it. She then removed it.

"Does it taste like sweet nectar?"

"Nah, it just tastes like curry."

She playfully punched him in his shoulder and stood up.

"Speaking of something sweet, what's for dessert?"

"I just had mine," he said.

"But what am I going to have?"

They looked at each other and laughed, both knowing what he wanted to say.

At that moment Winston walked into the living room.

"How did he get out of the bedroom?"

"When you dozed off, I let him out. I felt sorry for him. I hope you don't mind."

"No, not at all." Myles thought it was kind of nice that she would be concerned about his dog. "What are you in the mood for?" he asked.

"Didn't I pass an Italian ice place a couple of blocks up?" she asked.

"Yeah, Rita's," he replied.

"Let's walk there. We can take Winston along."

Myles snapped on Winston's leash, and they made their way downstairs. Marisa brought the CDs she borrowed from Myles with her, which she wanted to put in her car so she wouldn't forget them. They stepped outside into a beautiful day. But as Myles looked around, he didn't see Marisa's Mercedes.

"Marisa, where did you park?"

"Right there," she said.

Myles's jaw dropped, but he didn't say anything as she led him to a shiny black Range Rover. She unlocked it and put his CDs into a case with hers. Myles noticed a garment bag hanging up, and an overnight bag in the backseat. It reminded him of Amir, who when he was single always kept extra clothes in his car in case he got lucky and spent the night at some female's place. He used to call it his "spare attire." Myles wondered what Marisa's extra clothes were for. What if they were for the same purpose?

"You going on a trip?" he asked.

"What? Oh, no," she answered, closing the door. "Let's go."

As they started toward Rita's, Myles's mind was racing. She sure wasn't one to volunteer information. Anybody else would say what the bags were for, unless they had something to hide. Hmm, maybe his initial impression of her was right. Maybe she had her stripping clothes in there and had a private party to do tonight. Yeah, and what's up with that truck, anyway? He knew how much one of those cost. Dammit, he'd had enough.

"Marisa, what is it exactly that you do?" Myles asked.

Marisa looked at him, puzzled. "You don't know what I do for a living?"

He shook his head.

"I don't know why I assumed you knew. I'm an attorney."

"Oh," he said.

"Do I detect relief in that 'oh,' Myles? How did you think I supported myself?"

"I, uh, oh, nothing. I mean, I had no clue, I figured a, um, you know, some kind of professional." Damn, you stuttering jackass! He pretended he was all of a sudden very interested in Winston and focused his attention on him.

She put her hand on his arm. "No, really. What did you think I did?"

"I told you."

She let go of his arm and they resumed walking. She remained unconvinced.

"Let me go back to our first meeting last Saturday. We had a nice conversation on the porch during the course of which I, admittedly, had been flirting with you."

That's true, Myles thought to himself.

"I knew you were a little confused as to why I was leaving the party so early. It was before ten o'clock, if I remember correctly. I could tell you didn't totally accept my explanation that I was just tired and wanted to get home . . ."

True, as well.

". . . and since you didn't accept my explanation, I assume you thought I was going someplace else, possibly to a predetermined rendezvous. Then you see me get into my car . . ."

She stopped walking again. He thought she was about to get it.

". . . a new Mercedes convertible and drive off. And now you see the truck . . . oh, my God!" she said, and looked at him.

"What?" he said, playing dumb.

"You thought I was a *puta*, didn't you, Myles?" She started laughing. "Admit it."

There was no doubt in Myles's mind about her skill as a lawyer. He thought she would be able to tell if he was lying, and she didn't strike him as the kind of woman who would tolerate being lied to well.

"Well, Marisa, you have to admit, that you were acting so mysterious, and the circumstantial evidence would have led a person to think that, yeah, maybe something was going on."

Marisa turned and started walking again. She dug her hands in her pockets and looked ahead. She didn't say anything as they crossed the street.

"Marisa, if I offended you—"

"No, Myles, it isn't that," she said with a casual flip of her wrist. "I was just thinking about my Aunt Esther, and how she would be spinning in her grave if she knew that I was somehow giving men the impression that I was a prostitute." She chuckled softly to herself.

Damn, she was getting a little too serious for his liking. "Marisa, it has nothing to do with you, it's me. You seemed so ethereal that night that I had to concoct something to bring you back to a level of tangibility. I suppose."

Marisa looked over at him. She seemed pleased by his unsolicited confession, but he couldn't tell for sure.

They had reached Rita's. As usual it was busy, but he was just happy that there weren't any students or their parents there. He didn't know how long Marisa was staying today, and he didn't feel like wasting precious time making small talk with anyone else. He had already wasted enough when he fell asleep.

Myles tied Winston to a small tree outside. He and Marisa were about to enter the store when the door swung open. Amir and Deja walked out.

"Hi!" Deja said excitedly. Her tongue was turning purple from the water ice.

"Hi!" Myles said, matching her enthusiasm. He looked over at Amir. He was already giving Marisa the once-over.

"Marisa, this is my brother, Amir. Amir, Marisa."

They exchanged pleasantries.

"And this," Myles said as he reached for Deja, "is my Deja-booboo-bear." He took turns acting like he was going to eat her water ice and kissing her cheek, while she tried to protect, both of them. "The sugar from your water ice or from your cheek, which is it going to be, Deja?" She started giggling as she tried to keep both away from his mouth. Marisa laughed at Deja's maneuverings.

"So, Marisa," Amir said, "do you live in Lawndale?"

Myles looked at him. Amir knew full well that as small as this town was, he would have remembered seeing someone like Marisa. He put Deja down.

"No, I'm not from the area."

Good, Myles thought. She didn't give him any more information than was necessary, either. He was relieved to know it wasn't a personal thing with him. She must like to keep everybody in the dark.

"Amir, where are Kenya and Jade?" he asked.

"They're at Mom and Dad's," Amir replied, still distracted by the mystery that was Marisa.

"Hi, Deja," Marisa said.

Deja said hi shyly and quickly hid behind her father's leg.

"You stopping by there?" Amir asked

On Sundays they usually went to their parents' for dinner. That's where Amir was probably heading to now.

"I might be by later. Did you go to church with them today?"

"Yeah, I went. I figured I might as well, since my fraudulent workout partner canceled on me."

"Good for you. It's good to be strong in mind, body, and spirit." In his case, two out of three wasn't bad.

Deja had come from behind Amir and was pulling on Myles's pant leg. She did this whenever she wanted to tell him something without anybody else hearing it.

He leaned down to her. "Yes?"

"I've got a secret," she whispered. At least she thought she was whispering.

"What is it?" Myles replied in an equally inept whisper.

She looked over at Marisa before speaking. "She's pretty."

"I know," Myles said.

When he stood up, he glanced at Marisa, who seemed to be embarrassed and blushing. No, she seemed to be embarrassed that she *was* blushing.

"I'm going inside. What flavor do you want, Myles?" Marisa focused her attention on the store's outside menu to avoid eye contact with him.

"It doesn't matter, just get me whatever you get."

She walked into the store. Deja went over to pet Winston.

"Damn, Myles. Where did you find her?"

"I just met her last week at a party, and we're just getting to know each other, so don't say anything stupid."

"What is she, Dominican?"

"No, she's Cuban. Can I give you the biographical information later?"

"All right, all right, I'm going, but I've already seen one bad move you made."

"What's that?"

"Never tell a girl, 'I'll just have what you're having.' You sound wishy-washy and too damn eager to please. A man makes a decision, a *man* has a preference. Next thing you know, she'll be telling you what movie to see."

Myles thought about the conversation he'd had with Kenya the previous night and laughed. He wondered if Amir had had to make a return visit to the video store.

"What's so funny?" he asked.

"You. Tell Mom I'll probably be by tonight."

"All right. Come on, Deja, let's go."

"Good-bye, Deja."

"Bye." She waved to Myles and then took her father's hand as they walked to Amir's truck.

As they were pulling off, Marisa handed him a pineapple-flavored cup of water ice.

"Sorry," she said. "They didn't have pink swimmingo."

"Are you serious?" Myles asked incredulously.

"What kind of mom and pop outfit are they running in there?"

"No appreciation for the finer things in life," she said snobbily. They both laughed.

After he untied Winston's leash and they started to stroll leisurely back to his apartment, it occurred to Myles that he couldn't remember the last time he'd had a day so enjoyable.

❧ Nine

Later that evening, as Myles drove over to his parents' house, he was still buzzing from his earlier hit of Marisa. After they had returned from getting the water ice, they played a game of Scrabble and listened to some music. There was an instant familiarity between them like they were old friends, not people who had just met. Her being so comfortable around him put him at ease, and stopped him from making a fool out of himself by trying to impress her.

The only puzzling part of the evening was when he took her to see the vacant apartment. She gave the place a cursory viewing, not even testing the appliances or water pressure. She seemed to have already made up her mind before she went over there and, apparently, was not taking the apartment. That may not be a bad thing, though, because he was definitely having second thoughts about suggesting the place to her. What if he was misinterpreting her level of interest in him and she just wanted to be friends? Then he would be privy to the cruel sight of seeing other men going to and from her place.

And if she decided to fuck somebody, he would practically be able to feel their gyrations. The last thing he needed was some fraudulent pretty boy showing up at his door: "Excuse me, brother, Marisa sent me over. Do you have any whipped cream, oh and something for back pain, 'cause yo, she 'bout to kill a brother, know what I'm saying?"

"You're just coming from over there?" Jackie asked.

"Yeah," Marisa answered.

"I figured you were over there, the way he was acting when I called."

"Mmm-hmm," Marisa answered, her thoughts elsewhere.

"What's wrong with you?" Jackie asked.

"Nothing," Marisa answered. "Jackie, when did you first start telling me about Myles?"

"Well, let's see. It's been at least four or five months now, when you first told me that you were thinking about changing careers and moving up here—which I'm so excited about! It's gonna be so much fun having you close, like we're back in college." Jackie looked at her friend uncertainly. "Why do you ask?"

"It's just that . . . I don't know. Is Carlos here? I want to ask him something."

"Yeah, he's upstairs. Carlos! Can you come down here, please?"

Carlos came down the stairs and into the kitchen, where he saw his wife and Marisa sitting.

"What's up?" he asked warily.

"I want to ask you something about Myles," Marisa said.

"Don't try to draw me further into you two's deception. I'm already uncomfortable with the role I've played, plotting on my boy. Used, and set up to take the fall when the truth eventually comes out." He said melodramatically, "I'm just a patsy, just a patsy!"

They laughed at Carlos's histrionics. Marisa could see why he and Myles were friends.

"I just need some more information," she said.

"Marisa, why don't you just get to know him and find out for yourself?"

That made sense, Marisa had to admit. She *had* just met him.

So why had she already decided that she was going to take the apartment despite its proximity to him, a man she barely knew, a man she knew wanted her sexually? However, if she were being perfectly honest, the fact was she also wanted him.

Still, she could have him in that capacity without living in the apartment right down the hall from him. What if he turned out to be some asshole, or a fucking nut? That was what had nagged her on the ride over to Jackie's. There were too many questions, and her only answer was a gut feeling that she really liked this man. A "gut feeling." Aunt Esther would have told her to take some bicarbonate.

"Carlos, I just liked the apartment and wanted to quell some logistical concerns, that's all. For instance, can I expect a steady flow of women going to Myles's place at all hours of the night?" Marisa asked.

Jackie and Carlos looked at each other and laughed.

"I told you he wasn't out there like that," Jackie said.

"Not out there? That's an understatement. Yo, I probably shouldn't be telling you this, but last year he skanked it up with some girl and felt so guilty that he swore off sex," Carlos said. "He called me early one morning boo-hooing. He sounded so fucked up that I got worried and drove there. I opened the door and went in, but he was nowhere to be found. When I heard water running in the bathroom, I got worried that he may have done harm to himself, so I went in there. There he was, in the shower, buck naked, saying he had to 'get clean.' "

Jackie and Marisa stared uncertainly at Carlos.

"Did that really happen?" Jackie asked.

"Well, I may be exaggerating a little," he admitted.

"Last year, huh? And there have been none in the interim?" Marisa said.

"None that I know of," Carlos said. "Believe me, he takes so much abuse from Brian and them about his lack of *chocha* that if he was getting some, he would've said something. Does that tell you what kind of quote 'player' unquote, he is?"

"Yes," Marisa said. She had little doubt of her ability to make him forget his vow of chastity if she wanted him to. "But my concerns were about noise and traffic on the floor late at night, not whether he was promiscuous."

"Yeah, right," Carlos said.

"What do you mean, 'yeah, right'? I'm serious."

"Come on, Marisa, you don't like him a little? You were over there for—like, what—six or seven hours?"

"Strictly due to compatibility. It's rare to find a person who can give me a run for my money in Scrabble."

"Was d-e-n-i-a-l one of the words you made?" Jackie asked.

"*Muy comica*, Jackie," Marisa answered.

"Don't worry, ice princess. Myles is a sweetheart. I wouldn't have introduced you to him if he wasn't. So take the apartment. It would be nice having your ass in town."

"All right, you convinced me."

"*Bueno*," Jackie said. "Now it will be easier for you two to get to know each other. Soon you'll be a happily married couple."

"I wouldn't bet on that, Jackie," Marisa said. "Even if I fall madly in love, I wouldn't want to give you the satisfaction of being right."

"As jaded as you are, I wouldn't doubt it. But who's being *muy comica* now? Try to picture yourself falling madly in love," Jackie said. "The only thing that you truly love about any man is the ease with which you can replace him."

Marisa was a little hurt by Jackie's characterization of her.

"If that's the case, and I'm such a bitch, why did you want me to meet him? Unless you want him to get his feelings hurt," Marisa said crossly.

"Isn't it obvious, Marisa?" Carlos answered. "She ran out of other girlfriends."

🌹 Ten

The next morning when Myles arrived at the gym, Amir was already there. He knew he was dying to ask him about Marisa. Last night, by the time he had got to their parents' house, Amir and his family had already left, so Myles knew he was full of questions.

"What are we doing today? Chest?" Myles asked. Amir was in his favorite spot, in front of the mirror, ostensibly stretching but really admiring his physique.

"Yeah. Let's max out today, I want to get to the shop early," he said, getting up.

"No problem," Myles said, putting on his lifting gloves. "Why are you going in early? If you need some help, I can call Dad and tell him not to expect me today."

Their father owned a barbershop, and during the summer when Myles was out of school, he often went in to help him cut hair, especially on Saturdays. When they were kids, their father had made sure that Amir and Myles learned how to cut hair because he figured it was a skill that could always earn them money. "Brothers are always gonna make sure they look good. They might not have a dime left in their pocket afterward, but they will pay the barber," Myles had heard his father say on far too many occasions as he forced Myles to accompany him to the shop. At first Myles's duties consisted of sweeping up hair and running errands, but gradually, as his skills increased, he earned his own chair.

Amir, on the other hand, had loved being in the barbershop when they were growing up. He always had a natural affinity for cutting hair and was making good money in their father's shop when he was barely in his teens. And given that barbershops were true magnets for trash-talking black men, Amir was definitely in his element. Whenever their father took a day off and left Amir in charge, the barbershop became his domain. He dispensed advice on a wide array of subjects. He would tell you who was going to win what athletic contests ("I told you boys that the Knicks were frauds"), and he gave out investment advice, clothing tips, grooming pointers, car-buying data, and so on. Who dared challenge "the 'Mir" when he dispensed his wisdom? And don't let the conversation turn to women, particularly what to do when having trouble getting or keeping one. He would listen for a while with a bemused look on his face until he could stand no more and would hush the place with a slight wave of his hand and say, "Listen, fellas, I've fucked more girls than all of you, so let me tell you how to handle this. Now, this situation requires some delicacy. What you gotta tell her . . . "

Five years ago, Amir had opened his own shop in Camden, a city about a half-hour's drive away. Myles wasn't sure how much he was making, but when he once told him what he made teaching, Amir looked horrified and said, "How do you survive on that?" So, Myles was pretty confident that he was doing well.

As a child, Myles had taken his father's advice one step further and also wanted to learn how to do female hair as well. Their mother ran a small beauty salon in the same building as the barbershop, and Myles often went with her to the salon. This caused his father a great deal of stress because he feared that he might have a fairy in his midst, but Myles honestly couldn't understand his worry. To him, it seemed natural to spend time in the company of women getting dolled up and looking and smelling good rather than to be shoulder to shoulder with a bunch of loud-mouthed, idle-ass brothers talking shit.

So a compromise was struck, allowing him to spend every other weekend with his mother. Ignoring Amir's sneers, he learned to wash, cut, crimp, weave, bob, braid, and style hair as well as any of the female hairdressers.

Myles just figured that if their father was right about people always being willing to pay for hair care, he definitely would rather be in the demand of women than men.

"You're offering to help me?" Amir picked up a plate and slid it on the bar.

"What's so hard to believe about that?" Myles said as he slid a plate on the other side of the bar.

"Well, I would've thought you had a busy day planned, you know, finding more thoroughbreds and hiding them from your brother."

"I wasn't hiding her, Amir. That's the first time I've had her over."

"Had her over what? A chair? A table?"

Wasn't it a bit early in the morning for this?

"No, Amir. I'm not even sure if she likes me."

"I think she does," Amir said as he slid under the bar.

Myles waited for him to get down with his warm-up set before he asked him, "Why do you say that?"

"I just got that vibe from her."

"Why, because her chin didn't hit the sidewalk when she saw you?"

"Exactly. I didn't catch her looking at my finger to see if I was married, either. So I figured she must be into you, or a lesbian," he said, laughing.

"Seriously, why do you think she liked me?"

"The way she looked at you, especially when you were playing with Deja. The way she hung on your words. The way I saw her laughing at whatever you were saying while I was at the light waiting for it to change. Her body language, that kind of stuff."

Myles digested that as he lay down on the bench for his warm-up set. For once he hoped Amir was right.

"So what's her story?" he asked.

He did promise him the biography. Myles was better equipped to give it to him now. He put the bar back on the stand.

"Her name is Marisa Marrero. She's an attorney

who practices in the D.C. area, is twenty-nine years old, and she graduated from Georgetown Law School near the top of her class. Four years ago, she was offered a position by one of the most prestigious firms in the city. Marisa thinks that the fact that she is Latin, black, and a female made her an attractive hire for them—you know, being able to kill three birds with one stone—but she was better qualified than most of the white men out there anyway. She says the money is very good, but the types of cases she's delegated and the work that she does isn't very fulfilling.

"So, last year she was a guest panelist on some local TV show in D.C. She caught the eye of some broadcasting company—she told me the name but I can't remember it—and they approached her about doing her own shows here in Philly, radio and TV."

"Like Springer or some shit?" Amir asked.

"No, I think it's more serious, a political-oriented show that would address issues of importance to the Latin community. You know that TV show *Conexion Latina* that comes on Saturdays at seven on channel ten?"

"Yeah, the one with that old dude with the toupee."

"Yeah, well, she's the new host. In addition, she's got a radio gig on WLAT, that new Spanish station in town. From five to nine Monday through Thursday, she'll be doing a call-in show. Interviewing politicians, fielding legal questions, talking with prominent members of the Latino community. Writers, artists, whoever is in town."

"No Fridays?" Amir asked.

"That's what I asked. On Fridays she'll tape the TV show. On Friday nights WLAT plays nonstop salsa and merengue."

"What about practicing law?"

"She's taking a year leave to see if this is something she'd rather do."

"Hmm. And her being so telegenic could only help her."

"And she's very well spoken. She has a good voice for radio."

"What about her family?"

"I think her mother and father are both deceased. She mentioned an aunt, but I know she's dead. I think the rest of her family is in Cuba."

"What about *her* family? She doesn't have any kids?"

"Nope."

"She don't have a man either?"

"Nope. Or at least none that she thought was important enough to mention to me."

"I don't know. That's a pretty girl not to have a man." Amir picked up another plate and slid it on the bar. "So, where's she gonna live up here? In the city?"

"Yesterday she looked at a vacant apartment in my building."

"In your building?" Amir looked at Myles and started laughing. "And how did she find out about the vacancy?"

"I told her. So what?"

"I know how your mind works, that's what. She'll

need someone to show her around . . . yeah, you'll be in close proximity, readily available, Mr. Handyman. You'll insinuate your way into her life as well as her heart."

Damn, he does know me, Myles thought. "Is there a point to this?"

"Yes, there is, Myles. I keep telling you that you can't expect relationships with women to unfold like some storybook romance. You start by planning these things out and get frustrated when the woman deviates from your script. Of course she's gonna deviate. She doesn't even know she's a character in your drama."

"You mean, romantic comedy," Myles said, laughing.

"No, I mean *drama*. 'Cause that's what is caused when they start to believe you're trying to manipulate them. Then it becomes a tragedy. Be honest. Even though you just met this woman, you've probably already pictured her as your wife and the mother of your children, haven't you?"

Myles had already imagined him and Marisa reenacting the scene from *Roots* together. The one where the mother gives birth and the father lifts their newborn baby up to the stars.

"Don't be silly, of course I haven't."

"Yeah, right. Your mind is so cluttered with poems and love songs—you're a romantic fool."

"Amir, please, I'm hardly that bad. You act as though I'm totally clueless. And what makes you such an authority, anyway?"

"Whatever. I don't know what I'm talking about, then. I've seduced many, many, *many* women, but I don't know anything about the way a woman's mind works. I'm happily married to a sweet, wonderful sister who loves me to death, but I don't know anything about sustaining a relationship. I've been your brother for almost twenty-nine years, but I don't know your failings and weaknesses. You're right, I'm no authority."

"Exactly," Myles said. Amir was getting pissed, as he usually did when he thought Myles wasn't listening to him. When this happened he became quiet, like he was washing his hands of him. Myles knew that Amir just had his best interests at heart, but he didn't always want to hear it.

"Don't act a fool with this one, bookworm," he finally offered. He lay down on the bench and finished his second warm-up set.

As Amir was getting up, Myles noticed Brian walking into the gym. They gave each other a "whatup" nod, then Brian headed into the locker room.

"So what are you trying to do today," Amir asked, wiping his face with a towel.

"Put four forty-five on there."

Amir looked at him over his towel. "Are you serious?"

"Yeah, we're maxing out today, right?" Myles answered casually.

"All right," Amir said, a little disbelieving. He put the additional plates on the bar as Myles sat down and rewrapped his wrists. The most Myles had ever gotten up cleanly was four hundred and five, and that had been a struggle. But today he felt strong for some reason. He went through a series of arm-stretching exercises as Amir waited.

"You ready?" Amir asked.

"Not yet," Myles said. He walked over to get a drink of water, and then came back and sat on the bench. He saw Brian come out of the locker room. Now he was ready.

"Let's go," he said, lying down. Amir went into position to give him a spot.

He heard the gym noise subside, and he knew it was because all eyes were on him. He wrapped his hands around the bar and took a deep breath. "On three," he said.

"Okay."

Myles took another deep breath. "One, two . . ."

He and Amir lifted the bar off the stand. The bar was bending because of the amount of weight on it. When it was positioned directly above Myles's chest, Amir let it go.

Myles brought the bar down to his chest and rested. Exhaling, he then began the surge upward, centralizing his power and exploding like Amir had taught him.

Under his great strain the bar moved up slowly. At one point Amir was tempted to grab it, fearing it was too much weight for him. But though the bar's rise was agonizingly slow, it was continuous. Myles straightened his arms, until he finally, triumphantly held the bar above his head. Amir took hold of the bar and helped him put it back on the stand.

"Daaaamn!" Amir said.

Myles sat up, completely exhausted. He looked around. The gym returned to normal as people resumed their workouts. A couple of guys gave him a thumbs-up. He spotted Brian sitting at the pectoral machine. So did Amir.

"Yo, Brian, come here," he called out.

Brian sauntered over to them.

"Did you see that shit, Brian? Damn! Four forty-five! Yo, I see five hundred pounds being a possibility down the road," Amir said.

Brian acted unimpressed. "Nigga *oughta* be lifting that much. Look how big he is."

"Yeah, but before it was just fat, now it's muscle," Amir answered.

Brian sucked his teeth. "I wanna see him pee into a cup."

"Don't hate, Brian. You know my boy ain't 'roided up."

"Yeah, right."

Myles didn't like them speaking over him like he wasn't there, but was still too spent to talk.

"It must be his new girlfriend."

He glared at Amir. If his arms didn't feel like spaghetti, he would've strangled him.

"What?" Brian suddenly perked up. "Who is it? Some desperate-ass spinster?"

"Nah. Myles has pulled himself a bad-ass babe."

"I don't know what he's talking about," Myles said, standing up. Damn, Amir had a big mouth.

"I didn't think so," Brian said, then looked at Amir. "Myles couldn't pull lint out of a dryer."

"Whatever," Myles said.

"He couldn't pull a muscle. The only thing he can pull is his pud!" He and Amir laughed heartily.

"All right, Brian, be on your way," Myles said. "You know I can only tolerate you in small doses."

"Peeeeace." Brian walked back to the pec deck still laughing.

Myles looked at Amir, waiting for an explanation. "What? I shouldn't have mentioned the girl? My bad. Remember, I'm no authority." He flashed a big, unapologetic grin.

☃ Eleven

Marisa hung up the phone. Myles hadn't been home, but she left him a message thanking him for dinner yesterday, and to tell him that she had decided to take the apartment. She got up from her desk and went to the window of her new office. So this was the City of Brotherly Love. She knew very little about Philadelphia, other than that the WLAT building was located in Center City.

Though her official start date wasn't for a couple more weeks yet, she had decided to come in today rather than drive back to D.C. Yesterday she had put a change of clothes in her truck before she drove up. She was going to crash at Jackie's, but decided she'd rather be alone and got a hotel room in the city instead.

"You busy?" Cassandra asked, knocking on Marisa's open office door.

"No, come in and have a seat."

"So how's it going?"

Cassandra Hildago had been introduced to her by David when she came up last week. She was going to be the producer of her radio show. Marisa was glad, because they had hit it off right away.

"Fine, thanks."

"I'm excited about the show, Marisa. We're going to have fun."

"You're excited because you're a pro at this. I'm mostly nervous."

"Oh, please, Marisa. You'll be fine. The company must think highly of you. They gave you the best producer they have."

Marisa laughed.

Cassandra looked around Marisa's office. "So when you gonna move the rest of your things in?"

"Like what?" Marisa asked. She figured except for a plant or two and maybe a little artwork, she was done.

"For one, you don't have any photographs on your desk. I know you're not married, but what, no *beau*?" she asked, saying it like a starry-eyed teenager and clasping her hands dramatically for effect.

Marisa laughed. "No, nobody special right now."

"Uh-oh, don't let that get around. There are a lot of sharks working here."

"Thanks for the warning," Marisa said.

"Warning nothing, I'm just letting you know I got dibs."

They both laughed.

An intern named Liz hurried into the office, looking flustered.

"Oh, I'm sorry to interrupt. Sandra, V.A. is here," she said excitedly.

"Speaking of sharks," Cassandra replied.

Another young intern whose name Marisa couldn't

remember poked her head in the door. "He's coming!" she said and rushed away.

"Where you going?" Liz called after her.

"To fix my makeup, girl. I don't want him to see me like this."

"Good idea." Liz ran out after her.

"Who's coming, for heaven's sake? They're acting like it's the second coming," Marisa said.

Cassandra laughed. "Victor Andujar. But don't compare him to Jesus. They both may walk on water, but Victor wouldn't be caught dead in sandals."

Marisa heard the sound of men's voices in the hallway. David stopped at her door.

"Marisa, you free?"

"Come on in."

David walked into her office. He was followed by a handsome caramel-colored man in an expensive suit. It was tailor-cut to accentuate what looked to be an extremely taut body. He had light brown eyes and curly black hair that practically invited a woman to run her fingers through it. Now Marisa could see what all the fuss was about. This guy was worth it.

"I'd like for you to meet someone. This is my fraternity brother, Victor Andujar. Victor, Marisa Marrero."

Victor stepped forward and gently took Marisa's extended hand into his, putting his other hand on top. "It's a pleasure to meet you, Marisa."

"The pleasure's mine," she said smoothly.

"And you remember Cassandra," David said.

"Of course, nice seeing you again, Cassandra," Victor said, still looking at Marisa.

"Victor," David said, "you're looking at the future

drive-time queen of Philadelphia. We were lucky
enough to steal her away from the legal profession.
Marisa, Victor here is also a hot-shot lawyer."

"Oh?"

"Yes, though I don't know about the hot-shot
part," Victor said.

"Don't let him fool you," David said. "In the
world of Philadelphia's movers and shakers, Victor
is a rising star."

Victor finally took his eyes off Marisa and looked
at David. "What do you mean, *rising*?"

They both laughed and Marisa allowed a smile. So
he had some substance to back up the looks.

"Well, ladies, we'll let you get back to what you
were doing," David said.

"Marisa, I'm president of the Association of Latino
Lawyers here in Philly. We'd love to have you as a
member, even if you're not currently practicing. We
should get together sometime," Victor said.

"Yes, we should."

Victor smiled at her again. He looked over at Cassandra for the first time. "Ladies, you have a pleas-
ant day."

"You, too," Marisa said.

Cassandra gave him a quick, halfhearted smile.

Victor and David left the office.

Marisa looked at Cassandra. Cassandra was holding up her index finger as if telling her to wait a
second. She got up and looked out into the hallway.
When she saw it was safe, she closed the office door.

"Marisa, can I speak to you off the record? You
know, like that lawyer-client confidentiality thing
you guys have."

"Sure, Cassandra."

"I can't stand that smooth-talking snake. He looks good, I'll give him that, but he's slimy as Jell-O."

There's always room for Jell-O, Marisa thought. "Yeah?"

"Yeah," Cassandra continued, hardly needing any prompting. "He used to date my cousin's friend—I met her once, a real sweet, pretty girl—who is a CPA over in Jersey somewhere, I think. Well, he wined and dined the hell out of her. I mean, they were real hot and heavy for a while, you couldn't tell this girl that Victor wasn't the greatest thing walking. Then one day he takes her out to eat at some fancy restaurant. I mean, the works, violinist, champagne, everything. She thinks that maybe, he might be popping the question. Then, *bam!* Out of the blue he ends it. Tells her some bullshit about her 'not being ambitious enough' for him. Do you believe that? The gall." Cassandra shook her head.

"Wow," Marisa said quietly.

"Yeah, my cousin says her friend still doesn't know what hit her. Here she was thinking she was in a relationship. Girlfriend didn't realize she was just auditioning for the part. I guess she just didn't make the cut." Cassandra looked at Marisa and grinned mischievously. "He seems to have taken a real liking to you, however."

Marisa clasped her hands together like Cassandra had done earlier. "Oohh, do you really think so?" she asked dramatically. " 'Cause my heart is just all a-flutter," she added, fanning herself and making them both laugh.

After Cassandra left the office, Marisa chewed the

end of her pencil. She wondered if Victor was as good at taking his lumps as he was at dishing them out.

Later that day Myles went over to Carlos and Jackie's house. After he had gotten back from the gym, he had received Marisa's message that she had decided to take the apartment. Despite his initial reservations, he decided he was happy that she was going to be so close.

Jackie was at work, and Carlos was watching some old movie on cable.

"What up, bro?" Carlos said, letting him in.

"Not much, what are you doing?"

"Enjoying my last few weeks of freedom before school starts."

"I hear you."

Myles sat down on the couch. He was dying to tell Carlos about Marisa. "Yo, 'Los, you know that girl I was asking Jackie about?"

"Yeah, her name is Marisa, right?"

"That's the one. Anyway, I saw her yesterday."

"Where?"

"She came by my apartment."

Carlos took his eyes off the movie long enough to look over at him. "Yeah? She drove all the way from Silver Spring just to see you?"

"You act like I'm not worth the trip! She also came by to look at the vacant apartment in my building . . ." Wait a second, Myles thought. He never told him she was from Silver Spring.

"Then what happened?" he asked.

"I'll tell you in a second. Carlos, you got anything to drink?"

"No, we're camels," he said sarcastically. "You know where the kitchen is."

Myles got up to go to the kitchen but instead came up behind Carlos's chair. In a flash he put him in a sleeper hold.

"What—damn, *cabron*, that hurts!"

"All right, cockmeat, how did you know that Marisa was from Silver Spring?"

He started laughing. "Ow, ow—you told me."

"That's bullshit."

"No, it isn't . . . the other night when you stopped by. Let go!"

"No, I didn't, you lying sack of shit." Myles applied more pressure.

"All right, all right, she was Jackie's roommate in college, now let go!"

He let him go.

"Damn, you trying to cut off my circulation?"

Myles was piecing it together. He knew that Marisa had gone to Georgetown Law School, but he didn't know where she went to college. He knew Jackie was from Baltimore and attended the University of Maryland. That's where she and Carlos had met.

"So Marisa went to the University of Maryland, too?"

"Yeah."

"So why all the deception?"

"Because Jackie didn't think you would be amenable to the idea of meeting another one of her girlfriends, and that even if you did agree to it, your attitude would've sucked from the start. I told you she takes her matchmaking seriously. But mainly, she didn't want you asking me a whole bunch of questions about Marisa's past."

That's valid, Myles thought. Part of Myles was dying to know, but he was too scared of what Carlos might say, because he already liked her so much. He decided he didn't want to know.

Carlos knew what he was thinking. "Now, I wouldn't let Jackie set you up with a total skank, would I?"

"I don't know, Brutus. Who knows the bounds of your treachery?"

"Don't get holier-than-thou on me. I wonder who it was that suggested to Jackie that she get me a beeper."

He had Myles there.

"But how were they gonna keep it a secret from me?" Myles thought back to the night of the party, when Jackie and Marisa had pretended like they hadn't seen each other in eons, and how each had lied to him about the extent of their friendship.

"Jackie felt that by the time you found out, you would be so into Marisa you wouldn't care."

She had a point. Foisting Marisa on somebody was like forcing somebody to eat filet mignon. "But what did Marisa have to gain by this chicanery?"

"She wanted to see what you looked like before she dated you. She doesn't trust Jackie's judgment. And as far as you eventually finding out the truth, I don't think she anticipated being involved with you."

Myles's heart started to pound as he prepared to

ask the million-dollar question. Carlos could be of some use after all.

"So, what does she think now?"

"Yo, bro, she likes you, I can tell. She came over here last night after she left your place."

"She did?"

"Yeah, man, listen. Jackie and I could both tell that she liked you, even though Marisa isn't the type to kiss and tell." He walked over to Myles and extended his fist. "Sorry about the deception, but to be honest, yo, I didn't think you would care if it worked out, and if it didn't, nothing was lost anyway."

"That's true," Myles said, giving him a pound. " 'Los, she's damn near a goddess."

The smile dropped off Carlos's face. "See, right there is a problem. Don't romanticize Marisa or go putting her on any pedestals. She has her baggage and bullshit with her just like any other woman. If you start worshipping at the shrine of Marisa, you'll get a kick in the teeth, trust me."

"I wonder how long it's going to take Marisa to reveal herself," Myles said.

"The way I see it, they can't keep it a secret for too long. They're gonna wanna hang out together and stuff. Just don't tell them you know. I don't want to hear Jackie's mouth."

"No problem. So you really think she likes me?"

"Yeah, and I was a little surprised at how she was acting last night. I thought maybe she went to some other man's place by mistake. What did you get, some kind of intravenous charm infusion?"

"Very funny, beeper-boy."

❧ Twelve

Miles was getting his mail when he bumped into Marisa coming down the stairs. In transit was about the only way he had seen her since she had moved into the apartment. She always seemed to be coming or going.

"Hello."

"Good morning."

"So you all settled in, then?" he asked.

"Yeah, I'm about done."

"I should hope so. With all these people I've seen delivering stuff for the past week, I thought the Queen of Sheba was moving in."

She smiled. "Hey, I like to be comfortable."

"So, where you headed now?"

"Over to the radio station."

"When do you start?"

"My first day on air is Monday. I'm going over to tape some more promos now."

"Oh, okay, I won't hold you up."

"You're not," she said, sensing he wanted to talk

to her longer. "So, Myles, I need someone to show me around town. Are you available?"

"Sure, whenever you're free."

She suppressed a smile. He had perked right up when she suggested they get together. "What about tomorrow?"

Damn, Myles thought. Tomorrow was the Saturday that he had promised to take the twins to the zoo. They had been talking about it all week. Maybe he could see Marisa afterward.

"Marisa, I'm taking my nieces to the zoo tomorrow, but I'll be free later."

"The zoo? Can I come?"

"You want to come to the zoo with us?" Myles was surprised.

"Are you kidding? I'd love it. Besides, I saw on the news how the Philadelphia Zoo had these white lions, and I want to see them."

"Well, you're most certainly welcome to join us."

"So what time are we leaving?" she asked.

"Ten o'clock. I'll come by and get you."

"Are you sure it isn't out of your way, coming by and picking me up?" she teased.

"A little bit. I'll have to leave early to allow time for that extra thirty feet I'll have to travel."

"Great, see you then."

"Yeah, I'll see you later."

She smiled sweetly, put on her sunglasses, and walked outside. Well, Myles, you definitely passed the "character" test, she thought as she disengaged her car alarm. Marisa liked the fact that he had been unwilling to disappoint his nieces to go out with a woman he wanted. Unless maybe he wasn't as

hooked as she thought. As she drove away, she subtly glanced over her shoulder. No, he was definitely
hooked. He was still standing there watching her. It
reminded her of the party, when he had gotten
busted staring at her ass. She smiled to herself. What
had he said that night? Oh, yeah, "I thought I misplaced my keys." Marisa laughed aloud.

Myles watched Marisa disappear, then decided
he'd better go upstairs. When he got to his apartment, he called Carlos to tell him that Marisa was
going with him to the zoo, so his services were no
longer required. After he got off the phone, he took
a deep breath. He was happy that Marisa was setting
some time aside for him. He knew that this was probably the first time to herself that she'd had since she
moved in, and he was happy that she wanted to
spend it with him.

When he entered Amir's shop, there were three
other barbers working beside him. One was an older
man named Willie. The other two were young guys
in their early twenties named Omar and Gerard. As
usual his brother had everybody laughing, and he
was playing to a full house because the place was
packed. He nodded at Myles when he saw him enter
but did not speak, lest he mess up his comedic flow.

". . . A good woman is like a tasty dish made with
many different spices. You want her to possess the
ingredients for motherhood such as patience, consis-
tency, knowledge, some tolerance, and so forth. You
also want her to have the qualities of a good wife—"

"Like being faithful," a customer said.

"Puh-lease, you know that. First and foremost is

fidelity. That's the main thing. Then, sprinkle in some understanding, dice up some devotion, classiness, add a generous spoonful of respect, and a smidgen of piousness. Chop off a huge piece of loving nature, add that to the mix, and stir repeatedly. Now, before you're done, you want to pray over it. You ask that God imbue her with the skill to be a wizard in the kitchen. And in the bedroom, you want a little—"

"Skank in her?" the customer offered.

"What! Are you crazy?" Amir gave the man an exaggerated double-take. "I was gonna say a little 'freak' in her, I don't want no skank in my woman! What do you think this is? I ain't trying to make no prostitute soup!"

The fellas in the shop fell out all over the place in laughter. Myles just shook his head, trying not to laugh at his silly ass.

"So you ready for school, teacher?" Willie asked Myles after the room calmed down.

"Don't remind me. Whether or not I'm ready, it's still coming, Willie."

"I don't know how you put up with those bad-behind kids. Worst thing they ever did was take corporal punishment out of school," he said.

"You know," one of the customers added, "if teachers and principals could whip those little bastards, all of these so-called discipline problems would be over."

"Hell, it's to the point where DYFS's got parents scared to death," another customer said.

Myles put in his two cents' worth. "One of my students told his mother that he would call DYFS on her if she ever tried to spank him."

The sound of men sucking their teeth and saying "shiiit" came from every direction. The opinions then came fast and furious:

"If a child of mine ever told me that he was gonna call DYFS, I'd help him pack. He'd have 'ward of the state' written all over his ass."

"You know, I hope he enjoys his foster parents!"

"I'll be damned if I'm gonna be held hostage by some ungrateful little fucker . . ."

"A nigga I'm feeding, clothing, and putting a roof over his head gonna tell me what I better not do?"

Myles let them go on and turned to Amir.

"Marisa's coming with me and the twins to the zoo tomorrow."

"Yeah?"

"Yeah, I bumped into her this morning."

"That's cool." He turned the chair of the man he was cutting to get a better angle. "What time are you coming to get them?"

"Ten o'clock."

"So you're not playing ball tomorrow?"

"Nah, I'll pass."

"I'll see if Omar or Gerard will take your place. Ten o'clock, huh?"

"Is that okay?"

"Yeah, it's fine. I was just wondering what time the girls would be gone, to see if I could chase Kenya around the house before coming in to work."

"You're such a romantic."

"Hey, I like to keep the magic alive in my marriage."

*   *   *

"Come in," Marisa said, smiling. She let Myles in and then went into her bedroom. "Wow," he said. Her place looked sensational, as if it was professionally done. Her living room set was off-white and made of a leather so soft that it almost seemed a sin to sit on it. She had a coffee table with thick marble legs and glass so clear that he could barely see it. Across the room was a huge television and stereo system inside an expensive-looking wall unit. A matching bookcase stood in the corner. He was too far away to read the book titles, but he recognized *Tar Baby* by its distinctive green cover. On the end table, which matched the coffee table, lying facedown was *Cien años de soledad* by Gabriel Gárcia Márquez. Marisa came out of the bedroom rubbing lotion on her hands.

"Your place looks amazing, Marisa."

"Thank you. I don't have much music here, so I'd like to borrow some more of your CDs, if possible."

"Anytime. I see you're reading *One Hundred Years of Solitude*."

"Rereading it. I haven't read it since college."

"Me either. Maybe I should reread it too. The English version, of course."

"That would be nice, then we could have a literary discussion." Marisa walked over to the couch and sat down next to him.

"So you said nieces plural, right? Does Deja have a sister?"

"Yes, a twin. Her name is Jade."

"You mean to tell me that there are two of those cuties? I'm so excited."

"You like kids?"

"Well-behaved ones."

"Well, you'll like these two, then. Kenya and my brother keep a tight rein on them. If it was up to me, they would be spoiled beyond redemption."

"I'll bet. So you ready?" She went over to the table and picked up her purse and sunglasses.

"Yeah," he said, standing up. Myles wondered what she had meant by that "I'll bet."

Jade opened the door for them at Amir's house.

"Hi, fairy-tale princess. Where are we going today?"

"To the *shooo*," she answered.

"Exactly," Myles said. In the living room, Kenya was putting the final touches on Deja's hair.

"Kenya, this is Marisa. Marisa, Kenya."

"It's a pleasure," Marisa said, extending her hand.

"Likewise," Kenya said. "Though I hope you'll still think so after a day out with these two kids, three if you include Myles—be still, Deja."

Marisa looked over at him and smiled. "I'm sure I'll be fine."

Myles gave Kenya a fake look of irritation.

"Hi, Deja," Marisa said, smiling down at her.

"Hi," Deja said softly.

"And this is Jade, Marisa." He picked her up and kissed her on her cheek.

"Hello, Jade."

"Hel-lo."

"You're done, Deja," Kenya said, finishing up on her hair. "You and Jade go get your lunches off the kitchen table."

They scurried off excitedly.

"Your daughters are adorable, Kenya. How old are they?" Marisa said.

"Thank you, they'll be four next month."

"Amir went to work?" Myles asked.

"Yeah, you just missed him. It's funny. He usually leaves early on Saturday. I don't know what he was hanging around for."

Myles was hoping that Kenya didn't think Amir was hanging around to see Marisa. For once, his brother was innocent.

The girls came running back into the living room.

"Slow down, please," Kenya said. "Myles, what time do you think you'll be back?"

"I don't know, about three or four, is that okay?"

"That's fine. Come give me a kiss," she said to the twins.

They went over to their mother and dutifully kissed her, but were clearly dying to leave. Myles smiled at the scene. It seemed like only yesterday that they would cry if she was going to be out of their sight for one minute.

"I know you're going to be good, right?"

"Yes, Mommy," they said in unison.

"Let's go, ladies," Myles said.

"It was nice meeting you, Kenya," Marisa said.

"The pleasure was mine. Hopefully, the girls won't disillusion you to the point where it'll be our only meeting."

When they got to the zoo, Marisa commented on how quiet the girls had been during the ride.

"They're just being shy around you. Watch, by the end of the day they'll be fighting for your attention."

When they got to the entrance, Marisa tried to pay for her own way. Myles was appalled.

"Marisa, you're here as my guest," he said as he handed his money to the attendant. "Two adults, two children please."

"The way I remember it, I pretty much invited myself," she said. "So, I should pay my own way."

"Marisa, you're killing me, you're really killing me."

She laughed at his apparent distress and finally relented.

They walked into the zoo and looked around. It was busy, full of respectable families enjoying one of the last summer weekends.

They started walking among the ditlerent exhibits. It didn't take long for the girls to warm to Marisa, and after a while they began asking "Ree-sa" about the animals as much as they asked Myles.

When they stopped at the petting zoo, Myles noticed the man working there checking Marisa out. That in itself was bad enough because Myles knew that the brother saw that he was with her, but this cat was leering so bad he wasn't paying attention to the animals he was supposed to be tending. It was like he was starving and Marisa was a plateful of buttermilk biscuits. Myles was hot. Damn, he thought, if the dude had to look, he could at least be discreet. He was disrespecting Myles by doing it so openly.

After some time of the girls watching the animals, Marisa watching the girls, the worker watching Marisa, and Myles watching the worker, the girls decided they had had enough. Marisa took them to the ladies' room to wash their hands. Myles took the opportunity to confront him.

"My man, what's up?"

The worker smirked, sucked his teeth, and derisively nodded his head at Myles. Which, as any brother worth his salt will tell you, is the international code for "check this fool out."

Myles had been holding out hope up to that point that maybe he'd misinterpreted the whole thing. He half expected a "Shorty with you? Oh, my bad, yo" or something along those lines. But no, this asshole *knew* she was with him and therefore was showing him zero consideration. Needless to say, his flip response pissed Myles off.

"What, pussy?! Don't make me climb this fence and drag your ass through that sheep shit."

The worker looked at Myles more carefully, to judge whether he was crazy enough to do it. Either he must not have been too sure, or he got a good look at Myles's size, because he strolled to the far end of the pen before answering.

"Man, go 'head somewhere."

"I'll tell you what, I'll go ahead. Just tell me what time you get off work. Bump all this talking, what time you get off work, zookeep?"

He didn't answer. Myles suddenly became aware that because of the distance between them, he'd been shouting. He noticed the horrified faces of the other patrons. They were giving him "did we walk into the middle of some gangster shit?" looks.

Myles gave the guy one more clenched-teeth, head-nodding, dirty look and headed over to the rest room area to wait for Marisa and the girls.

The gorillas were next. The exhibit was set up so that they had a choice of either watching the gorillas from outside in their faux natural habitat, or watching them from inside through a thick pane of glass. They decided to go inside, where they could get a better look. Just a few feet away was a female holding her baby. The baby was chewing on what looked like lettuce.

Much to the delight of the twins, Marisa started mimicking the baby gorilla. She chewed in an exaggerated manner, matching the animal's mastication. She then put her mouth about an inch from the glass and kept on chewing. The baby gorilla leaned over to the glass and put his mouth up against it.

Marisa puckered her lips. The gorilla did likewise, and it looked like they were kissing. Myles thought it was disgusting, the shreds of lettuce and saliva dripping down the gorilla's chin. But the twins screamed with joy at the sight of the gorilla trying to kiss Marisa. It was pretty funny, Myles had to admit. Maybe he was just jealous. (Was it possible to be jealous of a primate?)

As he had predicted, the twins really took to Marisa. They were soon clamoring to be boosted in her arms for closer looks at things. Marisa impressed Myles with how she took the time to explain things to them and helped them with their pronunciation of the different animals. She really seemed to enjoy the girls' company, because she was in no hurry to leave.

The last exhibit they saw were the much ballyhooed white lions. There were two cubs along with a mother, and they were eliciting "oohs" and "aahs" from the people passing by. The twins didn't ask

Myles or Marisa any questions, but instead huddled together near the barrier. Myles thought that he saw Deja ask Jade what they were and she told her. He liked the way they got along, the way they looked out for each other.

When they left the zoo, it was nearly two o'clock and all four of them were hungry. Myles decided to drive to a Colombian/Cuban restaurant in North Philly, which would take at least another thirty minutes to get to. The girls were already starting to grouse with impatience, so Marisa sat with them in the backseat to unpack and help serve them their lunches so they wouldn't convert his car into too much of a disaster area.

The restaurant was not crowded during the day but was very busy at night, particularly Fridays and Saturdays when the club upstairs played salsa and merengue. By the time they were seated by the hostess, Marisa was already swaying to the song on the restaurant's sound system.

"How did you find out about this place?" she asked.

"I read a review of it in the *Inquirer* when it first opened last year. This is my fourth time here, twice with Carlos and once with Sylvia."

"Who's Sylvia?"

"A Puerto Rican secretary at my school. I only come here if I have someone with me who can speak Spanish."

"So, Sylvia, huh?" She looked at him suspiciously.

"Strictly platonic, I assure you."

"Mmm-hmm, I'll bet," she said. "Isn't that right, Jade? I'll bet."

"I'll bet," Jade said, and Marisa laughed.

A pretty waitress named Esperanza came over to take their order. Marisa got the steak with black beans and yellow rice. Myles ordered the same (after of course insisting that they have *empanadas* as an appetizer), and they ordered some ice cream for the girls. After Esperanza took their menus away, Marisa looked at him.

"Speaking of Carlos, I have a confession to make."

"Yes."

"I went to college with Jackie and Carlos. In fact, I was one of the bridesmaids at their wedding."

He gave her his best tortured, tormented man act. He looked at her, he looked off into space, he looked back at her, and then he looked skyward as if he was imploring the heavens to give him the strength to get through this shocking revelation.

"But, Marisa, why? . . . *Why?*" he asked in a deeply pained voice.

She wasn't buying his dramatics. "So Carlos told you, huh?"

"I thank God that one of you conspirators had a thimbleful of character."

"Myles, I—"

At that point the waitress came back with the girls' ice cream and everybody's beverages. Marisa thanked her before turning her attention back to Myles.

"Myles, I apologize. What can I say?" she said, playing along with his "pain."

"Secrecy and deception is no way to start a relationship."

"You're right," she said. "I tell you what, my life

is an open book. Ask me anything and I promise I'll be forthcoming and truthful."

A very intriguing proposition indeed, but Myles wasn't interested. If this girl wasn't an angel, he wasn't about to forfeit his God-given right to believe that she was.

"No need for that, Marisa. However, this is a very serious setback in your quest to become 'good peoples.' "

"Noon, Myles, not that!" she cried. "Let me make it up to you."

Myles scoffed at her suggestion. "What could you possibly do to make up for such an offense?"

He felt the instep of her foot sliding up his calf under the table.

"You're probably right," she said dejectedly, "but let me know if you think of something." She coyly looked up from taking a sip of her drink.

Satisfied with the surprise that lit up his face, she slipped her foot back in her shoe and turned her attention to Deja.

"So, did you have fun today?" she asked.

"Yes," Deja said, in between spoonfuls of her ice cream.

"Which animal did you like the best?"

Deja mulled this question over. "I liked the white tigers, but their stripes fell off," she said sadly.

Marisa and Myles looked at each other and laughed.

"That was a lion, baby," he said. He gave Deja a hug and wiped her mouth with a napkin. "They don't have stripes."

"See," she said to Jade, "I told you you was lyin'."

*   *   *

When they dropped the girls off, Amir was home. Myles thought they had walked in on something because Kenya's hair was disheveled and they both were acting a little happy. He figured that Amir had chosen to chase Kenya around the house as soon as he got off work.

Deja came in and hugged her father excitedly. She was the textbook definition of a daddy's girl. Jade went to her mother and started talking animatedly about the different animals she had seen at the zoo.

"So, Marisa," Kenya said after telling the girls to put away their lunch boxes, "I see you're still standing. You must be a gamer."

Marisa answered, "Your girls are so mannerable and sweet." She then looked at Myles and smiled. "I really had a good time today."

"That's good," Amir said, "because we were wondering if you wanted to go to a function tonight."

"What kind of function?" Myles asked, a little irritated. Amir could have pulled him aside and told him about it before asking her.

"Progressive Lawndale Men is having a get-together at the Ramada in Cherry Hill. Me and Kenya thought we'd go check it out."

Oh yeah, Myles did remember him mentioning something about it last week in the gym. He had told Amir he wasn't interested in going, so now he was asking Marisa because he knew that if she wanted to go, Myles's ass would surely follow. Progressive Lawndale Men, or P.L.M. for short, had started out as a group of friends who used to deejay parties back in high school and college. Then they were known as "Bumrush Productions," but as they got older (and after attending the Million Man March) they changed their name to the more mature and civic-minded P.L.M. Now they were involved with a number of projects around Lawndale, like volunteering at the boys and girls club, checking on the elderly, and literacy programs.

But their original deejay proclivity still reared its head now and then, and they would throw these socials, or functions, which professed to be for professionals to mingle and network, but were really just more opportunities for them to shake their asses and party.

"Carlos called over here looking for you, Myles," Kenya said. "He told me that he and Jackie are going."

"Well, it sounds like fun, but I think Myles may have already made other plans," Marisa said dejectedly.

Myles could tell in her voice that she wanted to go. It was thoughtful of her to at least give him the option of changing his plans. You could tell that Marisa was raised right. A less classy woman wouldn't have given him a second thought when given a golden opportunity to dress up, show out, and get her drink on at a party.

"I can give you the guided tour anytime, Marisa. Let's go there instead," he said.

"*Bueno*," she said slyly, as if she knew all along that he was going to do just what she wanted him to.

"It'll give you a chance to meet some more good peoples," Myles offered as the reason for changing his mind, to give the pretense that he was still in charge. "I'll stop by Vince's on the way home to pick up some tickets," he said to Amir.

"No need for that, my man." Amir walked over to the dining room table and picked up two tickets. "When he dropped by earlier to give us ours, I bought two more off him. Here you go," he said, handing Myles the tickets.

How considerate of him, Myles thought. Like Jackie, he and Kenya didn't think he got out and socialized enough.

"How can I ever repay your kindness?" Myles asked dryly, taking the tickets.

"By repaying me for the tickets," Amir said, holding his hand out.

When Marisa and Myles got back to their building, it was almost five o'clock. She told him that she was going to her apartment to take a nap and that she would be ready at eight to leave for the Ramada. Before she went in, Myles hinted to her that Winston needed walking, but she just looked at him as if to say "Negro, please." She went into her apartment and closed the door, leaving Myles in the hallway.

After walking Winston, Myles called Carlos's house. Jackie picked up the phone. He decided to take the opportunity to mess with her. She was the final member of the treacherous trio and the only one who didn't know he was on to them.

"What up, Jackie? Is 'Los there?"

"No, he went to the store."

"Well, all right," he said, pretending he was getting off the phone and knowing that she would stop him.

"Wait, are you going to the thing at the Ramada tonight?" she asked.

"Yeah, I thought I'd check it out," he replied. She paused. She was waiting for him to provide additional information, which he had no intention of doing.

"So, you're going alone?" she finally said.

"Yes. Should I be going with somebody?"

"No . . . no." She then took a different approach. "So, where have you been all day?"

"I took the twins to the zoo."

"By yourself?"

"What, you don't think I can handle them by myself?"

"When Carlos called Amir's looking for you, Kenya said you were with Marisa."

"Oh, yeah, I was. I figured she wasn't worth mentioning, since you barely know her."

"Oh." Jackie clearly suspected that he knew something but wasn't quite sure. "So, why don't you ask her to go to the party?"

"Why don't you ask her, or don't you know your own bridesmaid's phone number?"

She started laughing. "You ain't shit!"

"Oh, I ain't shit?"

"Who told you?" she asked.

Myles decided not to give Carlos up. "Marisa told me today."

"Oh, so what do you think of my girl? She's the bomb, ain't she?"

He wasn't going down that road with Jackie.

"She's very nice, Jackie. She's coming to the party with me tonight."

"Where is she now?" she asked. Myles decided she was going to try to get more info from Marisa.

"She's taking a nap," he said.

"There?"

Please. If she was lying down here, she wouldn't be sleeping, that's for damn sure.

"No, at her place."

"Well, I won't bother her, then. You just better not act like an asshole."

"Jackie, would you tell a wolf not to chase sheep? Would you tell a reverend not to preach the gospel? Would you tell an infant not to suckle? No, you wouldn't. So why tell me not to be an asshole? It's what I do, it's my nature," Myles said.

"You are so simple," she said, laughing.

While Marisa was still in slumberland, Myles was in his place deciding what he was going to wear. Shouldn't he be the one sleeping while she obsessed over her clothing selection? Wasn't it traditional for the woman to take everything out of her closet, lay it out on her bed, try everything on, and then say disgustedly, "I don't have anything to wear"?

He finally chose an olive green suit and a soft cream-colored shirt. He then lay down and set his alarm for seven-fifteen, which would give him enough time to shower and primp before it was time to leave. *Primp?* Wasn't that also something women traditionally did? *Groom* was the word he was looking for. It was the very essence of masculinity, i.e., bridegroom. He would shower and groom before he left. That was better. No, it wasn't really, because he was still lying in bed plagued by trivial, stupid thoughts instead of sleeping. He was behaving like a prepubescent schoolgirl going to her first cotillion. Geesh, he thought, if he became any softer, the Guardians of Manhood were gonna come and foreclose on his dick.

He could imagine the auction, straight out of the *Antiques Road Show*:

"Our next item is a male organ procured from a man who too often forgot about the expected behavior and responsibility that comes with the possession of a penis. As you can see, it's a swarthy negro dick, of a good size and in mint condition because of its rarity of use. Do I have a bid . . . ?"

"Do the balls come with it, Johnny?"

"Yes, they do. They've had a very unfortunate existence as the owner relinquished sovereignty of them to whatever girl he was involved with at the time . . ."

♟ Thirteen

Myles knocked on Marisa's apartment door at exactly eight o'clock. She opened it partially, hiding her body behind the door.

"Hi," she said.

"Hello," he replied.

"Nice suit," she said.

"Thank you." Was she going to let him in or what?

"I really like that shirt."

Oh yeah, he had forgotten that she liked cream. "Thank you. I'd return the compliment, but I can't see your outfit because you are blocking the door."

"I'm just soaking in all of your finery."

"Well, that's understandable, take your time." He then started striking a number of different body-building poses, each one more ridiculous than the one before. She stifled her laughter.

"Get your silly self in here," she said, opening the door.

She was wearing a short, sleek, fire engine red backless dress with matching pumps. The dress was cut to accentuate her small, well-formed breasts. She had two bracelets on her right arm and a watch on her left.

"You look . . . presentable," he said matter-of-factly.

"Thank God," she said, wiping her brow dramatically. "I was hoping I wouldn't embarrass you. Come in and sit down, I'll be ready in a minute."

Myles came in and quickly took a chair that would afford him the best view of her as she walked by. She went to the end table and picked up a pair of diamond earrings and then headed toward her bathroom.

"Myles, did you misplace your keys again?" she said from the hallway, not even bothering to turn around.

Damn, what, did she have eyes in the back of her head?

"No, actually, I was looking at your *culo*."

From the bathroom, she laughed at his bluntness. "Well, you better stop. You don't want anything popping out again," she said. Then she returned to the living room, adjusting one of her earrings. "True that?"

"True that. So, you ready?"

"Yes." She went to the closet and pulled out a red (damn, more red? she wasn't playing around) and black shawl and put it on.

"You want me to drive?" she asked.

"It's up to you."

She handed Myles her keys and said, "You drive."

"So, is it me?" Myles asked. He was doing about seventy on the interstate in Marisa's Mercedes.

"Oh, definitely," she said. "You have the regal bearing of a man born to drive a Benz. It's just . . . it's just so you," she said.

"So when can I drive the Range Rover so you can tell me how good I look in it?" he asked.

"It's in my garage back home. I'll go get it in the fall," she said. "So what kind of music do they play at this place?"

"Club music mostly. Some dancehall, and rap . . . sorry, *chula*, no salsa. Maybe you and I can go to a Latin club some other time."

"You like salsa?"

Myles gave her a double-take. "What? Don't make me turn this car around and go get my red sports coat."

"Can you dance salsa?" she asked.

"Can I dance sal—your homegirl Jackie didn't tell you? Why, in some quarters I'm known as Myles Magnifico, the salsa maestro." He had to take salsa and merengue dancing lessons for four months last winter, but she didn't need to know all that.

He turned off at the Cherry Hill exit.

"Wow, you're full of surprises, aren't you?" she said.

"Let me help you out. What I think you're trying to say is that I'm a Renaissance man, the quintessential *paquete toda.*"

"Total package, huh? That remains to be seen," she said as she fixed those luscious eyes on him. She should have to register them with the District Attorney's office, Myles thought, because they were lethal weapons. He was melting under her gaze.

"It's hot in here," he said. "How do you turn on the air conditioning?"

"Air conditioning?" she said incredulously. "Myles, we have the top down."

When they arrived, people were already swarming into the building. Myles pulled up to the front and handed the keys to the valet. Before he could get to his wallet, Marisa gave the young man a tip.

She waited for Myles to walk around the car and extended her hand to him. He quickly accepted it, and they walked into the ballroom.

Myles had to hand it to Vince and his crew. They had gone from deejaying house parties when they were kids to putting together professional, fully catered, classy affairs. They were smart enough to hire people who knew what they were doing instead of trying to do everything themselves. The place looked magnificent. It was packed, too. It looked like all of Lawndale and half of Camden was here.

"C'mon, I love this song," Marisa said, almost yanking Myles's arm out of the socket as she pulled him toward the dance floor.

They were playing a remixed version of "That's the Way Love Is" by Ten City.

They reached a spot acceptable to Marisa and she started to move.

Her entire body seemed to turn into a beguiling tool of subtle enticement. She rhythmically twisted, bounced, and bobbed in ways that would be illegal in at least five Southern states. At certain points she turned around and gave him a little, just enough to tease him, but didn't let him push up on that ass she knew he liked so much. But Myles especially enjoyed when she draped her arms around his neck and locked him under her gaze while jiggling her slim hips to the beat.

After a couple of songs, they went to get something to drink in the adjoining room where the food and beverages were served. There, they bumped into Carlos and Brian Boyd.

"Hey, fellas," Myles said.

"What's up," Carlos said. Brian mumbled a greeting but was too distracted by Marisa to say anything intelligible.

"Marisa, this is Brian," Myles said in a perfunctory manner.

"A pleasure to meet you," he said, trying to be suave. Myles looked at him. If his dumb ass tried to kiss her hand, there was gonna be a brouhaha in here.

"Likewise," she said. "So, where's Jackie?" she asked Carlos.

"And Tracy?" Myles added slyly.

"They went to the ladies' room," Carlos said, chuckling at Myles's sudden concern for Tracy's whereabouts.

"Speaking of which, where is it?" Marisa asked.

"I'll tell you if you promise to save a dance for me," Brian said, trying his hardest to make eye contact with Marisa. Myles glared at him.

"It's down that hallway on the left, Marisa," Carlos said.

"Excuse me," she said. "I'll be back."

"I'll count the seconds until your return, Lady in Red," Myles said.

She liked that, as he knew she would. A woman

always likes when a man is willing to embarrass himself in front of other men for her. She smiled at him before walking away. When she was out of earshot, he turned his attention to Brian.

"You're gonna learn to stop playing with me. How you learn is up to you, but trust me, you'll learn."

"What, your date can't dance with anybody but you?" he asked innocently.

"She can dance with everybody else in this place except you, okay?" Myles said. Damn, this guy could push his buttons. Myles had always felt that the only reason Brian went after Tracy was because he knew that Myles had some interest in her. Brian was probably tiring of her by now and looking to move on. If it could be once again at Myles's expense, so much the better.

"Can't you guys chill for one night? This is our last week off before school starts, and I want to enjoy it. I'll tell y'all one thing: much as these tickets cost, if y'all get me kicked out over some bullshit, it's gonna be three of us fighting," Carlos said.

"Hey, ain't nothing wrong with me," Brian said. "I don't know why he's getting upset."

Myles decided to ignore him. He knew Brian always had a lot of mouth when there were other people around. The thought of Marisa coming out of the ladies' room and seeing security dragging him out was enough for Myles to let it go.

Brian smirked at him.

Carlos, anxious to change the subject, asked Myles if he had seen Amir and Kenya.

"No," Myles said, looking around. "I've never seen one of these so crowded."

The D.J. was mixing in the club version of "As." Myles knew Stevie Wonder sang the original, but wasn't sure who did this version, which he liked a lot. He had to remember to ask Vince.

Jackie and Tracy came back into the room. They were with Marisa, but she went to the opposite side to get something to drink.

"Hello, ladies," Myles said as Jackie and Tracy joined their group.

"Hey, Myles," Tracy said.

"Hel-lo," Jackie said sweetly, like she had something on him. Myles wondered what Marisa had told her in the ladies' room.

"So you ready?" Brian asked Tracy.

"Yeah."

"C'mon, Jackie, I like this song," Carlos said.

"Okay. See ya later, Myles." They all left.

Marisa walked over and handed Myles some punch.

"Five hundred and two—thank you," he said, accepting the punch.

"*Que?*"

"Five hundred and two, the number of seconds you were gone."

She blushed. "Just drink your punch, Romeo."

He sipped it. "No pink swimmingo?"

"Nope, up until I found that out, I thought this was an upscale event."

He laughed.

The D.J. announced that it was time for a "Lumberjack Welcome Home Dance," and the room quickly emptied as the people hurried to the ballroom.

Marisa asked him, "What did he say? A lumber-jack what?"

"A Lumberjack Welcome Home Dance," Myles said, quickly taking a sip of his drink.

The pounding bass line of the club song started to reverberate through the walls.

"What is that?" she asked.

"You don't want to know," he said.

"But I do," she said, and pulled him toward the door, almost making Myles spill his punch. Marisa couldn't believe her eyes. Tsk, tsk, Myles thought. Shock was often the first reaction when the uniniti-ated peeped at the mighty spectacle that was the Lumberjack.

Spaced out along the perimeter, all the females formed a huge square. Inside the square were the men. Directly in front of each woman was her indi-vidual man. They faced each other, the woman with her back against the wall. The men then collectively marched backward four steps and then forward four steps to the beat of the music and in step with each other. All the while pumping their arms and balled fists like "lumberjacks" (but really Myles always thought it looked more like the walk that the seven dwarfs from *Snow White* did), hence the name. Now the women danced in place. Their man would ap-proach (four steps forward), then retreat (four steps backward). Approach, then retreat. Every fourth ap-proach, the women would turn around to face the wall. The D.J. would "break" the song with a series of scratches, and the men would freak their ladies from behind while they did the "give it up" along the wall (hence, the "welcome home" part of the dance's name). The D.J. would say, "Now, break!" the song would kick back in, and the couple would resume their original positions.

Some of the couples were creative. Some of the women would act like they were stirring a pot when the men were marching to and fro. Some would act like they were shelling beans, taking clothes down off a line, or some other household chore. Some men would steal a kiss every time they approached. Some of the more shameless men (as if all of it wasn't hedonistic) would turn their backs to their woman and let themselves get felt up. The "hotter" the couple, the greater the degree of debauchery. Kenya, for instance, would have her palms pressed against the wall, and Amir would have her backside up in the air during the breaks.

The D.J. was the key. Early in the song the breaks were short, and the couples would barely have time to "get their freak on." However, the closer the song came to the end, the longer the breaks became. Then the D.J. would exhort the couples to act even more frolicsome.

"C'mon, ladies, your man's been working hard all day . . . You have been too. The kids got on your nerves, you say . . . you know what you need . . . ya need, ya need, ya neeeed . . . Some recreation, some recreation . . . recreation . . . *recreation* . . ."

Recreation? Some of the more adventuresome couples looked like they were aiming for procreation. Myles snuck a peek at Marisa. She was mesmerized, but he couldn't tell whether she was titillated or appalled. No harm in asking, he figured.

He cleared his throat. She didn't budge. He cleared

it again, but still no response. "Ahem," he coughed out louder this time.

"Are you trying to get my attention, or is there something wrong with your throat?" She folded her arms and looked at him agitatedly.

"Uh, my throat. It's just a little dry," he said sheepishly.

"Well, I would suggest you go get something to drink, 'cause I just *know* you're not asking me to participate in this tawdry display."

"Uh, of course not."

"Humph," she said, not convinced. "Well?"

"W-what?"

"Go get something to drink, then!"

Feeling scolded, Myles was obediently turning around to go get something to drink when he spotted a glint in her eye. She quickly turned her back to him.

"Marisa?"

"You still here?" she said, refusing to turn around and burying her chin in her chest.

She was playing with him.

Damn, he was embarrassed. Why did he have such trouble reading this girl?

"I'm through," Myles said, storming away. "Where's the door so I can escape this madness?"

She followed him. "Wait, Myles, I apologize," she said, laughing.

"Oh, you sound soooo contrite," he said sarcastically as he walked through the lobby, Marisa in hot pursuit. "I'm going home."

"How?" she asked.

"I'm driving," he said.

"But it's my car," she protested.

"Don't bother me with trivial details." He opened the front door and went outside, after taking care to hold it long enough so it wouldn't close on her. "I know one thing, you can forget about being 'good peoples.' I'm gonna tell the membership committee to remove your name from consideration."

"No!" she yelped, and finally caught up. She got in front of him and blocked his path.

"What can I do to get back in your good graces?" she asked repentantly.

"*Nada.*"

"Oh, please." She wrapped her arms around him and put her head against his chest.

Aaah, sweet nirvana, Myles thought. Must be strong . . . though, she feels so good . . . don't give in, it's another ploy . . . but her hair is so fragrant . . . still, must hold out for more.

"Sorry, I just don't think you're redeemable." It would have been more convincing if he dramatically pushed her away when he said this, but he didn't have the will power.

"How about for a kiss? Can I still be under consideration, for a kiss?"

"Maybe."

She tilted her head up and leaned forward to kiss him. She paused about three inches from his mouth so he could feel her breath.

"Maybe?" she whispered.

His mouth started to water, but he didn't succumb.

"Maybe," he said.

She leaned in even closer. "Maybe?" She flicked his top lip with her tongue.

Myles could no longer resist. He cradled her face

in his hands and kissed her, trying to draw the sweet syrup from her lips.

She pulled back slightly and looked inquiringly at him. He wondered what she was thinking.

"Kiss me again," she said.

No problem. This time he took it slow, gently touching her top and bottom lip separately, before kissing her fully.

He could tell by the look on her face that she liked that. He could also feel her shivering, so he took off his suit jacket and set it over her shoulders.

She looked alluring in the moonlight. Her beauty had a romantic, lyrical quality, like a timeless work of art.

"Let's go back inside," he said, only because he thought she wanted to.

"Let's go home instead."

Who was he to argue?

During the ride back from Cherry Hill, Marisa was subdued. She leaned her seat back and stared out the window. She seemed to be deep in thought, and Myles was tempted to ask her what it was but thought better of it. She held his right hand in her left, leaving him only one hand to drive. Myles gave her hand a gentle squeeze. Whenever he held the hand of a woman he loved, it always made his heart sing. Damn, he thought, did he just say he loved Marisa?

He pulled into the parking lot of their building. Marisa still wasn't talking. She got out of the car and waited for him to come around. When he joined her, she took his hand again.

At her door, Myles hesitated, but Marisa nudged

him along to his place. "I want to listen to some music," she said, finally breaking her silence.

They went inside. "What do you want to drink?" he asked.

"Do you still have any of those coolers left?" she asked, sitting on the couch.

"Yes. You can turn on that lamp, Marisa." Myles went into the kitchen and pulled a cooler out of the refrigerator. In its light he saw Winston sleeping on his favorite blanket in the corner. Some watchdog.

Marisa had turned the lamp to its dimmest setting.

"*Baseball Tonight* is on," he said, handing her the drink and glass.

"Nah—thank you, not tonight." She set it on the table. "Come sit next to me."

He came around the table and sat on the couch. She shifted her weight so that she was leaning against his shoulder.

"So, Cuban girl, why are you so quiet?" he asked.

She nuzzled her head against his neck. "I don't have anything to say."

"Do you still want to hear some music?"

"That would be nice."

"Anything in particular?"

"You choose," she said, tilting so that he could get up.

Myles went over to the CD rack. Nothing too obvious, he thought. Something understated but romantic. He chose some classics; L.T.D's "Concentrate on You" and "Overjoyed" by Stevie, and put them in the five-disc carousel. As he pondered what else to pick Marisa squeezed in between him and the CD rack and pressed the Play button on the system.

Myles put his arms around her and started kissing her hair.

She must've *really* liked that because she immediately jerked back and leaned the weight of her body against him. She sucked her bottom lip and exhaled hard, and wrapped her arms around the back of his head while he slid his around her waist. So, like Samson, her hair was her weakness. Myles made a mental note.

With her writhing and heaving up against him, Myles's erection was threatening to really make its presence felt.

"What's that?" she asked.

"L.T.D., Jeffrey Osborne's old group."

"No," she said, turning around and facing him. "What's *that*?" She slid her hand down and started massaging his penis through his pants. She leaned in close and whispered in a kittenish voice in his ear, "What's *that*, huh, Myles? What's that?"

He was incapable of a response.

"What are you gonna do with *that*, huh, Myles?" She wrapped her arms around him, untucked his shirt, and slid her fingernails up and down Myles's bare back. She used her thigh in place of where her hands had been, rubbing it against him.

"What do you want, Myles?" she whispered, licking his earlobe.

He'd had enough. He pulled her down on the carpet, narrowly missing hitting his head on the edge of the coffee table.

After letting Myles devour her neck, chin, and shoulders, she sat up, unbuckled his pants, and slid them and his boxers down to his knees and pulled them off. She then sat astride him and slowly swayed her head side to side so that her hair brushed along his face.

"Do you have a sheath for your sword, babe?" she asked.

Damn, Myles thought. Now his stupid ass was going to have to go to the store. What if she was in the mood for *Baseball Tonight* by the time he got back?

"No, I'm sorry, I don't."

"Don't worry about it."

Marisa reached into her purse on the coffee table. She ripped open the box, pulled out a condom, unwrapped it and put it on him. Myles tried to slide her dress over her head, but she pushed his hands away.

She stood up, her feet still on either side of his hips. She slid her dress over her head and threw it on the couch. Next came her panties, which she took off and tossed aside, all the while she kept her eyes riveted on his. She then put her right foot on his chest, and Myles slid her pump off. They repeated the same with her left foot. Myles then tried to sit up so he could put his hands on her, but she put her foot in his chest and forced him back on the floor.

Marisa just stood over him with her hands on her hips, in all her splendid, naked magnificence with a devilish look on her face, never once losing eye contact. She slowly swayed her hips side to side while Myles held her ankles, the only part of her body that was within his reach.

She shook her legs free and stepped up to around his chest, her feet just beneath his armpits. Myles

moved his hands to her calves and held on for
dear life.

"Hi," she said. She was standing over him like
some tigress who had just stalked and caught her
prey, but refused to put it out of its misery.

"Hi," he said, leaving his mouth open to catch any
stray drippings on his tongue.

"So how you been?" she asked.

"Fine. I met this girl that I'm absolutely loco over."

"Absolutely and completely?" She started swaying
again to the music, this time touching her breasts.

"*Si*," Myles panted, feeling like he was going to
implode.

She turned her torso around and looked at his
penis, standing at full attention and motioning for
her to come back and play.

"I see," she said, then quickly locked her eyes back
on his. "You are *loco por me!*"

"That's what I've been trying to tell you," he said,
urging Marisa down on him by bending her knees.

"Uhn-uhn," she said, again shaking her legs free
of his hands. "First, tell me those three words that I
want to hear."

Was that all? No problem, Myles thought.

"I love you." He tried to sit up so he could grab
hold of her hips.

"Please," Marisa said scornfully, and put her foot
into his chest with such force that Myles hit his head
on the carpet. "No, Myles. I want you to tell me what
I am."

"Umm, you're incredibly beautiful?"

She sucked her teeth. Wrong answer.

She stepped back and sat down on his beckoning

erection. It was a luxurious, sweet fit. Myles knew it felt good to her too, because she closed her eyes, temporarily releasing him from her steady gaze.

"Oh, Myles," she whispered, rotating her hips.

Myles put his hands on her hips and thought how amazing she felt, how lucky he was.

"Tell me I'm good peoples," she said.

"You are *definitely* good peoples. You're such good peoples," he panted.

She leaned forward and kissed his mouth and started thrusting faster. She was damn strong for being small.

"No, tell me . . . I'm . . . gooooood peoples," she said between breaths.

"Oh God, Marisa, you're gooooood peoples," he repeated frantically.

"No." She pushed herself up off his shoulders and stood over him again. Myles thought he was going to cry.

"Say it like you mean it."

"Marisa, as God is my witness, as sure as I am of my love for my mother and my as yet unborn children, I hereby declare unabashedly and unequivocally that you are the very embodiment of good peoples! Please, have mercy on me, I beg you not to stop again!" Myles yelled, no doubt disturbing everybody within a twenty-mile radius. A tear actually rolled from the corner of his eye and onto the carpet. She had broken him.

"That's better." She smiled slyly and slid him back into her. She leaned all the way forward so she could whisper in his ear while gyrating.

"Mmm . . . this is so . . . nice."

The scent of her hair was intoxicating.

"Marisa, why do you smell so good, huh?"

She raised her face directly above his.

"Because I do," she cooed and swirled her tongue in his mouth.

"Oh, Marisa, why do you taste so sweet?"

"Because I do." Her breathing was getting more and more rapid as were her thrusts.

"But why do you feel so *perfect*?"

"Because I . . . do!" Marisa cried and collapsed on top of him. When she realized Myles hadn't ejaculated yet, she concentrated on him, working him over while he tried to hold out. He lasted a good thirty seconds.

She fell back on top of him. Myles stroked her hair and kissed her forehead gratefully.

Sometime later, they moved to the bedroom. After making love again, Myles lay on his back with Marisa stretched out on her side, gently tracing a rhythmic pattern with light fingers over his chest.

"What's that from?" she asked, touching his scar.

Myles hated having this conversation with women, but he figured it was best to get it over with.

"I was born with a heart murmur. When I was a child, I passed out in school. The doctors discovered that there wasn't enough blood going to my heart, so they had to go inside and widen my aortic valve."

He girded himself for the inevitable question: "Are you okay now?" or "You're not gonna die on me, are you?"

Marisa said neither. Instead, she rolled over on top of him.

"Poor Myles, born with a broken heart." She leaned down and kissed his scar. "Do you want me to fix it for you?"

He smiled at her. Maybe she really was an angel.

Myles rolled her onto her back, went under the sheets, and they proceeded to fix each other.

♘ Fourteen

David excused himself from the table to call home. The meeting was winding down. The topic had been *The Marisa Marrero Show*, which was set to make its debut that Monday. Cassandra looked at Marisa and smiled.

"They sure are giving you a lot of leeway as to how the show runs, Marisa."

"I just hope I justify it," Marisa said, taking a sip of her coffee.

"You're still worried? Marisa, John Lopes hasn't gotten where he has by being wrong. A couple of weeks from now, you're gonna wonder what all your concern was about."

Marisa smiled at her. She really liked Cassandra.

"So what are you doing with the rest of your day, Cassandra?"

"I think I'm going to go over to the—" Cassandra stopped short and looked toward the front of the restaurant. "Oh, Lord."

"What?" Marisa asked, turning around to look in the same direction. She saw David talking to Victor Andujar.

"I gotta get out of here," Cassandra said, getting up from the table.

Marisa laughed. "He can't be that bad."

Cassandra looked at her. "He can't? I'll see you later."

"Bye."

She headed for the exit just as Victor and David started walking over to the table. David stopped Cassandra on her way out to say something, while Victor kept walking toward Marisa, striding like a man full of purpose.

"*Hola*, counselor." He smiled at her.

"Hi, Mr. Andujar." She returned his smile. Marisa noticed that the eyes of every woman in the restaurant had followed Victor across the room.

"Please, Marisa, Mr. Andujar is my father. I'm Victor." He sat down.

"How's the food?" he asked.

"Good, especially the home fries," she answered. Victor was wearing a gleaming all-white outfit and looked damn good in it. David walked back over to the table.

"I'm gonna head out," he said, gathering his notes.

"You're leaving?" Victor asked.

"Sorry, Vic," David said, "my daughter has a recital."

"I was hoping that I had lucked into having some company," Victor said. He looked at Marisa. "You don't have anywhere you have to run to, do you?"

"No, I can stay a little longer."

David told Marisa he would see her at the station and said goodbye. Victor went up to the buffet table to fix himself a plate.

When Marisa first saw Victor she had suspected a setup. When she saw the look that he gave her when she didn't leave with David, she knew her suspicions had been confirmed. Marisa looked at her watch. She was supposed to be meeting Jackie to catch a matinee.

Victor returned to the table with a plate of French toast and sausage. "So, Marisa," he said, sitting down, "the Association of Latino Lawyers is having a fund-raiser Friday. It would be nice if you could make it."

Marisa was too involved in watching Victor eat to answer. He had cut up his stack of French toast into four perfect squares and separated them, creating space in the middle of his plate, where he moved his sausage. Then he cut up each of the four square stacks of bread into smaller, identical ones. He picked up the syrup and poured the exact amount on each of the four small stacks. Any excess syrup ran toward the sausage in the middle of the plate to flavor them. She had never seen anyone eat breakfast so neatly.

"So?" he asked.

Marisa realized that Victor was waiting for a response. But Marisa knew she hadn't heard a question.

"Pardon?"

"The dinner Friday, Marisa. It's a formal affair to raise money for programs for at-risk youth, so the money goes to a good cause. It's five hundred dollars a plate, which is probably chump change to you."

Marisa wondered where that came from. She hoped that David hadn't been so unprofessional as to tell his friend what her salary was.

"I have to tape the TV show Friday, Victor."

"But won't that be done by around three o'clock? The dinner doesn't start until seven . . ."

So she was right, he was getting inside information.

"C'mon, Marisa, it's for a good cause. You wouldn't deny the *ninos*, would you, Marisa? They're our future. Aren't they worth the investment?" he said, jabbing his fork in the air for emphasis.

Marisa smiled. He sounded like a politician on the campaign trail. A real "go-getter" as her Aunt Esther used to say. In fact, Victor was the type of man that Esther always wanted for Marisa. He was ambitious, smart, and successful. And his good looks only added to his appeal. "Okay, Victor, I'll go."

"There you go," he said casually, like it had been a foregone conclusion the whole time. Well, he certainly doesn't lack confidence, Marisa thought.

He took another bite and put his fork down. He stood up. "Thanks for staying with me, Marisa."

Marisa looked at his plate. He had barely eaten any of his food.

"You're finished?"

"I have somewhere to be," he said, and flipped a twenty-dollar bill onto the table. He flashed a sly grin at Marisa. A grin that Marisa took to mean that his work here was finished. "May I walk you out?"

"Sure," Marisa said, gathering her purse.

When they reached the parking lot, Victor deactivated his alarm. He had parked his Ferrari right next to Marisa's car.

"Would I be wrong to guess that you have aspirations for a higher office someday, Mayor Andujar?"

"Yes and no, Marisa," Victor said, sliding into his car and closing the door. He turned it on and rolled down the window. "I do have plans for a higher office, but it most certainly is gonna be a higher office than mayor," he said, checking his appearance in the rearview mirror. "I'll have my secretary call the station with the details about Friday, okay?" He started backing up.

"That'll be fine," Marisa said, stepping back.

"Goodbye, Marisa."

"Bye, Victor." She watched as he wheeled his car around to the exit and drove off, quickly accelerating.

He always seemed to be in a hurry, Marisa thought as she slid into her car. She decided that come Friday, she was going to wear something that would make him slow down and take notice.

As her mind raced to the different dresses in her closet, she caught herself. She had just spent the night—a wonderful night—with one man, and she already had a date with another? "Investment in the children," her ass. She had a good idea what was on Victor's mind. And what of her? She could've easily made a donation without attending the dinner. She put the key in the ignition and feverishly worked to collect her thoughts.

She decided that it was a positive thing for her to go to the dinner with Victor. One, because she would be able to network and meet some of Philly's most influential people and policy makers, many who would probably make good guests on her show. Second, and on a personal level, it would probably be a wise thing to hedge her bets as far as Myles was concerned. Be cautious. She knew her hot ass had probably made a mistake in giving it up already, but there was nothing she could do about it now. Besides, that shit had felt *right*. She turned the key and started the car. Well, since she *had* already given it up, there was no reason for her not to take advantage of that particular aspect of what Myles had to offer, with him living right down the hall and everything. They are two consenting adults, after all. She laughed at herself, knowing she was trying to justify reasons to continue sleeping with Myles.

She wheeled her car out into traffic. Hell, she didn't know how any of it was going to play out, be it the new job, new city, Myles, Victor, whatever. She decided she would let the different scenarios unfold and react to them accordingly.

Jackie opened the door for Marisa. "What happened, did the meeting run late?"

Marisa decided not to tell her about Victor. "Yeah," she replied as she walked in and sat down. "Where's Carlos?"

"He went to some car show over at the Civic Center in Philly. So, where the hell did you disappear to last night? As if I didn't know."

"It's not like that at all. Get your mind out of the gutter."

"Yeah, right, like I don't know you. You had that hot look about you last night."

"That was your imagination. It was your saucy ass I saw doing that Lumberjack Dance."

"Yeah, but I was in a room full of people. You just waited until you got home before you started slinging wood. Look at you, it doesn't look like you slept a wink."

"I was up all night talking to Myles."

"Yeah? What type of conversation requires those condoms I saw in your purse last night?"

Marisa laughed. In the bathroom of the Ramada last night, Jackie had asked to borrow some lipstick, and Marisa told her to go in her purse and get it. She had forgotten that they were in there. After she and Myles had gotten back from the zoo, she hadn't really gone to lie down but had stepped out to go to the pharmacy. Her stated purpose was to get lotion, nail polish and other toiletries, but the first thing she went for when she got there were the condoms. She had a strong inkling that she was going to want to screw his brains out that night and wanted to be prepared, just in case he wasn't.

She had liked the fact that he wasn't prepared. Since Carlos had told her that Myles wasn't sleeping with anybody, then why would he have condoms? Nor would she have wanted him to buy some for her. Nothing turned her off quicker than a man who was expecting her to put out.

She had thought about leaving them in her apartment instead of putting them in her purse, but she knew better. She might decide to pull over somewhere and do it in the car, under the stars, against a tree, whatever. She could be impetuous like that.

"So, just because a woman has prophylactics in her purse doesn't mean she used them," Marisa said.

"True. Isn't that the same purse that you had last night? Why don't you let me see those pristine, unused Trojans?"

"Go to hell, Jackie," Marisa said, laughing.

"That's where you're going, you hoochie mama. You ought to be ashamed, giving it up already. You're lucky your Aunt Esther has passed, because she sure as hell would be getting a call from me about your scandalous ass."

"Ha, ha."

"So how was it?" Jackie asked.

Marisa smiled. "Tremendous."

"Tremendous? That means he let you be in charge, then."

"I'm not some selfish control freak. I can be . . . giving," Marisa said. She chuckled to herself at her choice of words.

"Marisa, I used to live with you. I know how you like to dominate men, torture them, reduce them to sniveling sycophants, probably because of some deep-rooted hatred of them, but I'm not sure."

"You're a social worker, not a psychiatrist, Jackie. Besides, I'm not like that," Marisa protested.

"You aren't? Let me ask you just one question, but you have to answer it honestly."

"What?"

"Did you, at any time, make him cry last night?"

"Shut up," Marisa said, suppressing her laughter.

"Thought so."

Myles walked into Amir's house. He found him getting ready to leave for work.

"Where is everybody?"

"Kenya took the girls to Storybook Land," he said, adjusting a pair of clippers he had in his hand. He then looked at Myles suspiciously. "You certainly didn't stay long last night. Me and Kenya didn't even know if you had come or not."

Myles shrugged. "Marisa wanted to leave."

"It wasn't her scene, huh?" Amir asked, testing the clippers. They made a loud, irritating buzz.

"No, that wasn't it." Myles paused. "She just liked the scenery at home better."

The buzz stopped. Amir looked at Myles, who was trying to contain his grin and doing a bad job of it.

"What you saying?"

He burst. "What I'm saying is that the girl is a stud-goddess! Do you hear me, Amir? She is not of this earth, I'm telling you! Je-sus Christ!"

Amir laughed at his brother and matched his enthusiasm.

"Yo, nigga! Give me details!" He turned his head off to the side and looked at Myles from the corner of his eye. "So tell me, is she a freak?"

"You know I don't kiss and tell," Myles said, knowing full well he had come over there to do just that.

"How would I know that? You ain't had nothing to tell in so long," Amir said. "I'm just surprised that you still knew how to use it. So, tell me, does she rank in your top five?"

"She's a woman, Amir, not a college basketball team," Myles said, leaning back on the sofa and acting superior.

"You just don't wanna answer 'cause you probably ain't had five."

"Even if that were true, number six, seven, or eight might never come, because I'm telling you, this girl is amazing."

"Whoa, whoa, now," Amir said, "that's just the pussy talking."

"No, I'm telling you, 'Mir, I might soon be off the market," Myles said.

"What! Myles, you were never *on* the market. Now me on the other hand, when Kenya snatched me up, there was rioting in beauty salons from here to Atlanta."

"Amir, I'm telling you, this is The One."

When Myles saw the look his brother gave him, he knew that was something he shouldn't have said, though it was exactly how he felt.

"Where have I heard that before? Hmm . . . I know, Elaine was The One."

"Amir—"

"No, I stand corrected, Marie was The One. No, wait a second, now that I think about it—"

"Your point is made, Amir. But that's ancient history."

"Oh? So now you know the difference between being in love and being in love with the *idea* of being in love?"

"Yep. What? Are you the only one allowed to show growth?" Myles asked, irritated. Why did he have to throw a damper on his exuberance?

Amir walked into the kitchen to get a screwdriver, then rejoined Myles in the living room. "All I'm saying is, just keep your head about you," Amir said without looking up. Before Myles could respond, Amir turned the clippers back on, and continued making his adjustments.

❧ Fifteen

Carlos, Brian, and Myles were in the teachers' lounge. It was the first week of school, before the students arrived, when teachers spent their time going to workshops, getting their classrooms ready, and sitting around doing nothing, which was pretty much what they were doing now.

The past week had been great for Myles. Marisa had started her job at the radio station, and even though he couldn't follow most of it because it was in Spanish, he listened to it avidly. Myles liked to listen to her voice. It made it seem as if she was with him in the room.

Every night she had got home around ten, and usually showed up at his door by ten-thirty. She would be exhausted. Myles had learned that failure was simply not an option with Marisa, which was why she devoted so much energy to making sure her shows went as smoothly as possible. She was taping her first TV show that afternoon and then had a charity function to attend. She told him she probably wouldn't be done until very late, so not to expect her. Which is why he was in no hurry to get home.

Like her, Myles now had two jobs as well. His second job was pampering Marisa, and he was on the clock the minute she came to his door.

She first ate a little of whatever he had made for dinner, and then Myles would bathe, massage, brush, powder, primp, puff, stroke, and kiss her until she fell asleep in his arms. She kept warning him that he was spoiling her and creating a monster, but he really didn't care. First of all, he didn't mind doing for a woman he was into. Second, he didn't think she understood how much he enjoyed holding her in his arms.

The lounge door swung open, and they were joined by Mike Gilliam, Ron Battle, and Tim Walker. Mike and Tim were college students who worked as aides at the school, and Ron taught eighth-grade social studies.

Mike and Tim were arguing about who was the better shortstop, Derek Jeter or Nomar Garciaparra. Everybody else had already gone home except for the secretaries, a security guard, and the custodians. Someone had left the radio on the easy listening station. No one had bothered to change the dial or was paying much attention to it until a particular song came on.

The man was singing to his girl, telling her that their love would overcome everything, including a lack of money. It was one of those songs that everybody knew the words to, but had no idea how they learned it. It certainly wasn't in any of their music collections, but Brian, Carlos, Ron, and Myles started singing along with the vocalist. When they looked at each other and realized they were all singing, it was funny. Carlos took the opportunity to call for a lyrical joust. The rules were simple; you had to change the lyrics to a song on the fly, while keeping pretty much the same meaning. You had to be creative and do it quickly, for there was a time limit. Extra points weren't awarded for vulgarity, though one would have thought so when listening to one of their contests.

"I'm in," Brian said.

"You want some, Myles?"

"No, leave me out of your indecent, sexist repartee," he said, acting like he was above it all.

"I got five bucks on Carlos," Mike said.

"A wise bet, lad," Carlos said.

"I'll cover that," Tim said.

"Your faith in me will be rewarded," Brian told him.

"Same as always, right?" Carlos asked Brian.

"Yeah." They shook hands to agree on their standard ten-dollar bet. "Ron, you be the judge."

Matthew Green, a security guard at the school, walked in. "What's going on?" he asked.

"Brian and Carlos are about to joust to the song that's on the radio," Tim said.

"We're coming to you live from the teachers' lounge at Lawndale Elementary School, where we are pleased to bring you the battle of Carlos 'The Puerto Rican Pontificator' Rrrrrrr-oque and Brian 'The Bawdy Backtalker' Booooooooyyyd," Matthew said, imitating an announcer.

Carlos won the toss but elected to pass, so Brian had to go first. He had fifteen seconds to come up with something. He was ready:

"Even though we ain't got dough,
I'm so in love with you, ho'."

Ron said, "Pass," so now it was Carlos's turn.

"Even though we ain't got bank,
I'm so in love with you, skank."

"Pass."

Tim and Mike chuckled at Carlos's entry. Matthew shushed them with a "quiet, please" like a tennis umpire would do. It was now Brian's turn.

"Even though we're not rich,
I'm so in love with you, bitch."

"Pass."
Carlos:

"Even though we need more
I'm so in love with you, whore."

Brian: "I challenge on the grounds that I-I already used the word 'ho'."

Ron: "Challenge denied. While ho and whore are in the same family, the deviation and distinction is acceptable. Pass."

Brian (after sucking his teeth, to voice his displeasure at the judge's interpretation):

"Even though we ain't got quick cash,
I'm so in love with your trick ass."

"Pass."

"Excellent. Brian just executed a two-syllable rhyme, always a difficult maneuver," Matthew said in a low voice like he really was calling a tennis match.

Carlos:

"Even though we might have wants,
I'm so in love with you, cunt."

"Pass."

Brian:

"Even though we ain't got coin,
I'm so in love with your loins."

"Pass."

Carlos:

"Even though we ain't got shit,
I'm so in love with your clit."

"Pass."

Now the pressure was building, as they started to run out of their lewd, demented entries.

Brian:

"Even though, we ain't got cash,
I'm so in love with you, gash."

An appreciative "ooooh" resonated throughout the room. With his use of "gash" Brian showed he had taken his skills to the next level and that he was taking no prisoners. Carlos was definitely on the ropes.

"Quiet, please. Thank you," Matthew said.

"Pass."

It was now Carlos's turn. Sweat was beading on his forehead, and the tension in the room was thick.

Carlos:

"Even though we ain't got loot-a,
I'm so in love with you, puta."

"I ch-challenge," Brian said immediately. "No *Español* allowed."

"Challenge upheld. Fail," Ron said.

"Why?" Carlos protested.

"No Spanish words."

"But *puta* is part of the common vernacular—"

"I've rendered my decision, Mr. Roque," Ron said authoritatively. "You have five seconds remaining."

"C'mon, Carlos!" Mike yelled.

Carlos was desperately trying to come up with something:

"Even though we ain't got a nickel . . .
". . . I still wanna hit ya where you trickle."

"Fail! Too much deviation from original song's intent. I declare Brian the victor," Ron said. Matthew went back into announcer mode:

"The Bawdy Backtalker has won! Roque never recovered from Boyd's brilliant use of the word gash . . ."

The wagers changed hands.

"Sodas for everybody, on me. Well, really on Carlos," Brian said, rubbing Carlos's nose in it, and showing his typical inability to win gracefully.

Carlos was still arguing with Ron about his decision to disqualify *puta*.

Tim and Mike were rehashing the "highlights" of the contest.

Matthew continued blathering, "Now, back to the studio. Good night."

Good night, indeed. Myles looked at the sorry lot around the room. If the entire school was drenched with gasoline, and their collective dignity was an ignitor, they wouldn't have been able to produce enough flame to light a cigarette.

Brian stood at the soda machine.

"Yo, Myles, you want something diet, right?"

"You're a funny guy, Brian, anybody ever tell you that? No? I didn't think so," Myles answered. While the rest of the men in the room resumed the Garciaparra-Jeter and now Rodriguez debate, Brian sidled over to where Myles was and sat down next to him.

He took a sip of his grape soda, looking at Myles over the can.

"So what's up with that shorty I saw you with at the party?"

"Not much." Myles shrugged, flipping through the *Baseball Weekly* that Tim had brought into the lounge.

Brian studied Myles for a moment, then snickered. "I didn't think so," he said.

"Meaning?" Myles asked, still paying more attention to his magazine than to Brian.

"That girl was way out of your league, son."

Myles looked at Brian. He was about to say something along the lines of "the next time I'm looking at her beautiful naked body, I'll keep that in mind," but decided against it. Why let Brian goad him into cheapening Marisa?

"You're right, Brian," he said. "I wish I was more like you."

"You're being sarcastic, but you really should be taking notes. Bitches love me."

"Oh no, Brian, you got me all wrong, I'm not being sarcastic at all. Evidently, Tracy saw something in you that I couldn't provide her."

"You said it, not me," Brian said, laughing. He stood up, comfortable in his mind that Myles was still the loser that he thought he was. Now that he had once again relegated Myles to his perennial role as a sad-sack, hopeless, no-pussy-getting failure, he decided to throw him a bone.

"You going to the gym tonight?"

Myles nodded his head.

"You've come a long way from the fatboy I remember."

Myles looked up at Brian. His condescension was annoying, but Myles decided to play along. "Thanks, Bri," he said gratefully.

"You just keep plugging away," Brian said as he left to rejoin the group.

Myles shook his head as he walked away. A bigger asshole never lived.

🎵 Sixteen

Marisa walked into the huge ballroom of the Ritz-Carlton, where the charity function was being held. She looked around the room. The exquisite chandeliers, the shiny, smooth marble floor, the men in their black and white dancing with ladies in colorful, expensive gowns, it all looked like something out of a fairy tale. The song that was being played was some standard that Marisa always heard at this type of affair. The orchestra looked like a stiff bunch, though. No hope for salsa tonight.

"That dress is stunning," a voice said from behind.

Marisa turned around and faced Victor. She was wearing a backless, beaded, black evening gown with a high slit up the side. It was form-fitting and showed off her butt, which Marisa wondered how long Victor had been staring at before he spoke. She quickly checked him out. He was wearing the hell out of his tuxedo.

"Thank you."

"As is the woman who wears it."

Marisa smiled.

* * *

Myles and Winston made their way down the steps of the apartment building. They were going to walk to the store to pick up a Sunday paper. When they reached the door, Myles said a quick prayer of thanks when he saw Marisa's car in the lot. Last night he hadn't been able to sleep. He was halfway worried that she had just been a fantastic, sweet dream and that he was just now waking up to his old, staid life. But no, she was real and she was back. "My dream girl has returned, Winston," he said happily. However, his exhilaration at knowing she was back home was tempered by the doubt over where she had been.

The last time he had seen her was early Friday morning when he left for school. He knew she had to tape her TV show and attend some charity thing, but she had never come home. When he had left Saturday morning to work in his father's shop, her car wasn't in the lot. He had called her apartment a couple of times from the shop, and she hadn't been there. After work, he went to Carlos's house. Carlos told him that Jackie had gone to visit her parents in Baltimore, so Myles knew Marisa wasn't with her. Myles hadn't told Carlos about Marisa's disappearing act because he was too embarrassed at his inability to account for her whereabouts.

Last night he was really worried and starting to fear the worst. It was strange because he did see her on *Conexion Latina*, which made its debut in its Saturday time slot. He gave a thought to the possibility that her workaholic ass might be at the station, but he didn't have her office number. And what? She couldn't call him? His emotions had run the gamut, from petty suspicion that she was out with somebody else to genuine fear that something had happened to her. Now that he saw she was home safe, he was grateful. But damn, where the hell had she been?

Marisa lay in bed staring at the ceiling. She heard a door shut in the hallway and figured it was probably Myles taking Winston for a walk. When she had gotten in early that morning, she had found the messages he left on her machine. He was probably wondering who she had been out screwing.

Her mind went back to the charity function Friday night. She felt like she had met every politician in the city of Philadelphia. She had been impressed with the ease with which Victor worked the room, moving about the various groups of people with the self-assurance of a man who knew he belonged. He had a presence that oozed confidence. As he led her around by the hand and introduced her to everyone, Marisa saw many of the women there gritting their teeth with envy as it looked like she and Victor were a couple.

She watched Victor the entire time she was there. He looked right, he smelled right, he danced right, and when Marisa found herself thinking about other things he probably did right, she decided she had better leave. She felt herself slipping fast and was afraid what she might do if she stayed until the end.

Victor walked her to the entrance while they waited for the valet to bring her car around. When he bent to kiss her good-bye, she somehow summoned up the strength to turn her cheek to meet his lips. If Victor was disappointed by this, he didn't show it and went back inside to resume his hob-nobbing.

Instead of going across the bridge back into Jersey, she hooked a left and went down I-95 to her home in Silver Spring. She needed to clear her head—she always found that she did some of her best thinking in the car—and wanted to be alone.

She had needed a couple of nights of sleeping alone, in her house, which she missed more than she thought she would. She had been up under Myles all week, and though her body enjoyed the attention, she was a little concerned about the effect such an arrangement would have on her mentally. The last thing she wanted was to become too dependent on a man for her happiness.

A door closed. That must be Myles coming back in. She suddenly felt the urge to see him.

As Myles unfastened Winston's leash, he looked at his clock: 9:30. He wanted to see Marisa, but decided that since she had apparently gotten in very late, he should let her sleep. They could talk later.

Myles sprawled out on the couch with the Sunday paper beside him on the floor. "Which section do you want, Winston?" he asked.

Winston ignored him and went to his spot in the kitchen and lay down.

"See, that's why you're uninformed. Look, right here, there's an article about the British. You can read what's up with your road dogs back in your motherland."

Myles's ears perked up when he heard a door shut

on the floor. It was either one of the other neighbors or . . .

"Myy-elsss," a voice sing-songed.

Marisa.

"Come in, Marisa, it's open."

She walked in wearing her pajamas and looking for all the world like an adorable little girl, albeit one with unkempt hair. Myles barely had time to move the sports page he was reading out of the way as she walked straight to the couch and collapsed on top of him.

Myles waited for her to say something, like explaining where she had been, but she didn't. She just lay there with her head resting on his chest.

"So, Marisa, where you been?"

"I went to D.C."

Damn, he hadn't thought of calling there. He waited for her to go on, but she apparently didn't feel the need to.

"Why? Is everything okay?"

She turned her head over onto the other side. "Yeah, everything's fine."

Myles looked down at the top of her head. That's it? Everything's fine? What manner of creature was this?

"Marisa, you couldn't call me to let me know?"

She sighed softly. It was early on in their relationship, but time to set ground rules. She decided to let him know right now that she would not be forfeiting any rights or freedoms, including the right to come and go as she pleased. "I'm not used to having to check in, Myles." She felt his heart race under her ear.

"Marisa, it's not about checking in. It's about showing consideration. I haven't heard from you in forty-eight hours and have been worried as hell that something happened to you. To have me sitting here afraid to turn on the news, when it wouldn't have taken you a good ten seconds out of your day to pick up a phone so I can go about *my* day without worry isn't too much to ask. I don't call that checking in, I call that being fair." He put down the newspaper and wrapped his arms around her, sliding her up his body so that he could rest his cheek on her head.

Marisa didn't lift her head to look at him. She had heard his voice crack and knew that he was trying to keep it together, so she didn't want to embarrass him. She could've kicked herself. She had figured that his only worry had been who she was out fucking, not that he may have been worried about *her*. Damn, girl, she thought, had it been so long that she had forgotten it was possible for a man to be concerned for her well-being without having a hidden agenda?

Myles was pissed that he had exposed himself, and was desperately trying to rein in his emotions, which he thought Marisa probably took as a sign of weakness. Too often he had tipped his hand too soon to women and had lost them to men who couldn't care less about them. Men like Brian. He was too easy, not enough of a challenge, or intriguing enough to sustain their interest. He had come to the realization that maybe if you let a woman know you're into them too soon, they assume they can do better than you, and move on to a man more worthy of them. A man they have to work to please. He was determined not to let that happen with Marisa, and here he was already falling into the same old patterns. Getting all worked up because he had been worried about her when any other man would be cursing her out for staying out.

"I apologize. I was wrong."

"That's okay, Marisa."

"No, it isn't. But I promise I'll make it up to you."

He kissed the top of her head. She gave him a squeeze.

Myles wondered whether she truly felt sorry, which was fine, or whether she felt sorry *for him*, which was the kiss of death. Who wants to be around somebody pitiful?

After wondering about this for a couple of minutes, he decided there was nothing he could do about it now. He reached down and picked up the paper to resume his reading. They lay like this for about twenty minutes, before she finally spoke.

"What's so interesting in that paper?" she asked irritably.

"I'm just reading the box scores, why?"

"Because you're ignoring me, that's why. You know our arrangement. I come over and you cater to my every whim, which at the very least requires the use of two hands. Sometimes it requires your lips, tongue, and other assorted appendages as well, but at the bare minimum it demands the use of both of your hands. Don't try to change up on me now."

"You didn't read the fine print. Our deal is null and void if you come in here with your hair looking every which way but done."

"Ouch," she said. "Well, let me go back to my

place . . ." She made a big production out of getting up.

"Nooooo!" Myles said, and dramatically tossed the newspaper aside and pulled her back on top of him. Grabbing her by her arms, he lifted her up in the air and brought her down to him and kissed her forehead. He was always worried about being too rough with her because she was so little. Marisa always wanted to roughhouse; her little ass was always challenging him to wrestle, or jumping on him. But Myles figured with the hours he spent massaging and caressing her, he could indulge her occasionally.

She giggled as he turned her over and hugged her tightly. Myles started stroking her hair.

"So, how you been, comely one?"

"I'm fine now."

She started to make the noise that she made whenever he did something that gave her satisfaction. It was a mix of a purr and a hum that emanated from the back of her throat. The combination of his stroking and her fatigue was also making her slumberous. When he thought she was asleep, he tried to pick up the paper to resume his reading, but she emitted a growl to let him know that she was still very much conscious and in need of more attention.

"Did you watch the show?" she murmured.

"Of course."

"So what did you think?"

"Well, first of all, I thought your skirt was too short."

She gave no reaction, but Myles could tell she didn't like that remark. During the segment when she was in the studio interviewing a Philadelphia councilman, she had been wearing a blue suit with a skirt that showed more than a little leg. The councilman had noticed too and had been flirting with her. Myles couldn't remember verbatim what the fraud had said, but it was something along the lines of:

"What the Latino community as a whole, and particularly our girls, need is more examples of positive role models like you, Ms. Marrero. Here you are, an educated, eloquent, gorgeous young lady."

Gorgeous? And if she had been homely, then what? She wouldn't have been a good role model?

"I did like the cooking segment," Myles said.

"I bet you did, *tu gordito*."

"I also liked when you"—somewhere in his mind, a brain cell was checking to see what *gordito* meant and found it, fatboy—"hey, what do you mean, *gordito*?"

"Well, you're certainly not skinny," she said, rubbing his stomach.

"Unhand me," Myles said, squirming from underneath her.

She laughed at him.

"Sure, laugh at my pain. I have spent endless hours in the gym transforming my body from the chubby mass it's genetically predisposed to be to carve out a presentable physique. Since I figured I'd never be skinny, I have spent years turning pliant flab into muscle, and here you come along and . . ."

She tried to put her arms back around him. He quickly removed them.

"Don't touch me! As I was saying, not all of us

are blessed to be born skinny like you, Ms. Marrero. Or to be born as eye candy like Amir."

"Ohhh, Amir," she moaned. "*Ahi, Papi!* Now you're talking!"

"Wh—what?! Is that what you like?"

"No, no," she said soothingly. "I like you. I mean, look at these broad shoulders, these biceps and pecs. You're a thick, meaty hunk of man, and that's the way I like 'em," she said in a salacious voice. She started rubbing his chest. Myles looked at her warily.

"And Amir?"

"Well, a girl might not be in the mood for steak every night . . ."

"Get out of my presence, you viperous woman!"

"I'm just kidding. Remember, us good peoples have a sense of humor. Amir is far too, um, too pretty for my taste," she said, purposely unconvincing.

Good girl. He let her lie back down on his chest. They started laughing. Myles didn't know why she got such a kick out of him acting silly.

"By the way, since I am now good peoples, how come I haven't been to any meetings yet?" she asked.

"I've been meaning to talk to you about that, Marisa. I'm under investigation for allegedly skirting the normal membership procedure and letting you in for personal gain. A cloud over my good name, can you imagine that?"

"I'm sure you'll be cleared. If not we'll just have to start our own *very* good peoples club."

Myles pulled her close to him. "I love you, Cuban girl."

Oops, he hadn't meant to say that. Idiot! Myles

berated himself. It was too early on for this shit. He didn't want to scare her off.

She didn't say anything, she just lay there with her head on Myles's chest, directly over his heart. It sounded three more thumps before she finally broke the silence.

"I know you do, Myles," she said softly.

He decided to change the subject.

"So, am I a *gordito?*"

"Nah," she said. She then propped herself up on her elbows so she could look him in the eye. "Was I really dressed too provocatively on my show?"

"Hell, yeah," he answered.

"Jerk." She proceeded to punch him in the gut. She made a mental note to wear something even more scandalous on next week's show.

ꝕ Seventeen

Marisa picked up the phone.
"Hello?"

"Hey, pretty lady."

"Hello, Victor. So how have you been?"

"Fine, I just received some great news," he said.

"What's that?"

"I just been retained by two of the families of the kids involved in the Turnpike shooting incident."

Marisa knew the incident he was referring to. Two white state troopers had shot at four college kids during a routine traffic stop. The kids were all either African American or Latino.

"Wow. That's gonna be a high-profile case," she said.

"High-profile? That's an understatement. We're talking national coverage. I'm gonna make my bones with this case, Marisa."

"As well as receive justice for the families? Expose the racial profiling practices used by state troopers? Reveal the systematic, covert racism that exists within the department and how it imperils minority drivers?"

"Of course, Marisa, and you know I'm gonna look damn good doing it," he said.

She laughed. "Well, you're gonna have to come on my show and discuss it."

"Which one, the TV or radio show?"

"Both."

"No problem. That is, as long as you do something for me in return."

"Isn't blackmail beneath you, Victor?"

"Yes, it is. That's why I call this reciprocity."

"What do I have to do?" she asked suspiciously.

"What's that tone of voice for, Marisa? What? You can use me to boost your ratings, but I can't ask you for anything?"

"Of course you can, Victor. Go ahead."

"Good. Let's say that in return for doing each show, you accompany me to dinner at the Four Seasons."

"Victor Andujar, there are about a billion women who would love to go out to a five-star restaurant with you. Why me?"

"I have my reasons. So what's your answer?"

"Okay, a dinner for the shows."

"Uhh-uhh. Two shows, two dinners."

She laughed. "How about one dinner and a doughnut in the green room?"

"That's cute, Marisa, but I didn't say it was negotiable."

"Everything is negotiable, counselor. Make a counteroffer."

"All right. A dinner and a lunch."

"I accept those terms."

"Good," he said. "And, Marisa, one more thing. No running away like you did last time."

The gall of this guy, even if there was some truth in it. "What would I have to run for, Victor? It's *just* dinner."

"True, but you might decide you want dessert."

Marisa rolled her eyes. This guy was too much.

After saying good-bye to Victor, she looked out her office window. Victor was an excellent contact to have in Philadelphia. He seemed to know and be known by everybody. Though she had promised herself that she was going to keep their relationship professional, she would be lying to herself if she didn't admit that he held some allure. *Some* allure? Who was she kidding? Men like Victor held a great deal of allure. They were used to nothing but success with women. It would be like a game to Marisa, to see if she could make a dog heel and make him pay for every woman he'd used and tossed aside.

But she also knew that the parts of her that were drawn to Victor were not the aspects that she should be listening to. They hadn't served her well in the past. Isn't part of growing up, she thought, doing not only what feels right to you, but what you know to be right for you?

Myles came inside the apartment and laid his briefcase on the table. It was full of tests he needed to grade and progress reports he needed to finish. He had stayed very late at school and still wasn't done with them. He usually was good about not letting work pile up on him, but he had been slipping lately.

He walked into the kitchen and poured himself a glass of grape juice. Myles looked in the sink, saw it was empty. That morning he had asked Marisa to take whatever she wanted out of the freezer before she left for work and he would make it for dinner. She must have forgot.

It was understandable, he thought. She'd had a rough night. Around three o'clock in the morning the sound of her voice had woken him up. She was saying something, but he couldn't make it out. In part it was because she was sobbing and also because she was speaking in Spanish. Her face was full of streaks from where previous tears had fallen and more were streaming down her face. Myles hesitated before he woke her up, not sure if he should, but the torment in her voice and grief etched on her face were more than he could bear.

After getting past the initial shock of being startled out of her sleep, she gave Myles such a blank, hollow look that it chilled him. He tried to write off her lack of recognition as residue from her nightmare, but the emptiness in her eyes lingered even after he returned from the bathroom with a damp washcloth for her face. He started wiping her face as she lay there. When he tried to speak to her, she didn't answer. Her only movement was the diminishing upheavals of her chest as her body slowly calmed down.

After a prolonged period of receiving no response from her Myles grew concerned. He sat upright, scooped her in his arms, and cradled her. Being in this position seemed to cause her a great deal of distress, because her shoulders slumped and she started crying again.

Myles turned her around to face him. Her body was limp and pliant, and Myles leaned her against him and clutched her tightly. Her arms dangled lifelessly by her sides.

At this point it selfishly became about him, too. He felt that whatever demons were tormenting her, they were pulling her in a direction away from him. She was receding into a place he wasn't permitted, and that thought scared him to death.

"Marisa, please tell me what's wrong," he pleaded, supporting the back of her head with his hand so he could whisper in her ear. "I adore you, I adore you, I adore you," he kept repeating over and over because he couldn't think of anything else to say.

Now both of them were whimpering.

She finally lifted her arms and wrapped them around his neck, her body's first voluntary movement since he had woken her. Myles was eternally grateful for this small token of affection and proof of acknowledgment.

"I'm in love with you, Marisa." Myles kissed her cheek and held her as tight as possible without killing the poor girl. "Please, don't ever leave me."

Had that been his imagination, or did her grip on his neck slip just a bit?

Myles took some boneless chicken cutlets out of the freezer and put them in the microwave to defrost. He looked at the clock: 6:19.

He turned on the radio, preset to WLAT. A couple of weeks ago, when Marisa had found this out, she messed with him: "If you were stranded in Mexico City, you couldn't speak enough *Español* to get yourself home. What are you doing listening to a Spanish talk station?"

As if she didn't know.

The show came back from a commercial to Marisa's familiar voice. She was laughing at something her producer said and was showing no ill effects of that morning. Myles knew she wouldn't. Her professionalism would never allow that. Her ability to separate the aspects of her life into distinct parts served her well on occasions like this, and probably in the courtroom as well. But he found this icy reserve more than a little off-putting.

Marisa's show broke for the bottom of the hour news update. As Myles walked over to the corner of the kitchen to mess with Winston, the phone rang.

"Hello?"

"Hey, *mi* big boy."

"Who's this?"

"Ha-ha, you can act a fool if you want."

"Hi, Marisa." The beeper went off on the microwave.

"What was that godawful sound? It better not be what I think it was."

"What, the microwave?"

"You better not be nuking anything to put in my delicate stomach. Negro, you get on your job and make me something good to eat."

"Relax, m'lady, I'm just thawing out some chicken for stir-fry. Someone, who will remain nameless but is of Cuban extraction, forgot to take anything out, though I asked her to early this morning."

"Speaking of early this morning, can we not talk about it when I get there?"

She didn't want to talk about her nightmare. Myles had been wanting all day to ask her about it.

"But, Marisa, don't you think you should—"

"Pleeeease . . ."

As if he was capable of saying no to her.

"All right."

"*Gracias*. I gotta go. Bye, babe."

Bye.

When Marisa got home, she was still in an upbeat, silly mood. Myles was sitting on the sofa finishing up the last of his progress reports when she climbed onto his back and wrapped her arms around his neck and her legs around his torso.

"Mush, you brawny, buck Mandingo. Mush, I say!"

She was always climbing on him. Myles swiveled her around so that she was facing him and laid her on her back on the couch.

"Lawdy, Lawdy, Lawdy, I'se declare. Is ya trying to defile me, Mandingo? Youse knows I'se a dainty fresh gal."

Myles laughed at her. "Speaking of African tribes, let me ask you a question."

"Go ahead."

"There is this little girl in my class named Cindy. She's Puerto Rican and about our complexion, if not a little darker."

"Okay."

"Well, anyway, some of the kids were arguing about whether Cindy should be considered black or Puerto Rican. Now, we know it's obvious what she is, but keeping in mind I have fifth-graders, tell me if you think I answered it properly."

"Go ahead."

"I told them to imagine that there were three sisters who grew up playing together. They were born in and lived in Africa, and they were black. They were very close and shared many enjoyable days running on the beach, swimming, and having fun. Then one day, while they were on the beach, a group of men came and kidnapped them and took all three sisters to separate boats. The boats then set sail for a faraway place. The three sisters looked out of their windows on their boats and could still see each other, they could almost reach out and touch each other, but they couldn't swim to each other because the water was full of sharks who followed the boats to eat the people that fell off. Well, the three sisters cried for days and never lost sight of each other, until the unthinkable happened; the boats separated.

"One boat landed on one island, another landed on a different island, and the third one landed on a big country. The sister on the first boat landed in a place called Haiti, so she learned to speak French. The sister in the second boat landed on Puerto Rico, so she learned to speak Spanish. The sister in the third boat landed in the United States, so she spoke . . ."

"English," Marisa said, raising her hand.

"Very good! English. Now, class, I ask you. Let's say those same three girls grow up and reunite years later. Who can tell me where these sisters were born?"

"Africa, Mr. Moore," Marisa said.

"Will they still be black?"

"Yes."

"Because even though they now speak different . . ."

"Languages."

"They are still . . ."

"Sisters."

"And if the three sisters have children, what will the children be to each other?"

"Cousins."

"Because even though the cousins were born in different . . ."

"Countries."

"And speak different . . ."

"Languages."

"And even though they weren't born in Africa like their mothers, they are all still of what descent?"

"African."

"Very good, Ms. Marrero. You get extra computer time."

Marisa clapped her hands excitedly.

"Because even though they might live on different islands and are separated by bodies of water, they are still related because 'blood is thicker than water.' That's where we get that saying from, class, 'Blood is thicker than water.' "

"Is that really the origin of that saying?" Marisa asked.

"I don't know. They're fifth-graders, you can tell them anything."

She laughed. "Continue."

"Just like there are black Americans, there are black Haitians, and black Puerto Ricans. A better way of saying this is Americans of African descent, Haitians of African descent, and Puerto Ricans of African descent. Mr. Moore is an American of African descent. Cindy is a Puerto Rican of African descent. Mr. Moore has a friend who is a Cuban of African descent.

"So, how was that?" Myles asked.

"Exemplary, very well put. Even if her parents are ignorant, self-hating *hibaros*, they shouldn't have a problem with that. But who is this friend of yours?"

"Just some Cuban girl I'm crazy about."

"Is she bigger than me?"

"Isn't everybody above the age of twelve?" he said, getting up.

She wrapped her arms around his neck and legs around his waist so that when Myles got up, she came along for the ride.

"I got enough *culo* for you, *papi*," she said, putting on her sexy voice.

"That's because your ass is out of proportion with the rest of your body, studgoddess." He started kissing her neck.

She started putting different parts of her body in the path of Myles's lips. Each time he kissed a different spot, she switched to a different word.

"Worship, worship, worship (forehead) . . . indulge, indulge, indulge (cheek) . . . pamper, pamper, pamper (mouth) . . . cater, cater, cater (chin) . . . revere, revere, revere (collarbone) . . ."

Myles wondered who would run out first. Him, with places to kiss, or her with verbs to describe his rapturous adoration.

". . . fawn, fawn, fawn (chest) . . . adulate, adulate, adulate (breast) . . ."

He didn't know, Marisa had a pretty extensive vocabulary. He guessed it would depend on how nasty he was willing to get.

Needless to say, she ran out first.

ℜ Eighteen

Marisa and Myles were just coming out of the George Theater in the Olde City section of Philadelphia. The George specialized in foreign and art-house films, the kind that Amir made fun of Myles for seeing. He always told him that if a movie enjoyed any kind of commercial success, then Myles automatically avoided it. Like if the masses enjoyed a particular movie, then Myles somehow felt it was intellectually beneath him and shunned it. Therefore, Amir would say, Myles insisted on finding the most obscure cinema possible and patronizing it. There was some truth in that, Myles had to admit. He just thought mainstream movies, for the most part, had stupid dialogue and were mind-numbing.

One Sunday, when they were over their parents' house having this conversation, Amir had said, "Myles, movies are supposed to be escapist. Why does everything have to be intellectually justifiable to you? I go to the movies to be entertained, not to be cerebrally massaged."

"Hey, if you don't mind contributing to the 'dumbing down' of society, that's on you. I just can't, in good conscience, be a party to it."

"What? You think you're better than me? See, Mom, I told you not to send him to that elitist, uppity college. The boy ain't been right since."

Marisa and Myles had been out for a Sunday of sightseeing when he remembered that *Guantanamera* was coming to the George that weekend. It was an acclaimed Cuban film that he had read about some time back, and it was just being released in the United States. It was shot entirely in different locales in Cuba. He thought it was funny, and laughed throughout the movie.

Marisa had sat through the movie in an almost hypnotic state. At the parts that Myles thought were hilarious, she allowed herself only a slight chuckle or two, and that might have been more a reaction to his infectious laughter than the movie itself.

"So what did you think?" he asked, grabbing her hand as they walked along a cobblestone path. It was a crisp autumn Sunday, Myles's favorite time of the year and his favorite day of the week. Autumn, because of its many colors and cool breezes, and Sunday, because it was the one day of the week he was assured of having Marisa to himself.

"I liked it a lot, Myles."

"You didn't seem to enjoy it that much."

"Well, I did, a lot." She then looked him in the eye. "I'm just not as emotionally expressive as you."

That stung him, because he knew what she really meant. Last night they had watched *Conexion Latina* together. On the show, Marisa had interviewed a Phillies player from the Dominican Republic and his wife. When Marisa began telling Myles what a good baseball player she had been as a kid, he laughed at her. It wasn't because he didn't believe her; it was because he just couldn't picture Marisa sliding into third base.

"I'm serious. In Silver Spring there's a batting cage near my house that I go to at least once a month. As a child I was very good. The only reason I had to stop was because I reached the age where the boys became more interested in grabbing my ass than playing ball."

Now, he had no trouble imagining that.

She refused to accept Myles's insistence that he believed her, and the next thing he knew, she, Winston, and him were at a nearby park underneath the lights on the basketball court. She was crouched in a batting stance, and he was standing sixty feet away with a supply of rubber racquetballs. To his surprise, in her apartment closet she had a ton of athletic equipment. It had taken a lot of convincing on Myles's part to get her to use these balls instead of the hardballs she had.

"This is silly and I'm cold," he complained.

She took the barrel of her bat and smacked it against the instep of her sneaker like baseball players do when they are ridding themselves of mud stuck in their cleats.

"Just groove me one."

Myles took one of the balls and half lobbed, half threw it over the "plate."

Marisa swung and hit it over the fence enclosing the basketball courts.

"There it goes," she said as the ball disappeared into the darkness. "Now, really pitch me one."

Myles threw one a little harder this time. Instead of swinging, she reached out and caught it with her left hand.

"Is that as hard as you can throw, rag arm?" she asked as she threw it back to him.

Now Myles was pissed. He threw the ball to her, harder than he meant to.

She swung and hit the ball on a line to his left. It smacked up against the fence. Winston went chasing after it.

"Marrero goes the opposite way, exhibiting excellent bat control," she said, imitating a baseball broadcaster. "It's nice to see a batter use all parts of the field."

Myles threw her another one. She swung and this time hit a screamer to the right of him. She imitated a crowd roaring and again brought back her broadcaster:

"This time Marrero pulled the ball, taking what the pitcher gives her. What a professional hitter! She should tour the country giving clinics on bat control."

Myles decided to throw her a brushback pitch, just to shut her up. He aimed straight for her ass. She barely moved out of the way in time.

"You can act a fool if you want," she said. "If you bruise it, you lose it."

"What was that? Did you say, 'If I bruise it, I can peruse it'?" he asked her. "Because if your ass should con-tuse, I'll be its mas-seuse," Myles said, rhyming like some erstwhile Johnnie Cochran.

"Just throw the ball, pervert."

Myles threw her another one. She hit a line drive up the middle that nearly decapitated him. He lost his balance and found himself ass down on the cold cement.

He looked at her, trying to discern whether she really had enough bat control to have done that on purpose.

"You okay, hon?" she asked innocently.

A little *too* innocently for his liking.

"I'm fine." Myles got up and nonchalantly started brushing himself off. When he thought that she wasn't looking, he ran at her.

Marisa squealed, dropped the bat, and took off running. After much effort, Winston and Myles finally cornered her on the tennis courts. Myles picked her up in his arms and pinned her against the fence and started ravenously pawing her.

"You brute, you savage thug, get your grubby mitts off me."

He put her down and stroked her cheek. "Marisa, I know you did that on purpose."

She grinned like an imp.

"You trying to kill me? Why do you have to resort to violence?"

"Because I do."

It was cold enough where you could see their breath each time they exhaled. Myles reached down to where hers was, "caught" some, and pretended to eat it.

"You are so silly," Marisa said as she led him to a bench that was put there to watch people play tennis.

Myles sat down and Marisa sat on his lap. She started kissing his neck.

"How come you're not complaining about it being cold now?" she asked.

"Because you put fire into my loins."

For some reason she just thought that was so humorous. She laughed that really ebullient laugh that she did from time to time. It was that same laugh that had warmed his *corazon* the first night he met her. Of all the wonderful sensations that she had ever given him, carnally or otherwise, it was when she laughed like this that gave him the greatest thrill.

"I'm in love with you, Marisa," he said.

This was the third time that he had let the "L" word slip out.

She stopped laughing, looked at him with a fake serious expression, and said, "As well you should be."

Myles smiled at her, trying to mask his disappointment, and said, "Come on, let's pick up this stuff and go back inside, slugger."

She said, "Okay" in such a soft voice that Myles knew that she could tell that he was hurt. But what really hurt was that she knew it and did nothing to help it. It was too one-sided for his liking.

In bed that night, she had gone wild on him. Myles figured that was her way of cheering him up or saying she loved him, or whatever.

So as they were walking through Olde City, Myles knew exactly what she meant when she said that she wasn't as "emotionally expressive" as he was. Damn, he thought, she made his feelings for her sound so clinical.

He also knew that whenever Marisa looked directly into his eyes, as she was doing now, she was watching to see if he would reveal something. She was big on eye contact, especially during lovemaking. She told him it was from years of dancing salsa, when looking your partner in the eye is expected.

Myles changed the subject.

"Marisa, you told me that you came over from Cuba when you were a child. How was that possible? It being a closed country and all."

"My father and I came over in the Mariel boat lift in 1979," she said quietly.

"Your father?"

"Yes, he died shortly thereafter. My mother died when I was younger, of cancer, when she was the age I am now, twenty-nine." She said it wistfully, like this was the first time that she had realized it. "So my father and I were going to live with my great-uncle Eli, my father was his favorite nephew back when he used to live in Cuba—and his wife, Esther. After my father died, it was just me that went to live with them."

"Wow, Marisa. Most people who use their horrible childhood as an excuse for their lives didn't have it one-tenth as bad as you. Yet you've accomplished so much and never let it hold you back."

"I probably would have, but my Aunt Esther wasn't having that," she said, laughing.

Later that afternoon, Marisa and Myles were in her apartment. They were both hungry and each was trying to pass the task of cooking off on the other person. Marisa went into her bedroom to check her machine. When she came out, Myles was on the phone.

"Barbecue ribs . . . macaroni and cheese . . . peach cobbler . . ."

Marisa assumed he was placing an order at some takeout spot. It sounded good to her and she damn sure didn't feel like cooking, so she thought nothing of it. She turned on the TV.

"Sounds good, Mom. Marisa and I will be over in a little bit."

Marisa had to fight the urge to throw the remote control at his head. Who the hell told him that she wanted to go over his parents' house? It was just like his manipulative ass. She knew what he was thinking; that the next logical progression in their relationship was Sunday dinner with the folks. And let's talk about "the folks" for a second. Myles's father gave Marisa the creeps. Much like his son, he evidently was a "butt man," because the last time she saw him, he spent the whole time looking at hers out of the corner of his eye. But unlike his son, he wasn't much on personality. Mostly he just sat there and leered. As for the mother, she was standoffish. One time Marisa had been out shopping with Jackie when they bumped into her. The way Mrs. Moore had reacted when she saw Jackie, you would have thought she was the daughter she never had. It was like a mutual admiration society, all huggy and happy. When she was finally done making sure every possible aspect of Jackie's life was going well, she smiled at Marisa and gave her a cursory "And how are you today, Marisa?" flashing her a toothy, phony smile.

Jackie tried to tell Marisa she was just imagining

things, that Mrs. Moore was the sweetest woman on earth. Maybe to her she is, Marisa thought, but Jackie isn't going out with her precious, tenderhearted *enamorado* of a son, either. Marisa almost wished his mother would come out and say what she knew she was thinking: "Look, bitch, I know you're gonna hurt my child. Why don't you just get it over with so I can begin picking up the pieces?"

". . . All right. Okay, bye." Myles hung up the phone. "Marisa, I told my mother we'd be over to eat."

"I heard," Marisa said. She changed the channel.

Myles looked at her. "What, you don't want to go?"

She clutched the remote tighter. *Now* he was asking her if she wanted to go?

" 'Cause I can call my mother back and say we can't make it."

Yeah, right. Marisa thought. So she can blame me for keeping mama's boy away and hate me even more? "No, I want to go."

Marisa stormed into her apartment and tried to slam the door behind her. She was unable to because it hit Myles.

"What's with you? What did I do?"

Marisa turned around and looked at Myles.

"I'm not in the mood for your clueless act, tonight, all right? You didn't do anything wrong. You *never* do anything wrong, okay? Just go to your place, I wanna be by myself."

Myles hesitated, then headed for the door, muttering under his breath, "All right, if you don't want to talk about it." A shoe crashed against the door six inches from his head.

"Oh, *now* you wanna talk? So, you've rediscovered your tongue, huh? When your family was grilling my ass for the past three hours, you didn't have shit to say then, did you?"

Marisa felt like she had been ambushed. Myles's mother, his aunts Roslyn and Dee, and his mother's friend, some woman named Joyce, had questioned Marisa on every aspect of her involvement with Myles. What was in their future? Don't you want to get married? Do you want kids? How old are you? Girl, you'd better get started. Everything but how often and in what positions, and Marisa was sure that Joyce's nosy ass was tempted to ask that. Not once had Myles come to her defense. He left her twisting in the wind. It was bad enough that she was going to eat with his parents. She didn't know it was gonna be a full-fledged family reunion. But Myles knew.

"What? I thought you did fine."

Did you now? So, you get to go over and stuff your face while I have to improvise a fucking tap dance on the spot and you think that's "fine." Marisa glared at him. She knew that no matter what he said, it would only make her angrier, and she was about two seconds away from saying something she didn't want to say. At least, not yet. She walked over to the couch and sat down and closed her eyes, hoping to God that he would be gone when she opened them. She composed herself before speaking.

"Myles, just leave. I'll talk to you later," she said

in a steady voice. Please let this man know that he'd better leave, now.

"All right. Good night, Marisa," he said quietly. She heard the door close.

When she opened her eyes they were stinging with tears. She hated when he did that. The way he would say her name with such reverence, like it was a privilege for him to do so.

She was mad. Mad at Myles and even madder at herself for crying. What the hell was she crying for? She wiped away the tears. After composing herself, she looked through her Rolodex and picked up the phone.

"Hello?"

"Hey, Victor." She quickly added, "It's Marisa."

Victor laughed. "There was no need for that. I recognized your voice."

"I just thought I'd help you out. I heard you have a full dance card."

"Don't believe all those rumors you hear about me, Marisa. You know hearsay isn't admissible in a court of law."

"But it is in the court of public opinion."

"True, but you're not the type to be clouded by other people's judgments. You're a lady that likes to find out things for yourself."

"Am I, now? And your extensive knowledge of me tells you this?"

"Or maybe I listen to hearsay, too. What, you think I'm the only one people talk about?"

"Good point." Marisa acceded. "So none of what I have heard about you is true?"

"I'm not gonna say all that, now. Some of it is true."

Marisa laughed. Her bad day with Myles was rapidly becoming an afterthought.

"Listen, Victor, I was just calling to confirm tomorrow. You didn't forget did you?"

"Are you kidding, Marisa? Lunch and then I'm doing your show. Do you really think I'd forget that I was spending the better part of an entire day with the lovely and talented Marisa Marrero?"

"You might," she said warily.

"I'll tell you what. Let's use the lunch as an opportunity for both of us to form our own conclusions concerning the other."

"It's a deal," Marisa agreed. She then heard a woman's voice in the background.

"You have company?" Marisa was embarrassed but not sure why. Maybe because she had been getting into this conversation with Victor, unaware that all along a woman was there waiting for him to finish.

"*Sí*, I should go now."

"Yeah. I guess you *should*," she said, deliberately sounding both impressed and critical.

"Hey, now. What was that for? I did tell you *some* of it was true."

⚘ Nineteen

Marisa and Victor walked into her office. She sat down, and he sat next to her on the edge of her desk. His radio appearance on her show was slated for later that evening. They were returning from their lunch together. Marisa made sure to leave her door open. She didn't want people in the office to think that there was something going on between them.

"Now, didn't I tell you that you'd have a good time?" he said.

"Oh yeah, maybe next time I can watch you berate the rest of the help."

"Hey, if I say I want my steak rare, I mean rare, not medium-well. I can't excuse that kind of incompetence. They're supposed to be an upscale restaurant. If they're gonna purport themselves to be such, what, I'm not supposed to hold them accountable?"

"I suppose you're right."

"You're damn right I'm right. Hell, they're lucky I was in such a forgiving mood. I'm tempted to make a few phone calls. By the time I was through, they'd be ruined, a zero star restaurant, on a par with Wendy's, maybe. They'd rue the day they heard the name Victor Andujar."

Marisa laughed heartily.

"I just hope our dinner goes better," he said.

Marisa smiled at him. She'd had a good time today. Victor wasn't interested in her meeting his parents. He wanted only one thing.

There was a knock on the door. Marisa looked around him to see who it was. Victor didn't even bother turning around.

Jackie was standing at the door. "You busy?"

"No, come in, Jackie. Jackie Roque, this is Victor Andujar."

Victor finally decided to acknowledge that there was somebody else in the room. He stood up, walked around the desk, and took Jackie's hand.

"A pleasure to make your acquaintance, Jackie."

"Likewise, Victor."

He turned his attention back to Marisa. "Well, since we have an hour before your show starts, I'm gonna go see what Rios is doing."

"All right, I'll see you in a little while."

"Nice meeting you," he said to Jackie.

"Same here."

"I'll close the door so you ladies can have some privacy," he said slyly, like he just *knew* that he was going to be the topic of conversation after he was gone.

As the door closed behind him, Jackie looked at Marisa with her eyebrows raised. "My, my, my," she said, fanning herself.

"Don't start, Jackie. That was nothing."

"I would hardly call *that* nothing. *That* is an extraordinary piece of manhood."

"You know what I mean. There's nothing going on."

"Really? So when is this dinner rendezvous?"

So she had heard that. Marisa looked at her. She knew what her friend was thinking, that she was staying true to form. Except this time she was fucking over her boy Myles. "I'm just having dinner with the man, Jackie. I'm not screwing him."

"So who's accusing you?"

"You are."

"I did no such thing," Jackie said, raising her hands defensively.

Marisa sighed. Why was everybody playing clueless with her lately?

Myles got home later than usual from school. He had had to make a stop at the home of one of his students. Marquis had been cutting a fool in class lately, which was bad enough, but in addition his grades were slipping. The look on his face when he saw Myles at his front door was memorable. His parents and Myles came to an agreement that Marquis would stay after school every day for extra help until his grades showed improvement. By the time Myles left, he felt sorry for him because he knew young Marquis was about to meet the business end of a belt.

There was a note on the fridge.

I won't be home until late, so don't wait up.
                                        Marisa

That was just like her, Myles thought. She knew that he felt bad about upsetting her last night, and now she was gonna make him suffer by not being available to him. He guessed she wanted to teach him a lesson. What, it's just a coincidence that she's not coming home the day after they had an argument? They hadn't slept apart but a couple of times in the past three and a half months. And what about how vague this shit is? "Won't be home until late" because of what?

He'd had all day to think about yesterday, and he knew that he had been in the wrong, letting his aunts terrorize Marisa. He should have stepped in and called off the attack dogs. It was his family, it was his place to do it. To be honest, the reason he hadn't was that he was as curious as everybody else to hear her answers.

Hell, she could try to be a little more understanding about where he was coming from. He hadn't said shit when she went to Baltimore to spend Thanksgiving with Jackie's family. He hadn't said shit to her about how tired he had been that night of answering the question, "So where's this girl of yours we've heard so much about?" and how foolish he had looked when he told them she was spending the holiday with her friend's family instead of her man's.

Myles flicked on the radio to her show. It sounded like she had an in-studio guest, because an unfamiliar voice was on with her. He was doing the majority of the talking, and Marisa's voice had an almost deferential quality when she addressed a question to him, like she was hanging on his every word. He decided to call Carlos.

"Hello?"

"What up. 'Los, you listening to Marisa's show?"

"Not now, but I caught a little bit of it in the car."

"Who is that with her?"

"You need to learn how to speak Spanish. It's Victor Andujar."

"Victor Andujar. Where do I know that name from?"

"He's the attorney representing those college kids from that turnpike thing."

Oh, yeah, Myles thought. Four college students, three blacks and a Latino, had been headed to some basketball camp last summer when they were pulled over by couple of state troopers, allegedly for speeding. Next thing you know, the officers had discharged their firearms, injuring several of the kids. It seemed to be a cut-and-dried case of excessive force by some overzealous cracker cop.

He had seen Andujar on the news discussing the case. He was in his late thirties maybe, and very well spoken. He seemed like the kind of guy that got on white people's nerves because he knew how to play their game better than they did.

"Why?" Carlos asked.

"Just curious," he replied.

Carlos laughed.

"What's so funny?" Myles asked.

"You."

Marisa was true to her word about not being home until late. In fact, she didn't come to Myles's apartment at all. As he was getting dressed for school, he looked out the window onto the parking lot and saw her Range Rover.

Myles had no idea what time she had come in, but he knew it had to have been very late. He decided to call her. Her phone rang five times before she answered it.

"Yeah," she said groggily.

"Good morning," Myles said.

"Uhhnn," she grunted.

"May I come over and see you before I leave?"

She didn't answer.

"Hello?"

"Huh?"

"May I come over before I leave for work?"

"I'm sleeping, Myles."

"C'mon, Marisa, real fast, let me come over. Let me have a kiss so I can start my day off right."

She exhaled with disgust, as if to say what part of "I'm sleeping" didn't he understand. Which pissed Myles off because she wasn't willing to allow herself the slightest bit of inconvenience for him. Hell, he never complained when she disturbed him out of his sleep with one of her nightmares.

"Jesus Christ. You know what, Marisa, just forget it. I'm sorry to bother you."

Myles heard her suck her teeth, the phone hit the floor, and then a door open on the floor. Seconds later he heard loud banging on his apartment door.

"Who is it?" he sang.

He was met with stony silence, so he figured he'd better hurry up and open the door. When he opened it, Marisa was standing in the hallway completely disheveled wearing a bathrobe and a pissed-off expression.

"Behold," he said, "it's the wicked witch of the West . . . Indies."

She ignored his attempt at humor and gave him a sterile, antiseptic, tight-lipped peck on the lips. Myles tried to put his arms around her, but she wriggled away. He was hoping to make up with her, and in the process find out where she had been last night. She turned around and walked back down the hallway.

"Thank you," he said to her as she disappeared back into her apartment.

The only response he got was the sound of her door slamming.

Marisa had been in a sour mood all morning. After Myles had woke her up, she had been unable to return to sleep, partly out of restlessness but mainly because she was so steamed. She had hated how manipulative he had acted that morning, playing on her sense of obligation. Like a big fucking baby.

"I want you to get up . . . Why? Because I want you to. . . . What? Fuck what you want . . . come see about my ego."

As if he had a right to do so after that shit he pulled at his parents' house, anyway. See, this is the bullshit I don't want to go through, she thought. Myles had been sweet, *almost* perfect, so far, but she knew better. Given enough time, a man will eventually be a man and show his ass. But something else bothered her beyond his lack of consideration and his manipulation.

She recounted the entire episode. What she didn't understand was why Myles had been so insistent on coming over to her apartment. Until something in her just clicked and it all came together.

She knew that Myles listened to her show every night, despite his inability to understand most of it. Last night her guest had been Victor Andujar. He had been all over the news recently because of his turnpike case. It was impossible to turn on the TV and not see him. So she knew Myles had to be familiar with Victor and have noticed that he was very good looking.

Now factor in that on the same night that Victor was her guest she didn't come home until very late. And that Myles already knew she was pissed at him about Sunday. And the fact that she left him a note saying she was going to be out late, like she just *knew* that she was going to want to give some to Victor, so don't wait up, *cabron*. Damn, did he really think she was that simple? That she would go fuck somebody else because she was angry at him? Apparently so. Not only that, but that she would bring him back to *her* apartment to fuck him. All his goddess-princess-angel shit was just that, fraudulent bullshit. He thought of her as a common *puta*.

She and some of the other ladies who worked at the station had gone out to eat and then to Cassandra's house for an evening of girl talk and acting silly. The other women who worked evenings at the station had been inviting Marisa out with them for weeks, and she was glad that she finally accepted because she had had fun. She particularly liked Cassandra's crazy, carefree ass. She was a riot. Well,

Marisa decided, maybe I should go out with them more often.

As Myles readied himself to go home, his thoughts turned to Marisa. At lunchtime he had almost called her. He knew she was upset with him and he was thinking that maybe he should offer some kind of balm of contrition. But he decided against it. Partly because he figured that she might still be sleeping and partly because he didn't feel that he had done anything so wrong. What had been his crime? Missing his girl? He knew she was already pissed at him, but what, he was a bad guy for wanting to see her before going another fifteen hours apart? And where exactly had she been last night anyway? With her secretive ass. Hell, a case could be made for him having an attitude about *her* attitude, if he wanted to pursue it. Which he didn't. What was to be gained?

Carlos walked into his classroom.

"What's up, 'Los?"

"*Nada*. Same ol', same ol'," he said. "How are things with you and Marisa?"

"Pretty good," he said, turning around from erasing his blackboard. Myles looked at Carlos and decided to tell the truth. "Actually, she's pretty pissed off at me right about now."

"Yeah? What's up?"

"We went to my parents' house Sunday. There was some family over, you know, some aunts and others, and they started digging into Marisa's ass pretty good, asking her a bunch of questions."

"About what?" Carlos asked.

Myles paused before answering. "Mostly about her future, and where I fit in it."

"And what were you doing while this was going on?"

"You mean, besides avoiding eye contact with Marisa?" Myles asked.

Carlos laughed. "Yeah, besides that."

"Nothing. I was too interested in hearing the answers. I just let my henchmen do the dirty work. I know I was in the wrong, 'Los. She probably felt like she had been set up."

"Not only that, Myles, but she probably felt betrayed. And, you gotta understand, she's kinda fragile about stuff like that. Think about it, she has no family to parade you in front of. She's alone."

Myles felt like shit. "Did she say something to Jackie?"

"Nah, not that I know of. I was just asking because when you called last night to ask me about Victor Andujar, I thought I heard something in your voice." He looked at Myles warily.

"Nah, I didn't give that dude a second thought," Myles said, lying.

"Good," Carlos said, probably knowing he was lying. "Then, just for future reference, I don't think Marisa is slimy enough to skank it up on you. She thinks too highly of herself to go sneaking around. Before she'll do that, she'll just give you your walking papers."

"That's a source of comfort."

"Relax," he said, laughing, "she likes you. However, may I issue a warning?"

"Please do."

"Christmas is right around the corner. I strongly caution you not to get too sentimental. You know how you can get. Being around Amir's family, you'll start thinking about how nice it would be to have a wife and kids of your own during the holidays. Next thing you know, you'll start waxing poetic to Marisa on how you think she'll make a great mother, getting all gushy and sappy on her."

"Geesh, most women want that," Myles said.

"Marisa isn't 'most women,' or haven't you noticed?"

Yes, Lord, he had noticed. And all this talk was making him crave her. He didn't have to tell Myles; Marisa Marreros didn't grow on trees.

"What I'm asking is, are you prepared to do whatever it takes to get the girl?"

"What exactly does it take?"

"That's hard to say with Marisa. I've never seen her 'gotten.' But I can still be of service, because I can tell you what *not* to do."

This conversation suddenly reminded Myles of how Carlos interacted with troubled students that got sent to his office for counseling.

"And what would that be, Mr. Roque?"

"To use baseball parlance: Don't crowd the plate, don't overextend or swing for the fences, take what the pitcher gives you, and be patient."

"Got it. Don't smother her, don't press her for an ironclad commitment, enjoy the little victories, and be patient."

"And lose your stubbornness, your preconceived notions, and be prepared for the possibility that you may have to eat a whole lot of shit in the interim."

"Hey, now you might be going a little too far."

"I agree, I wouldn't do it. But then again, I'm not the one in love with her. So once again I ask, are you willing to do what it takes to get the girl?"

Myles was about to offer some fraudulent argument about his use of "in love," but Carlos gave him a look that said don't even try it.

"Yeah, 'Los."

"Look at it this way," he said, holding his hands out like he was admiring a work of art. "Picture Marisa's lovely visage. Imagine waking up next to that from time immemorial. Years from now, will it matter to you that you had to ingest a little *caca* in the beginning?"

Myles shook his head. "No, it wouldn't."

"Hey, you don't think Jackie made me eat shit? You don't think your mother made your dad eat shit? You don't think that Kenya made Amir eat shit?"

They looked at each other and laughed.

"Okay, maybe Amir's a bad example."

"Yeah, that's the man."

"But my point is that every man who truly loves a woman has to eat shit sooner or later. You might try to flavor it with weak justifications, or sauté it with denial to allay your pride, but you're still just eating shit. The greater the prize is, the more you value the woman, the more you feel that she is essential to your happiness, the more shit you're gonna have to be willing to take. Agree?"

Myles nodded. Carlos was making a lot of sense.

"Jackie and I were talking last night. Do you know that there are parts of Marisa that Jackie still doesn't know about? Think about that. They've known each other for twelve years, and she's still an enigma to her. I mean, I think Marisa is basically a good person, but just from what I have gathered in bits and pieces, she had a pretty fucked-up childhood, which of course would affect anybody deleteriously."

Deleteriously? What, did he swallow a dictionary along with Jackie's shit?

"She's always struck me as having, you know, potentially loose wiring in the basement. But it's so well hidden, it's hard to identify and address."

Damn, Myles thought, he was saying she was "potentially" a basket case. But he knew exactly what he meant. She was so mysterious. Sometimes when he was with Marisa, he felt that she revealed to him only her outward shell: an attractive, glossy, epidermal casing. What he wanted to do was flip her over to expose her vulnerable underbelly. He'd have to have her heart too, before he'd be satisfied.

"Just remember one thing, Myles. She might not always be fair, but then again, she doesn't have to be. *You* want *her. Entiende*?"

"I understand."

"Good."

"Though I've always envisioned a scenario where the two people take each other at face value and decide to love from the onset. Therefore they don't have any hard feelings to throw in each other's faces later," Myles said.

"Yeah, Myles, but down here on earth, it doesn't happen that way."

Marisa put the key Myles had given her into the door of his apartment. She had been meaning to give him her spare but kept forgetting. She had her game face on and was ready for warfare.

As she opened the door, what she saw brought to mind a feeling the direct opposite of fighting. In fact, the only conflict in her mind was deciding who to hug first.

Before her stood Deja and Jade, with their cheeks painted rosy red and wearing matching plaid pajamas. On top of their heads were pointy green elf hats.

"Hi, Reesa!" they exclaimed in unison, their faces beaming with delight.

"Hi!" Marisa answered. Unable to choose, she knelt down and hugged them both at the same time.

"What are you two doing here? Besides making my day?" she asked.

"Un-kel Myles came to get us," Jade answered.

"Oh, he did, did he?" Marisa said. "Let's go see what he is doing."

She got up, took each of the girls by the hand, and walked to the bedroom.

Myles was sitting at his computer, hurriedly closing a program and shutting it down. She wondered what he had been working on. He was wearing a Santa's hat. On the floor next to him was Winston, wearing a hat with felt antlers protruding from it.

"Hi, sweetheart," he said tentatively.

You'd better be cautious, she thought. "Hi," she said coolly. "What are you working on?"

"Just some grades," he said in a dismissive manner. "So, I see you've met Santa's little helpers."

"Yeah," she said, smiling down at the girls, "and I see that you got Winston pitching in."

At the mention of his name, Winston peered up at

her with a look of chagrin. He knew damn well he was a dog, not a reindeer.

"Here, Reesa," Deja said, going over to the bed and picking up a red Santa hat, "we got one for you."

Marisa put on the hat. "Look, girls!" Myles said. "Mrs. Claus is definitely in the hooouuuse!"

The twins started cheering, taking their cue from their silly uncle. Winston even threw in a bark or two.

Marisa tried to roll her eyes at him but couldn't help it. A smile had formed on her face.

Later that evening Myles told the girls a bedtime story. They snuggled next to Marisa on the bed to listen to it. It was already way past their bedtime, so he told them a quick one that he had made up some time back and committed to memory. The standard fare, a little princess who finds true happiness kind of thing.

After they said their prayers, Myles kissed them both good night. Marisa did the same, but lingered a while, smiling down at them. What's that sound she heard? Was it her biological clock ticking? Her maternal instinct rearing its formidable presence?

Myles was about to say something along the lines of "Do you want one?" to her, but then he remembered the conversation that he had with Carlos and kept his mouth shut. He left her in the bedroom and went into the living room.

Myles spread a blanket on the floor and took the pillows from the couch. The girls had been watching his *Emmitt Otter's Jug Band Christmas* videocassette for the zillionth time. Myles reached over and took the reindeer hat off Winston, who seemed to be relieved to be free of it.

Myles stretched out on the blanket, closed his eyes, and yawned. When he opened them, he was eye level with Marisa's feet. She was standing over him.

"You're a fraud, St. Nick," she said.

"St. Nick a fraud?" he said, raising himself onto his elbows. "Oh, you must still be upset about that pony you wanted last year, little girl. See, what had happened was, we loaded it on the sled, but somewhere over Albuquerque, me and the reindeer hit some turbulence, and unfortunately—"

"You went and got the twins because you knew you were in for it."

"What? Marisa, I went and got the girls because Kenya and Amir had tickets to see a show in Atlantic City."

"And your mother couldn't watch them?"

"Well . . . I suppose, but I figured that you wouldn't mind having them over."

"Mmm-hmm." She wasn't buying it. "Why don't you pull out the sofa bed?"

"I'd rather sleep on the carpet than sleep on that uncomfortable thing. I figured you'd be sleeping in your apartment tonight, anyway, so I didn't mind giving up the bed to the girls."

"Why do you think that I'm going to sleep in my apartment tonight?"

"Because you're mad at me."

"Why would I be mad at you?"

"Because of Sunday at my parents' house. I left you out there."

Marisa looked at him but didn't say anything.

"Which I was wrong to do. Marisa, you should never feel like you're alone when I'm with you. I won't let that happen again."

The only sound was Winston rustling in the kitchen. Marisa finally spoke.

"Myles. I'm tired. I'm gonna go to my place. I'll talk to you tomorrow, all right?"

"Okay. Good night."

"Good night."

She didn't seem in the mood, so Myles didn't ask for a good night kiss. When she got to the door, though, he did say, "Oh, Marisa."

She didn't turn around. "Yeah?"

"I did just want to see you this morning."

She nodded, shut the door, and left.

♘ Twenty

On Christmas morning, Marisa and Myles exchanged gifts. She had bought him a nice leather trench coat (it felt like it was made out of the same soft leather that her couch was made from), a thick silver link bracelet, and some CD-ROMs for his computer, and she bought Winston a new chew toy. Myles, with his typical lack of understatement, practically bought her a whole store. He wrapped the gifts in different boxes and hid them in places where she would find them. The idea being that for days after Christmas, she'd still be finding presents. He gave her three gifts on Christmas Day and hid the rest. He hid them in the back of her truck, in her closets, in her desk at work (Jackie assisted him with that one), in her gym locker (also thanks to Jackie), everywhere. Myles told her that he had thought about hiding some in her kitchen but didn't, because he did want them to be found eventually.

He didn't want to think about how much he spent on her, but needless to say, it would behoove him to spend a couple of Saturdays doing hair at his mother's salon.

Myles especially liked when he was with her and she found one of his hidden gifts. Her face would light up, and she would magically be transformed into a little girl. She would leap in his arms, and he would carry her around while she smothered him with kisses, squeezing him like she couldn't possibly squeeze him tight enough.

He liked this so much that soon he began helping her out. He would ask, "Marisa, can I borrow that flashlight in your truck" or "Could I have a couple of racquetballs for the kids at school" so that she would find his hidden gifts and reward him. With his assistance, she found all the gifts by the 28th.

She liked them all, especially the leather-bound complete works of Gabriel García Márquez, the Celia Cruz box set, and a year's subscription to *Beisbol Semanal* (the Spanish *Baseball Weekly*). She had balked when he gave her the tennis bracelet on Christmas, saying it was too expensive, but finally accepted when Myles told her it was non-returnable.

Myles violated his pledge to not pressure Marisa only one time. It was the night when she found his last gift, the Celia Cruz CDs, and she was feeling especially amorous. They were in her apartment, and she was playing one of the CDs. She kept telling him, "Kiss my hair, Myles, kiss my hair," which always drove her crazy, but this night she was enjoying it even more than usual.

When the action started getting a little too heavy, she was still conscious enough to reach into her purse on the nightstand and pull out a condom. She

handed it to him. Myles took it from her and opened
the package. But he didn't put it on. Instead, he sat
up in the bed. After a while she realized he wasn't
making an effort to put it on. She had assumed that
he was just fumbling in the darkness.

"What's wrong?" she asked, sitting up alongside
him.

"Nothing, Marisa. I was just thinking."

"About what?" she said, irritated. She was in the
mood for "Buck Mandingo," superslayer of *chocha*,
not the musings of "Introspective Boy."

Myles hesitated, knowing it was something he
shouldn't say.

"How nice it would be to not require a sheath for
the sword."

She exhaled loudly and fell back onto the bed. She
rolled onto her side away from him. He took this to
mean that she was thinking, "Does he know how
many guys would love to be in his position, and he's
balking over using a fucking rubber?"

And that pissed him off. Fuck it, he could be one
of "those guys."

He put on the condom and lay down next to her.
He kissed her shoulder and stroked her hair. She
kept her back to him and didn't say anything.

Myles put his left hand around her waist and
started slowly tracing along her belly button and her
pubic region. He nuzzled the back of her head, sepa-
rating her hair into different places for him to kiss.
He pressed up against her backside.

She was still silent, the only acknowledgment of
his presence that her breathing grew a little louder.

Myles slid his hand farther down to her inner

thigh, careful not to touch her vagina, saving that for later, and parted her legs, prepping her for a rear entry. She reached in between her legs to feel him and make sure he had on the condom.

Yeah, Marisa, you can rest easy, I got it on, he wanted to say but didn't.

She then positioned and poked out her ass in such a way as to give him maximum exposure of her pussy.

Myles slid his other hand underneath her so that he now had both of his hands situated on her inner thighs, so he could better control the force of his thrusts.

Marisa wasn't talking to him. Usually, the only time she talked more than Myles did was during lovemaking. It would be the standard stuff. If he went down on her she might say, "You can't stop eating my *chocha*, can you?" or if he was pumping her, she'd whisper, "You like being in me, don't you, Myles," or "You're filling me up, baby," and start moaning as to how she was too little to withstand such a pounding.

Myles rolled her onto her stomach, forcefully grabbed her by the hips, and lifted her up into the air until she bent her knees. When he finally put her down, she was hunched over on all fours. Though Marisa was damn near as bright as a rocket scientist, she didn't need to be to know what his intentions were.

Myles went behind her and pressed her hands flat on the bed with his palms. When he was comfortable that she was going to keep her hands there, he moved his to her breasts and started massaging them, while he licked and kissed the entire length of her back. At the same time he rotated his hips to let her feel his penis circumnavigate the entire expanse of her ass.

Usually Marisa would say something like "What are you gonna do with that?" but she was still. All she said was "I know you want me" in a barely audible whisper.

After Myles was finished orally traipsing up and down her back, he put his hands back on her hips and inserted his thigh in between her legs, spreading them farther apart. With his hands he pushed down on the small of her back so that her ass was even more in the air.

He moved the tip of his penis around the entrance of her forbidden input. When she didn't even flinch, he gave a second's consideration to taking her butt but thought better of it.

She kept saying, "I know you want me . . . I know you want me."

You got that right, Myles thought. He mounted her, putting his organ into the more traditional receptacle, and commenced to riding.

Marisa moved her hands off the bed and grabbed the rungs of her brass headboard. Once again she repeated her mantra.

"I know you want me . . . I know you want me . . . I know you want me . . . "

Her voice seemed to be filled with too much torment to be her normal sex chatter, like she was in pain. Myles pulled out before he wanted to and turned her over so he could see her face. He put his face close to hers. Her eyes were brimming with tears, and his anger about the condom was quickly forgotten.

"Did you finish?" she asked.

"Yeah," he said, lying, "what's wrong?"

She turned over on her side, again away from him.

Myles pulled her close to him. She felt his still erect penis against her leg.

"Liar, you didn't finish," she said, trying to force a laugh.

"To hell with that. Marisa, what's wrong?" He rolled her onto her back. She was trying her best to smile, but when she saw the look of concern in Myles's eyes she started crying again. She put her hand up to his face and stroked his cheek.

"What is it?" Myles asked her again.

She turned her face to the ceiling. Her eyes sparkled because of the tears.

She pulled him down on her so that she could whisper in his ear. Myles felt the moisture from her eye on his cheek.

"Myles, I *know* you want me. Understand? I know . . . I do."

Oh, now he got it. Therefore, he didn't need to keep reminding her about his issues of permanency and how she wasn't addressing them. Myles realized that this must make her feel like shit. Carlos was right. All he was gonna do was drive her away.

"All right, Marisa, I'll calm down."

Through her sniffles, she chuckled in his ear.

"No, baby," he said, moving so he could see her face. Myles couldn't resist. He traced her lips with his tongue. "I'm serious. We'll just take it day by day, I promise."

She looked at him earnestly. Myles could tell she really wanted to believe him. But he wasn't sure if she did.

She wrapped her arms and legs around him, her cue that she wanted to be held. Myles sat up holding her. For a long time. She finally whispered to him, "Listen, I know what you're worth, okay? So you can relax."

He kissed her cheek.

"Now, why don't you finish what you started?" she said.

"Happy to oblige, ma'am," Myles said, laying her on her back with the care and delicacy that she deserved. "Never let it be said that Mrs. Moore raised a son who didn't finish a job."

Myles reached over for Marisa and felt nothing but sheet. He looked at the clock: it was 3:14 in the morning. He sat up and saw that the bedroom door was closed and the light from the TV was emanating under it.

He walked into the living room. Marisa was sitting in her usual late-night pose, an upright, fetal position hugging her knees. At least this time she was looking at the TV. There had been times over the past couple of weeks that Myles had caught her sitting like this staring at a wall.

"What's wrong, Marisa?"

She looked at him, startled. Myles realized that she hadn't even known that he was in the room.

"Nothing. I'm fine."

Myles sighed and walked into the kitchen. He knew it was useless trying to press her to tell him.

But lately these periods where she'd been comatose were getting more frequent, and he was worried about her. He poured himself a glass of milk.

"Come here, Myles."

Myles walked out of the kitchen and into the living room.

"Sit down," she said.

Myles walked over to the couch and sat down. Marisa moved onto his lap. She rubbed her cheek along his, which she knew he loved because her skin was so soft. She had long ago figured out that whenever she allowed any part of her body to touch Myles, it soothed him. Forget the obvious like breasts, butt, or lips; it could be an arm, a shoulder, or a foot. It didn't matter. As long as some part of her was rubbed up against him, he was good to go.

Whenever he was worried about her, like now, she would use physical contact to soothe him. But Myles wasn't of a mind to be placated.

"Marisa, you don't have to go through this alone. If you have a nightmare, wake me up."

"Myles, you have to work in the morning, I don't. You should be sleeping right now," she said, kissing his neck.

Myles pulled away so he could look at her. "You get these often, don't you? What do you do? Crawl back in bed right before my alarm goes off so I won't know about them?"

"Myles, the reason I don't want to bother you is because I don't want you to worry or think you're doing something wrong. It's not you, it's me, understand?"

Myles looked at her. He knew she was trying to

reassure him, but she was missing a vital point, something that Myles had known for a while. For him, happiness exclusive of hers had become an impossibility.

ℛ Twenty-one

"Marisa!" Cassandra said, peeking her head into the office. "The *viejo* is here."

"Who, Mr. Lopes?"

"Yeah. I'm making myself scarce," she said as she left.

It wasn't often that the big boss came around, though he always seemed to know everything that went on. Since Marisa had been hired by Lopes personally, many people at the station thought she was an informant.

Marisa heard commotion on the floor, and soon Mr. Lopes, David, a couple of men that Marisa didn't recognize, and a sheepish-looking Cassandra, whom they had caught making her escape, were in her office. After exchanging pleasantries, Mr. Lopes asked Cassandra and Marisa to take a seat.

"Ladies, I'm not going to take up a lot of your time. I know you have a show to do in a half hour. You are aware that the latest Arbitron ratings came out today."

"Yes, we are," Marisa said. She looked at Cassandra, who was pale as a ghost.

"Well, ladies, I just thought I would personally stop by to tell you that the company is extremely happy with your performance. It's astounding how meteoric the rise has been, isn't it, Rios?"

"Yes, sir, it is," David replied.

"But then again, I knew what I had on my hands the first time I saw this young lady," he said, smiling at Marisa.

"Thank you, Mr. Lopes," she said. She looked at Cassandra, who was regaining the color in her face. "I couldn't have done it without Cassandra," she said.

He turned around to face her. "Ah yes, I've heard the show. You make an excellent tandem."

"Thank you," Cassandra said.

"Which is why I wanted to speak to both of you, to offer what I believe is a unique opportunity. Your sister station in D.C. has been underperforming in the drive-time slot, and we're going to be looking to make a change down there in the spring. So what we would like to do is simulcast *The Marisa Marrero Show* to D.C. Of course, your salaries will reflect this."

Marisa and Cassandra looked at each other. Both were trying to maintain their composure. Lopes looked at Marisa.

"Of course, if it would be preferable for you, you could work out of the D.C. studio. As a matter of fact, the company would prefer that you be a visible presence down there, at least until we gain a foothold in the market."

Marisa couldn't believe her ears. They were going to pay her *more* money to move back home.

"And as far as your TV show, Marisa, I think

you've seen enough of the facilities in D.C. to know they are state-of-the-art, so that wouldn't be a problem. But I know it's a lot for you to take in, so I don't want you to rush your decision. Take your time and think about it."

"We'll do that, Mr. Lopes," Marisa said. She wanted to make sure they knew she and Cassandra were a team.

"Ah, yes," he said, preparing to leave. "Once again, congratulations, ladies, and keep up the good work."

"Thank you," Cassandra and Marisa said in unison.

Cassandra shut the door behind them after first making sure the gentlemen were a safe distance down the hall. They squealed and hugged each other.

"What are the men in D.C. like, Marisa?"

"Fine, Cassandra. As long as you stay away from congressmen, athletes, and Cuban contractors who do shitty work."

That evening after Marisa was finished with her show, a bottle of champagne was delivered to her. It had a note attached:

Congratulations, drive-time queen. Sorry I had to cancel last time. I'm very much looking forward to that dinner you still owe me, so I can toast you personally.

V.A.

Marisa entered the apartment in an excited state. Myles and Winston had been watching an old Cary Grant movie, *That Touch of Mink*, when she barreled in. She was holding a bottle of champagne.

"Do you know who you are looking at?" she asked exuberantly.

"The apple of my eye?" Myles answered.

"Besides that," she said, smiling.

"A skinny Cuban girl with an apparently well-hidden alcohol problem?"

"Wrong again, my good man," she said, still beaming. "You are looking at the main reason behind WLAT's jump from number nine in the marketplace to number four, according to this quarter's Arbitron ratings."

"Yeah?"

"Yes, sir. And do you know how I know this?"

"How?"

"Because I was first in the city in my time slot!" she yelled.

"*Numero uno*, Marisa?"

"Well, second behind the all-news station, but they don't count," she said. She was so effervescent that Myles didn't know what was more bubbly, her or the champagne.

"Marisa, I'm so proud of you." The last quarter's Arbitron ratings had shown WLAT gaining slightly, but nothing like this. There was a high Latin population in South Jersey and Philadelphia that had been previously untapped, which WLAT now served, and apparently quite well.

Myles had firsthand knowledge of her burgeoning popularity. She was often recognized in public, and he had begun to lose count of how many cameras he had been handed to take pictures of Marisa with her fans.

She set the bottle on the coffee table and lay down on the couch, putting her feet on his lap.

"You're my hero," he said.

"That's understandable."

"But hell, your eventual victory was never in doubt. It was just a matter of time."

"But you *know* this."

"I'm gonna call the people at the *Guinness Book* with a new entry for the shortest list in the world: The things Marisa Marrero can't do."

"Get those frauds on the phone."

They laughed.

"This calls for a 'Marisa Day.'"

She perked up. "Yeah?"

"Yep. I was saving it for Valentine's Day, but we can have it early. How about Saturday?"

"But that's three days away," she whined.

"Hey, in order to do a Marisa Day true justice, it takes preparation."

"I know," she sighed. "I guess I'll save the champagne for Saturday." She got up to go put the champagne in the fridge.

Myles decided that he'd better get another bottle in case she wanted something to drink this weekend. Because come Saturday, that bottle was going to be poured all over her body, with his amoral, shameless ass slurping it up.

She came back into the living room and stood smiling at him.

Myles wanted to tell her he loved her but remembered his promise. He knew he should wait for her to say it before he said it again.

"I am proud of you, Latin love affair."

"Thanks, Myles. Why don't you show me?"

In Myles's pants, Mr. Happy raised its head attentively as if to say, "Yo dog, she's calling us out!" But he quelled him.

"I'll wait until Marisa Day."

Marisa rolled her eyes to the ceiling. Myles didn't know whether that meant "Get your mind off debauchery for one second" or "Please, like if I wanted to seduce you right now, you'd have the will to fend me off." He could never be sure if he was reading her right.

"No, I want you to dance a jig for me," she said, her voice full of mischievous anticipation.

One Saturday a while back, they had been lying down watching TV. Myles was clicking channels and stopped on a dated movie with black actors portraying stereotyped characters. He had stood up and started to imitate their dancing and even made up a song. When Marisa caught his act, she was too through.

Myles took a deep breath and shook his head. "Marisa, Marisa," he said wearily.

"Please, *mi chulo*, please do it for me," she begged.

"Do I have to sing the song, too?"

"Please. For me, baby." She puckered her lips.

Myles hesitated. "Okay, but only because it's such a big day for you."

She quickly slid the coffee table out of the way, sat in the chair, and started her contribution to the "jig" or—as it's also commonly known—the "buckdance." Her job was to clap her hands and stomp her foot. Myles stood up and went to the middle of the living room to assume the position. He first tucked his arms in like a chicken, putting both thumbs in his armpits. He then puffed out his chest and poked out his ass. Next it was time to "step lively." Myles leaned back, picked his knees up high, bobbed his head slightly, and pranced and preened around in a circle, always taking care to land gingerly on the balls of his feet.

Marisa started roaring. She loved to see him cut the fool.

"Don't forget to sing the song," she said.

"I'se jus' doin' a jig,
like a happy kid
my dawg's dun got him a bone,
and I got me sum corn-pone."

Marisa fell onto the floor convulsing. Her rib cage was heaving so wildly that it looked frightening. Myles decided to finish the second verse, though his tempo keeper was no longer doing her job.

"I'se jus' doin' a jig,
I might zag where you zig
I don't care cuz I'm grown,
and I got me sum . . ."

"Corn-pone!" Marisa shrieked from the floor, then literally started rolling around laughing hysterically.

Myles looked down at her and smiled. If he was willing to debase himself like this to please a woman, you couldn't tell him he wasn't in love.

He decided to go into the kitchen to get something to drink. Cooning it up made a brother thirsty.

From her spot on the carpet Marisa watched him

walk away. She sputtered a few more giggles before she finally stopped laughing. No one could make her laugh like Myles. She reached up and grabbed a pillow off the couch and slid it under her head.

As she stared at the ceiling, she knew that she had become very attached to Myles, despite her efforts not to. She would be lying to herself if she said she hadn't. Truth be known, she had accepted her position as Myles's woman without much of a fight. Damn, that simply was not like her, to be so *content*.

She rolled onto her side and looked into the kitchen. Myles was roughhousing with Winston. He makes you happy, she told herself. That's why you willingly relinquished sovereignty of your body, time, and space to him. That's why you haven't told him about the D.C. offer, because you don't want things to change between you and him. Because he makes you happy.

To Marisa it all seemed too good. The part of her that was expecting the other shoe to drop and have Myles reveal himself as a fuck-up was growing smaller by the day. She knew he thought too highly of her to do something stupid and risk losing her. If they were to stay together or part, it looked more and more like it was going to have to be her doing. In short, *she* would have to be the fuck-up. It was a responsibility she hated having.

Twenty-two

After Myles came back from the store, he began sweeping up the rose petals that were strewn out in the hallway. The only down side to a Marisa Day was the cleanup afterward. Marisa came out of her apartment. She walked over and gave him a kiss.

"You need any help?"

"Marisa, you can't clean up after a Marisa Day. That would be like making the Yankees sweep up after their ticker-tape parade."

She came into his apartment and sat down. She watched him sweep the petals into the apartment and vacuum them up. She had told herself that she was going to break the news of the D.C. job to him, but kept delaying it. It never seemed to be the right time.

He had just returned from his mother's salon, where he picked up some items he needed to braid Marisa's hair. He had also stopped by the store. He was putting away the groceries when she spotted a big bottle of hot sauce that he took out of the bag.

"That jumbo-sized bottle of hot sauce reminds me of a story," she said.

"Yeah?" Myles replied from the kitchen.

"Yeah, it was when I was sixteen or seventeen. I had been working all summer as a baby-sitter for some of the families in the neighborhood. With some of the money that I had earned, I went to the mall and bought an expensive designer outfit. It was the kind of outfit that my aunt never would have bought for me. One, because of the price; second, because she would have thought it too revealing. So, I took it home and put it in the back of my closet.

"Well, on a rare Saturday night that Esther let me go out with some of the other girls from the neighborhood, I decided to wear my new outfit. When I saw my friend's car pull up, I came down the stairs. I bumped into my aunt, who had been in the kitchen frying chicken. She had heard the car pull up too and wanted to see me off. Needless to say, my aunt was appalled when she saw my outfit.

"She asked me where it came from. I told her I bought it at the mall. She then said she hoped I still had the receipt because it was gonna go right back. When I asked why, she said because I looked like a whore and that she was raising me to be a proper young lady, not the kind of woman that men wipe themselves on. She then told me to go upstairs and take it off."

Marisa paused. Myles looked out from over the breakfast nook so he could see her face and waited for her to continue.

"I told her to look outside and see what my friends were wearing. That the only time I was allowed to dress like my friends was when I was wearing my school uniform. Aunt Esther told me that she couldn't speak for them, and then I raised my voice and said, 'And I'm tired of you always speaking for me!' "

"Uh-oh," Myles said.

"You know," Marisa continued. "My aunt had this stunned look on her face as if to say 'Whose ungrateful little heifer is this that stands before me?' "

Marisa heard Myles stifle a laugh. She ignored him and kept going.

"I heard my friends honk the car horn again, so I asked my aunt could we talk about it later. She said, 'Sure, but that outfit needs a splash of color, try this.' She lifted up the big bottle of hot sauce that she had been using to flavor the chicken and started pouring it on my outfit. 'There, that's better,' she said. So I pushed the bottle away and ran out the front door wearing my now stained, brand-new outfit. My aunt yelled after me, 'That outfit goes well with your lack of decency, and you can't get your money back for that either.' "

Marisa didn't tell Myles that her aunt's ruining the outfit wasn't what had bothered her the most at the time. The red fluid running down her clothes had reminded her of her father's blood. He had died in Marisa's arms when she was a child.

She noticed Myles looked visibly shaken.

"Hey, Myles, it wasn't that bad, I survived."

"You? I'm mourning the loss of the hot sauce. I mean, the *hot sauce*? Was your aunt black? What was wrong with her, wasting food like that?"

Marisa burst out laughing. "See, I try to share my childhood pain with you and you mock me. I'll remember that."

"I was feeling you, too, kid. It's just that I was

prioritizing. You know me, first the food, then the girl. Speaking of which . . . " He went back to putting away the groceries.

"So that's the way it is? Let's see you snuggle up to a plate of ribs tonight."

"It wouldn't be the first time."

She laughed. "Is it easy being this silly, or do you have to work at it?"

"Look who's talking. How about you letting me walk around thinking that the bracelet you gave me is silver?" The fellas at school had tipped him off to the fact that it was white gold. Of course, Brian had to rip him for not knowing what he was wearing.

Marisa laughed. "Hey, you seemed so happy that it was silver, I didn't want to burst your bubble. I figured you just weren't ready for truly aristocratic leanings, despite my best efforts to instill in you some class."

"Hey, hey, now, we know I got class."

"Yeah right. Monday through Friday from eight-thirty to three."

"All *right*. Marisa made a pun. Isn't she the clever one?" Myles said, using the rhyme he said whenever one of his fifth-graders used a pun successfully.

After washing and drying Marisa's hair, Myles was getting every thing together he needed to braid it.

"What's this about?" Marisa asked, holding up a videocassette box.

He looked at her like she was crazy. Surely, she had to be kidding.

"You've never seen *Sparkle*?"

"Can't say I have. Is it good?" She turned over the box to read the back.

"It's in my collection, isn't it?"

"Yes, but is it good?"

"What have I shown you that hasn't been a cinematic tour de force? Everything I own has been perused by a team of exacting film historians—most notable among them me—and has stood the test of time. They have endured the most rigid scrutiny imaginable before being allowed membership into the sacred and most estimable canon that is my video collection. Why, scholars from all over the world still call to ask me about any recent works that I may have added. By the way, you haven't forgotten to give me any of their messages, have you?"

"Yeah, I got the one that asked you to shut up," she said lightly, loading *Sparkle* in the VCR and sitting on the floor in between his legs.

Myles started combing her hair. When he had first suggested that she let him braid her hair months ago, he was going to add some extensions. But her hair had grown so much in the interim that now she didn't need them.

She began watching *Sparkle* as Myles moved on to braiding her hair. As he made the initial part in the back and started working his way up, he figured they were in for at least a three-, maybe four-movie afternoon because he was going to take his time to make sure he did her justice.

Myles wasn't paying any attention to the movie, other than listening to the songs, because he had seen it many times. But Marisa was riveted. During the scene where they were at Sister's funeral, Marisa leaned her head against his knee.

"You okay?" Myles asked, moving the big hair clip he was using to hold her hair out of the way so he could see her face better. She looked as though she was about to cry.

"Yeah," she said sadly, raising her head.

He scooped up some African Pride to grease her scalp, but before he applied it he kissed her head. She kissed his knee to reassure him that she was fine.

Marisa didn't move once during the whole movie. When Myles got up to get something to drink, she still remained there, transfixed. After the youngest sister's triumphant performance and the movie finally ended, Marisa rejoined him in the realm of the living.

"So what did you think?" he asked as the credits were rolling.

"Excellent movie, and music. Do you have the soundtrack?"

"No, I don't think they made a cast soundtrack. They do have one with Aretha Franklin singing the songs, though."

"Well, it certainly deserves a place of prominence in your vaunted film archives."

"Yeah. So what did you think of Sister, huh? Typical ho-bitch who got what she deserved, right?"

Why did he say that? He didn't think she really deserved to die. It was just an off-the-cuff remark meant to elicit dialogue about a movie. But . . . why did he say it?

Marisa spun around so fast that her clip came off and fell on the carpet. She had a look in her face that went beyond pissed off. It was a combination of anger and revulsion that altered her pretty face almost unrecognizably.

"What kind of stupid shit is that to say?" she snapped.

The intelligent thing to do at this point would have been to realize that maybe he had touched a nerve and to clarify or rephrase his statement. But Myles chose not to.

"What's so stupid about it? Look at the facts. When she met Satin he was with another woman, who he unceremoniously discarded when he caught sight of Sister. Sister saw him do this—hell, she damn near encouraged it. A classic bitch maneuver if ever there was one. What? She didn't think he would mistreat her as well? Second, you see how fast she forgot about her man when Satin came along? No explanation given to him, he just walked in and saw her naked ass getting skanked out. Add to that how she ignored the advice of her mother, and the callousness she showed her sisters, and there's only one finding I see. Ho-bitch," Myles said, punctuating the air with his index finger on each syllable.

"See? You don't see anything except that which your myopia allows you to. Your analysis is the equivalent of someone looking at the ocean's surface and thinking that is all there is to it, though you know nothing about it personally. Did you happen to notice the abject poverty that she was raised in? You have no idea what that kind of poverty can do to a person's self-worth—what have you ever had to go without? And, did you see a father in the house? Was a father ever mentioned in the story? Who do you think is a child's first teacher as far as men? Where do you think that a daughter should first learn how to differentiate between assholes and men? What type of man to look for and how to hold one accountable, if not from her father? I didn't see any evidence of any central male figure in those girls' lives."

Myles had never seen her this worked up, and she wasn't finished.

"And as far as her mother's warning, of course she's gonna dismiss it. Where was her mother's man? And she probably felt a woman without a man had no value. All her esteem seemed to be tied up in the fact that men found her attractive, which is awful because it's fleeting, it diminishes you, and you're dependent on them for validation of your worth. Here was this man, older and more sophisticated, who showed her a bit of attention, that she wasn't equipped to think was anything but love. She didn't know the difference between a loving, decent man and a sick, twisted, sadistic sorry ass fucker—an inability that cost her her life, I might add. Her naiveté was so gross, she was easy prey. Her self-worth was so low that she tolerated that animal beating on her. She needed her father. We hear all the time how much boys need their fathers, and they do, but what is often overlooked is how vital a father is in a daughter's life. I know if I had had mine, I wouldn't have let a third of the cavalcade of idiots get through my door, much less in my bed, that I did."

Myles looked at her wide-eyed. She returned his eye contact, but not with the usual intent of extracting information. This time there was a cold, piercing steeliness.

"What's the matter, you surprised to hear that your princess is damaged goods?"

Marisa went into her office, closed the door, and sat down. As soon as Myles had finished with her hair, she got away from his ass. Damn, he could get to her like no one else. How could a man be so opinionated about shit he knew nothing about?

She was aware that he hadn't meant to upset her, but, hell, that just made him all the more ignorant. Dangerously ignorant, she thought, because he doesn't know he's ignorant and therefore doesn't think before he opens his mouth. With his judgmental ass. The man has had it easy all his life and is gonna comment on shit he doesn't know about? Until he can give someone a frame of reference beyond Lawndale, he needs to shut the fuck up.

There was a knock at the door.

"Come in."

Victor Andujar walked in wearing a softball uniform. "Hey, drive-time queen." He sat in a chair facing her.

"Hey," Marisa said, "what are you doing here?"

"*Aspira* had a charity softball game today. I drove Rios back to the station. I heard you were in your office—wow, your hair looks nice."

"Thank you."

"Going afrocentric, huh?"

"Something like that. I wish they had told me about the game. I would have had some fun today."

Victor looked at her. "What's wrong, Marisa? What are you doing here on a Saturday anyway?"

"I have some things on my mind and went for a drive. I ended up here."

"Is it anything I can help you with?" he asked, with a look of concern on his face.

Marisa studied Victor. Right about now there was *something* he could help her with, but it had nothing to do with him pretending to give a damn about how she felt. And she bet he wouldn't complain about using a condom either. Or insist she meet his parents. Or pressure her to tell him how much she loved him. Or make her feel like garbage. No, Mr. Andujar was in the pleasure-giving business. She knew Victor didn't respect women and could give two shits about her, which was fine because she cared even less than two shits what an asshole like him thought of her anyway. When she was younger, she made the mistake of falling hard for Victor Andujars. Now she knew better than to put herself out there like that. Still, Victor used in his proper role could serve a purpose. Hell, she might still have some fun today yet.

"Well? Is there anything I can do?" Victor repeated.

How about a hassle-free stiff one? Marisa thought.

"No, thanks for asking." She decided to change the topic. "So you still gonna be on next week's show?"

"But of course. 'Puerto Rico—Independence, Commonwealth, or Statehood?' One of my favorite topics to discuss. Of course, you still owe me a dinner for the last time I was on discussing the turnpike shooting."

Marisa laughed. "Victor, you canceled on me, remember. Mr. 'Something's-come-up' . . . "

"It did, I couldn't get out of it."

"I don't wanna hear that. You had me get all dolled up with no place to go," Marisa said.

Victor leaned forward, resting his elbows on his knees, and grinned. "Yeah?"

"Yep. And you blew it, mister."

"So tell me, Marisa. Was it anything like that black one you wore to the A.L.L. dinner?"

"Maybe. Why?"

"Because if it was, you would've seen something else come up."

Marisa gave him a knowing look. He had never been that forward with her before, but evidently now he felt he had license to be. She knew why. Victor was a skilled pussyhound. He had picked up her scent of vulnerability.

Myles sat down on the bench in the gym's locker room and tried to figure out what the hell had happened earlier. Marisa hadn't said a word to him for the rest of the time he took to finish her braids. She went back to her apartment, and then out. Usually, if she was in her apartment and was going out, she'd come over and ask Myles if he needed anything. But he knew today was about what *she* needed, which was to put some distance between her and him.

He wasn't quite sure what had pissed her off so badly. Was it simply his lack of understanding? It could have been that she was mad at herself for getting so worked up over his idiocy. Or it could be that Marisa was pissed that she had made the admission that she had been "out there" in a previous life.

Myles hoped that wasn't it, because then he could be in trouble. No woman worth a damn wants to be around a man she doesn't think respects her. Something Amir and Carlos always warned him about was holding women up to an ideal that was too unrealistic. Putting women on pedestals seemed good in theory, but not in practice, because they have no room to maneuver (after all, pedestals are for statues) and will eventually fall off.

He hoped Marisa didn't think that he somehow thought less of her, because then she'd rid herself of him and he'd be back to languishing in the solitary existence he had before she entered his life. He used to think that it took strength to be alone. Since Marisa, he knew that it wouldn't prove anything except that he could be lonely.

"Damn," he said quietly. The thought of not having Marisa around was something he didn't even want to imagine. He rested his head in his hands.

"What's with you?"

Myles looked up. It was Brian. He had just finished his shower and was toweling off. Myles stood up and opened his locker. "Nothing."

"How's Marisa?"

Myles turned around to face him. Brian had his back to him and was applying deodorant.

"Why?" he asked, annoyed.

"Damn, Mr. Sensitive, my bad. I was just wondering if Marisa had a sister or a friend, you know, somebody else that has her exotic look, because I'm about to fire Tracy."

"Brian, did I just hear you say you was about to fire Tracy?" Amir said, walking in and putting his gym bag down.

"Yeah, so?"

"So? Nigga, you ain't got that kind of clout. You better take what you can get. Where do you think you're at, a Benz dealership or something, where you can just trade her in? You? Your Ford Pinto ass? You believe this nigga, Myles? Talking shit about firing somebody . . ."

Marisa raised her eyebrows when she stepped from the elevator into Victor's penthouse apartment. He noticed the look on her face.

"There's no crime in living well, is there?" he asked. He led Marisa into a sunken living room. "Make yourself at home, Marisa. Would you like a drink?"

Marisa sat down on the couch. "No, thank you."

"Let me get out of this uniform and take a shower. I won't be long."

"Do you need to make reservations for dinner?" she asked.

"Reservations?" he scoffed.

"Oh, you got that kind of juice," Marisa asked teasingly.

"I got more juice than the state of Florida, Marisa." He started unbuttoning his softball jersey. Marisa quickly turned away toward the fireplace. Above it was a huge portrait of Victor striking his best *GQ* pose.

"Interesting subject," she said.

"Thank you," he said. She heard his voice trailing

off, so she knew he was making his way to the bedroom and it was safe to turn around.

Victor's penthouse was fabulous. It looked like something out of *Lavish Living* magazine. While he was showering, she looked around. There were Roman columns, a majestic fireplace, marble floors, and oriental rugs. Besides the vainglorious picture over the fireplace, there was artwork everywhere, pieces from all over the globe. Everything looked in its perfect place, without looking cluttered. He had excellent taste.

Now, how did your silly ass get here? Marisa thought. She then decided not to beat herself up. All she was doing was waiting for a man to get dressed. If he was gonna try something, they wouldn't be going *out*. Not when he already had her on his home turf. Victor called out:

"Marisa, did you notice the African masks? I picked them up last summer in Ghana. The detail is remarkable."

Marisa spotted three masks along a far wall. She hadn't noticed them before. She went over to them for a closer inspection. While she was looking at them, she glanced to her left down the hallway. Victor's bedroom door was open, and he was walking around naked. Marisa looked back at the masks, but found herself sneaking another peek down the hallway. Victor's profile was stunning. She went back to the couch.

"Marisa, I'm a little sore from the game earlier. Do you mind if we order in?"

Marisa heard herself say, "That'll be fine," though she knew she had no business saying it. A song by

Marc Anthony came on. Marisa looked around for speakers, but they must have been those kind that were hidden in the wall.

A couple of minutes later, Victor walked out wearing a red silk set. He walked over to the bar to fix himself a drink.

"I ordered a couple of lobsters, is that okay?" He walked over to Marisa and handed her a drink. He sat down next to her and put his arm around her, massaging her shoulder.

"Damn, you're tense. You know, I have a Jacuzzi if you want to relax."

"No, I'm fine."

"You certainly are, Marisa Marrero," Victor said, leaning toward her and putting his other hand on her leg. He began to nibble on her ear.

"Victor, I'm seeing somebody," Marisa said, and removed both his hands. It wasn't nearly as difficult to do as she thought it would be.

He picked his drink up. "Marisa, when I said make yourself at home, I meant it. I'm not interested in a one-night stand."

She looked at him suspiciously. "What are you saying?"

"I'm proposing a merger, Marisa. I think we'd make an excellent team."

She was incredulous. "Victor, you barely know me."

"But I like what I know, and I know what I like."

"Yeah? Tell me, what do you like about me?"

"Huh?" he said, taking a sip.

Marisa wanted to laugh at him but didn't. She knew he hadn't planned on this. According to his way of thinking, she was supposed to throw herself in his arms, grateful as all hell for being chosen by him, and get carried off into the whirlwind world of being Lady Andujar. That is, until he got tired of her. Or found somebody "more ambitious," or some other lame excuse.

"You heard me. Why me?" she asked.

Victor seemed to think the question was preposterous. "I don't understand. Why not you?"

All of a sudden Marisa found herself missing Myles. She patted Victor on the leg. "Well, as I said, I'm seeing somebody."

He stood up. "I know, your schoolteacher," he said derisively.

Marisa stood up with him. "You spying on me?"

"Marisa, I've done a little research, that's all." He walked over to the bar to refresh his drink. "Don't get me wrong. It's kind of quaint, you and your working man."

"Victor, teaching is an honorable profession. Every other Latino on the face of this earth feels that way except you and your bourgeois ass."

"Hey, I know. Somebody has to do it, and I'm sure he loves the little kiddies. But, Marisa, you're kidding yourself if you think he's enough for you. You need to be with someone that deserves you."

"Like you, right? Victor, you just want something that looks good on your arm. I suggest you buy a Rolex."

"I already have three."

"My only value to you is that I'm new and exciting. But unfortunately, you can't throw me on a far wall when you're tired of looking at me. I'm bound to depreciate with age, Victor. I'm human."

"Marisa, you can't tell me you're satisfied. He doesn't make enough to pay your taxes. It's a bad match. Me and you, on the other hand, we match."

"Now, that's downright insulting."

Victor laughed. "Methinks the lady doth protest too much. But that's cool, Marisa, defend your man. I like your fire. I'm a patient man, I'll wait."

"This is a waste of time," Marisa said, gathering her keys and purse.

"Just don't make me wait too long. There are many others who want your spot."

"Bye, Victor." She headed for the elevator.

"You're not gonna stay for dinner?"

She pressed the button. "I'm sure you can eat for two. You got ego enough for ten."

"Well, I'll still honor *my* commitment and appear on your show next Saturday."

The elevator door opened. Marisa stepped in.

"You're gonna outgrow him, Marisa. It's sad but true."

"Maybe, but at least it'll take another thirty or forty years. I'd have to regress in order to be compatible with you," she said as the doors closed.

Myles put some braid spray in Marisa's hair and tied it up in a scarf before they got into bed. She slipped in under the covers without saying a word. He looked at her. She was facing the wall, keeping her back to him.

Earlier, after her diatribe against Myles's lack of

empathy and short-sightedness, it seemed it was all she could do to muster up the will to be in the same room with him, much less let him touch her so he could do her hair. Myles had to coax her to let him finish her braids, and he put in the Poitier/Cosby comedies to try to bring some levity to the room. She did laugh a little—it's impossible not to laugh at those movies—but still, her skin seemed even redder than usual, and Myles knew it was because her anger at him was still smoldering.

Since Marisa had gotten back from wherever she had gone earlier, she had said nary a word to him.

"Thanks for doing my hair. I've already gotten some compliments on it," she finally said, keeping her back to him.

Myles was going to ask who gave her the compliments or where she had been, but he knew better. So soon after a conversation where her virtue had come up would have been almost implying that he didn't trust her.

"You're welcome . . . Marisa?"

"Yes?"

"I didn't mean to upset you earlier."

"I know, Myles." She grabbed his hand and let his arm drape loosely around her waist. Myles recognized the move. You can touch me, but I don't want to talk about it.

Not placated, he decided to press the issue.

"Marisa."

"Yeah," she said, a little more wearily than before.

"Just one thing about what you said earlier, about your past."

She didn't say anything, but Myles could feel her hackles rising.

"I was just wondering . . . how . . . I mean, how . . . what I'm saying is, w-what kind of *fool* walks away from you?"

She tried to stifle a laugh but couldn't. Myles seized the opening.

"You're laughing? You're no better. What did you say before, 'damaged goods'? Don't you know you can't damage a diamond? And a brilliant red diamond, of which you happen to be, is the rarest of them all."

She turned over to face him. Myles slid his arms around her waist and pulled her close to him. She was searching for something in his eyes. Myles hoped it was sincerity, because she would find that he meant every word of what he had just said.

She must have found it because she then got on top of him and stretched out, which she knew drove him crazy. When she began kissing his ear, Myles started babbling incoherently, which made her laugh.

"I want to go home tomorrow and drop the truck off and pick up my car. Will you go with me?" she asked.

"What kind of fool says no to you?"

She squeezed his waist with her thighs. "Do you mind if I stay up here tonight?"

Mind? Myles was always asking her to sleep on top of him. She seldom consented to it, saying it was too uncomfortable. Myles always offered to put a pillow on his face, but she thought that he was silly to risk suffocation just so he could, frankly, cop a feel all night.

"You gonna be okay, with the braids and all?" Myles asked.

"This is true," she said. "I know, hand me that pillow . . ."

ꙮ Twenty-three

Myles couldn't believe how opulent Marisa's house was. He wasn't sure what she was pulling down, but he knew it was way out of his stratosphere. If this was the luxury she was used to living in, he wondered why she had taken the apartment in his building.

He was tiring of watching the Sixers beat the hell out of the Wizards, so he decided to go upstairs to see what she was up to. He went into her bedroom and found her lying down sleeping, looking all the world like the angel he said she was when he first met her. Myles stood there admiring her, certain that whatever happiness he was going to have in the rest of his life rested in the hands of this sweet figure.

Myles went over to her and lightly stroked her hair, careful not to wake her. It was nice to see her sleeping so peacefully. He knew her nightmares still plagued her occasionally, though he only knew about the ones that woke him up.

There was no way to describe all that she meant to him, but he was willing to give it a try. He sat

down at her bedroom desk. It was older and looked
out of place with the rest of her furniture. Myles had
asked her what its purpose was, considering that she
had a home office downstairs. Marisa told him it was
for jotting down thoughts that came to her in the
middle of the night.

Myles quietly took a legal pad out of her drawer
and just wrote what he was feeling. The words
flowed out, the pen being the substitute for his
tongue. When he finished, he looked it over. He was
glad to be able to get his thoughts out, but he decided it was too mushy to give to her. It violated his
"day by day" promise.

As he was putting the finishing touches on it, as
if on cue, Marisa started stirring out of her sleep.
Myles quickly stuck the pad in the desk drawer and
went over to the bed. His *princesa* was awaking from
her slumber, and he wanted to be nearby in case she
decided to bless him with a kiss.

Marisa woke up to find Myles sitting next to her
on the bed.

"Hi," she said, yawning.

"Hi."

"What you doin'?"

"Just taking in this castle you got here."

"There's no crime in living well, is there?" Marisa
asked, stealing Victor's line.

"No, not unless a person has to resort to a life of
crime to live this well," he said.

Or to keep his lady living like this. Marisa knew
what he was thinking. She didn't think Myles realized how much he had to offer a woman. She was

starting to, however, which was why she had brought him down to see her house, though she still hadn't told him about the D.C. gig. She knew one thing—he doubted himself too much.

"Myles Moore, when have I ever made money an issue?"

"Of course it's not an issue to you, Marisa. You're the one that has it."

Marisa thought about men like Victor and Ruben and how they couldn't begin to approach Myles as far as quality and substance. For all of Myles's faults, and there were more than enough of them, she knew beyond a shadow of a doubt that he adored her. And valued her. Ask any woman what she would be willing to pay for that. Marisa reached out and took his hand.

"Myles, it's not about what you make, it's about how you treat me. That's the true measure of a man." She squeezed his hand.

He gave her a thin smile.

"Besides, you gave me something precious the first night I met you," Marisa said.

Myles looked at her, puzzled.

"Your heart. What? You don't remember? 'You're carrying precious cargo, my heart.' Hello? Boy, am I disappointed. That was some good shit. I thought you meant it."

He beamed. "I did. I just can't believe you remembered it."

"I remember more than you think I do, Myles. You don't give me enough credit."

"What do you need credit for?" he said, looking around. "You can afford to pay with gold bullion."

"All right, Myles made a pun, isn't he the clever one?" she said.

They both laughed.

She looked down at their clasped hands. She rubbed her thumb along his ring finger. "So, what are you saying anyway? That I should feel guilty, living alone and having a house this big?"

"No, I'm not saying that. You earned it."

"Damn right I did." She chose her next words carefully. "I'm sure you could get accustomed to living like this real fast, couldn't you?"

Myles hesitated, then smiled. "You got that right. If only they had joints like this in Lawndale, me and the twins could have some *hellified* games of hide-and-seek."

ॐ Twenty-four

Carlos and Myles were at the studio, where they were watching Marisa wrap up a taping of her television show. She had concluded a panel discussion on the topic of Puerto Rico and whether it should retain its commonwealth status, or vote for statehood or independence. She had served as moderator, asking pointed questions to panelists representing all three sides of the argument. She was professional as always, never tipping her hand as to what side she leaned toward.

The plan was for the three of them to go meet Jackie, who was in the city on a Saturday for some reason (Carlos was being mysterious as to why), and go out together.

"Hey, boys," Marisa said, coming over to them. She gave Myles a long, passionate kiss.

"Wow," he said, startled, when she finally let him up for air.

"See, Marisa, you need to talk to Jackie. That's the proper way to greet a man," Carlos said.

"So what did you guys think?" she asked, taking Myles's hand.

"You know us. We think that Puerto Rico should be out from under the heel of the white man," Myles said.

"Yeah, bring that fraudulent, wannabe EuroRican panelist, so dead set against independence, over here so I can spit on him," Carlos added.

"Now, that would have made for some compelling television. I should have had you on the show," Marisa said, laughing. Just then she saw a man with a headset on motioning for her to come over. Marisa signaled to him that she'd be there in a minute.

"How much longer are you gonna be?" Myles asked.

"Gimme about twenty more minutes. Where are we meeting Jackie?" she asked.

"At the Bourse," Carlos answered, checking his watch.

"All right, let me finish up here." She headed toward the studio tech who had beckoned her.

Carlos's beeper went off. Myles snickered.

"Shut up, *pendejo*," he said as he and Myles walked toward the pay phone they had passed in the hallway. "Where's your silver bracelet, anyway?" They left the studio.

"Was that kiss for me?" Victor asked as he came up behind Marisa.

"That kiss was for my man."

"Regardless, Marisa"—he leaned in close so he could whisper in her ear—"my offer still stands." She shook her head as she watched him walk away. A bigger asshole never lived.

Marisa parked her truck in the indoor parking lot at the Bourse. It was a huge building that encompassed offices, restaurants, shops, and a theater that ran specialty films. It had been Jackie (who else?) who beeped Carlos, telling them to meet her in the lobby of the movie theater.

When Carlos had finished talking to Jackie on the phone, he seemed very happy, like he had just received some good news. When Myles asked him what was up, he had been evasive.

As soon as Carlos spied Jackie through the plate-glass window, sitting at one of the lobby's little circular tables, he left Marisa and Myles in his dust. When they caught up to him in the lobby, Carlos was sitting beside Jackie, kissing her so passionately it was like they hadn't seen each other in three to five. Myles wondered what was up.

"Whoa," Marisa said. "Those two oughta get a room."

When they got closer, they saw that Jackie was crying and Carlos was a little misty, too. This could only mean one thing, Myles thought.

He was right. Next thing he knew, Marisa was hugging Jackie, calling her "mommy," and he and Carlos were plotting his yet-to-be-born son's eventual rise to center fielder of the Yankees.

"How do you know it's gonna be a boy?" Marisa asked.

Carlos and Myles looked at each other dumbfounded, as if to say, "You mean, there's another possibility?"

When Marisa and Myles got back to his apartment, after toasting the expectant couple with well wishes and non-alcoholic drinks, he went into the kitchen to hang up her truck keys. Marisa kicked off her shoes and collapsed on the sofa. "Take a hike, *perro*," she said, brushing Winston away. "These shoes cost too much for you to be slobbering on."

Myles laughed at Winston's reaction. He was looking like, "No, Ms. Think-she-the-shit didn't just put her hands on me."

"Jackie's the closest thing I'll ever have to a sister, so I guess I'm going to be a *tia*," she said, her face buried in a pillow.

"You don't necessarily need siblings to be an aunt. For instance, you might marry a man who already has too-cute twin nieces," Myles said, violating his ban on talking long-term.

"I might," she said, her head still facedown. She rolled over and saw Winston still staring at her. "What? You got a 'tude? By all means, if you're feeling froggy, then leap."

Winston turned his ass up at her and walked away.

"Good job, Winston. It takes the bigger man to walk away." Myles moved Marisa's legs so he could sit down. She put them on his lap. He picked up the remote and began searching for basketball.

"It was nice to hear about Carlos and Jackie, huh?" Myles said, bringing up motherhood and marriage in a span of less than two minutes.

"Yeah, they had been trying such a long time."

"You know, I was starting to think that your girl was barren."

"Puh-lease, you know it was Carlos shooting blanks."

"Watch it now, you'd better still that tongue of yours, woman."

"I have a surprise for you as well."

"I'm gonna be a daddy, too?" Now he had brought up fatherhood, thus completing the trifecta.

"Not unless you've been out skanking it up."

Myles started changing the channels real fast, pretending he was hiding something. She kicked him in the shoulder.

"Marisa, I've told you about putting your hands on me in anything other than a loving manner. Well, that goes for feet, too."

"Do you want to hear about my surprise or not?"

"Not."

"Well, you're gonna hear it anyway. I'm taking my vacation at the station to coincide with your spring break."

"A whole week of lounging with my baby? That is good news. Why, this is truly the Lord's day!" Myles said, kissing her instep.

"It gets better," she said, enjoying his exuberance.

"That isn't possible."

"I've rented us a house in Brigantine for that week."

"Marisa, that sounds expensive."

"It wasn't that much. It's still off-season."

"But still."

"Myles Moore, let me worry about my finances."

"I'm not *worried* about your finances. I know you have mucho disposable income. It's just that I feel so kept, like a male mistress . . . a himbo."

Marisa had decided she was going to break the news to him about her taking the D.C. job during this Brigantine trip. She had no idea how he was going to react, but she could guess that it probably wasn't going to be too well. She wanted to be able to enjoy him and wanted him to have a good time as well which is why she decided she would tell him on the last day of their vacation. She didn't know whether her pronouncement would signal the beginning of a beginning or the beginning of the end. Nor was she quite sure which outcome she preferred.

"You mean so much more to me than that. You hear me? You do. Now, kiss the other foot, and be quick about it."

🎀 Twenty-five

"**G**et up."

It was the crack of dawn on Saturday, the sixth and next-to-last day of their stay at the beach house down at the shore. Marisa was waking Myles up so that they could go to the beach again to watch the sun come up. Myles failed to see what the big deal was. After all, excepting for when it was overcast, it happened every day, didn't it? But since Marisa derived a great deal of serenity and satisfaction from watching the sunrise, he had to see every one of them as well. Today he decided he was going to make a stand.

"I think I'll pass, Marisa," he said groggily.

"Come on, Myles, get up."

"I'll see it tomorrow, I promise."

"Tomorrow's not promised to anyone, babe."

"Marisa, the sun will come up tomorrow. You can bet your bottom dollar."

"I'm the orphan girl, not you."

"It's a hard-knock life, huh, Cuban girl?"

"Come on."

Myles would, he thought, but the bed felt too good. They had gotten in late last night from Atlantic City, where they had gone to see N'Dea Davenport perform. Myles don't know how Marisa did it, but mere mortals like him needed sleep. He rolled over, turning his ass to her.

"Won't you be sorry—correction, you're already being *sorry*—won't you regret it if some madman whisks me away because you were too lazy to come with me?"

Myles said nothing.

"Well, won't you?"

"That depends. Who gets the Benz in the event of your untimely demise?"

Myles heard her suck her teeth and storm out. Geesh, he thought, where was her sense of humor? He got out of bed and hurriedly got dressed. The thought of her alone on the beach this time of the morning did fuck with him, which she knew it would, which is why she said it.

Myles finished putting on his sweatshirt and grabbed a blanket, because it was chilly this time of morning and he wasn't sure if she had one. He opened the door and bounded down the steps, his eyes searching the beach for a solitary figure.

"Did you remember the blanket?"

Marisa was leaning against the house with her arms folded and a smirk on her face.

"Why do you always have to win?" Myles asked.

"Because I do," she replied. She grabbed his hand and started leading him to some predetermined spot on the expanse of sand that she was comfortable with. When they sat down, he wrapped the blanket and his arms around her. This wasn't so bad.

She began humming "Tomorrow" and then chuckled softly.

"When I was a child, that was my favorite movie. I thought Daddy Warbucks was the man!"

Myles didn't know why he chose that moment to satisfy his curiosity. Maybe it was because he had his arms wrapped so tight around her that he felt she couldn't squirm away. He decided to ask about her father.

"How did your father die, Marisa?"

Surprisingly, she didn't hesitate, as if she knew that particular question was coming out of his mouth.

"When we first arrived in Florida, we were put into an internment camp while we waited for my father's uncle and aunt to pick us up. During what was to be a short stay for us there, a man touched me in an inappropriate way, and I told my father about it. When my father approached him about it, he called me a *mentirosa*. My father knew I wasn't lying and nearly beat the man to death. The next day another man knifed my father in the back in retaliation. So instead of picking up his nephew and grandniece, my Uncle Eli picked up me and the corpse of my father."

Already knowing his next question, she continued. "The perpetrator was never brought to justice. It was then I decided I wanted to go into law."

She had recounted this story as matter-of-factly as if she were detailing a shoe shopping spree at the mall. She had been sparse with details. Myles tried to pull her closer to him, but while she didn't resist, she made it seem as if it wasn't really necessary. She changed the subject, to the one she'd been avoiding for so long.

"Myles, the company has decided to put my show on the D.C. station," she blurted out.

"Yeah?"

"Mmm-hmm. And since it will be the same show syndicated to both stations, they would prefer I move back home and do the show out of D.C."

Myles's heart began to race. "What did you tell them?"

"I told them I would do it. Hell, I miss my house, and I miss the area."

Not one word about what or who she might miss from this area. What was with her? Myles thought. Though he felt his chest tighten, he didn't say a word. He didn't want to sound the pathetic, universal lament of the discarded: "What about me?" Her silence with regard to "their" future spoke volumes. Myles was too disappointed and hurt to be angry. He lightly brushed her hair with his lips.

They sat quietly for a long time. Each waited for the other to say something. Marisa finally broke the silence.

"Look, Myles, here it comes," she said, pointing at the horizon.

When they came back inside, Myles decided he wanted to spend as much time away from Marisa as possible. He left her under the pretense of going to the gym (there was one down the block where he and Marisa had gone a couple of times during the past week) and he did go, but only to shower and change his clothes. Instead, he caught the bus to the city. Once there, he went to see Mike, an old college roommate of his who lived in Ventnor, and spent the day with him and his daughter, Yorla. She was having trouble with conversion of fractions, and Myles spent the afternoon tutoring her. That evening the three of them went to see the Atlantic City-Camden basketball playoff game at the convention center. By the time Mike dropped him off in Brigantine, it was well past ten o'clock.

When Myles walked into the condo, Marisa looked like she wanted to throttle him. He saw her glance up at the clock as he came in. Of course, Myles was prepared for the vitriol that he knew was forthcoming, having already rehearsed what he was going to say: Since you're apparently moving back to D.C., I figured I better get used to life without you. No time like the present, I always say.

Apparently, Marisa must have seen something in his face and decided to change her tactics, for her whole countenance changed.

"Did you have a good time today, honey?" she asked in a saccharine voice.

Momentarily taken aback, Myles stammered, "Yeah, I—I did."

"That's good. There's some food on the stove if you're hungry."

"No, thanks, I already ate."

Marisa was sitting on the couch and immersed herself in the book that she had brought along, *Drown* by Junot Diaz. Myles sat down in the adjoining chair and marveled at her show of indifference. Not only had he rehearsed what he was going to say to her, but he had also gone over *her* lines. Myles had expected her to ream him out for not calling her to let her know where he was, for wasting her time by having her sit around all day waiting for him, or even making her worry that something had happened to him. Hell, even for wasting the money that she had spent for them to be together on what was the last full day of their vacation. But she just sat there engrossed in the book, ignoring him.

Myles furrowed his brow and slipped into "uncommunicative brooder" mode, but she refused to look up, or even acknowledge his presence, for that matter. Jesus Christ, he thought, what manner of creature is this? Aren't women supposed to want to "talk about it"?

If men were from Mars and women were from Venus, then Marisa must be from the icy environs of Pluto.

The only sound that emanated from her were little giggles whenever she reached a funny passage in the book. Enough of this madness, Myles decided.

"Marisa, I—"

Just then she really started laughing. "Myles, this book is *hilarious*. There is this part where he turns on the light and the cockroaches are so bold they tell him, 'Hey, *puto*, turn that shit off.' "

Myles wanted to tell her that he had already read the damn book. That he was the one who had recommended it to her. But he put on a thin smile and decided to wait for her to stop laughing before he tried to speak again.

She didn't afford him the opportunity. Instead of coming down from her laughter high slowly like normal people, she stopped abruptly and said, "Well, that's enough silliness for one evening. I'm turning in."

As Myles wondered what silliness she was talking about—the humor of the book or the delight she was taking in messing with his head—she walked over to him and gave him a peck on the cheek. "Good night."

Myles pulled her onto his lap, which for the look of surprise she gave him you would have thought this was the last thing in the world that she had expected. He raised his eyes to her. He couldn't believe she was actually going to go to bed without finding out what was wrong with him, or at the very least where he had been all day.

She returned his gaze for a second and then feigned a look of recognition.

"Oh," she said. She then brought her face to his and gave him a long, soft kiss on the lips and stood up. "Is that better?" she asked sweetly, pretending that that was what he had wanted.

"Yeah," Myles mumbled, "thank you." *Just take your cloying ass to bed or to whatever cavern you slumber in, you heartless demon bitch.*

"*De nada,*" she said as she pranced into the bedroom.

It sure wasn't. And it was becoming more and more evident to Myles that this was pretty much the energy she was willing to exert to make their relationship work.

The next afternoon as Myles was driving back to Lawndale, Marisa slept in the car. Actually, she wasn't sleeping. She was resting her eyes and recounting the events of the past twenty-four hours. Yesterday, after waiting for three hours for Myles to return, she had called the gym. When she found out that he had left hours ago, she suspected he was up to something. After several more hours passed without a call from him, she knew for certain that something was wrong.

It obviously must be her mentioning that she was moving back to D.C. Could he really be that simple? His woman, whom he professes to "love," tells him about a golden opportunity in her career and he sulks like a selfish eight-year-old? Was that his brand of love he prattled on so effusively about? He couldn't for one instant be thrilled for her without thinking about the impact it would have on him? Why, because his source of *chocha* would not be so readily available as it was now? What a big fucking baby, she thought. He can shuttle his ass down I-95 whenever he feels so inclined.

Or, he could relocate with her. Believe it or not, she wanted to say, there are schools down there, too, and rumor has it that they require teachers as well. Why should she be expected to stunt her career happiness for him?

But she sure wasn't going to be the one to bring that up. It was a hell of a thing to ask a man to do, to move with a woman to another city into *her* house, especially when he was already insecure about their differences in income. Besides, she wasn't sure if taking such a big step with Myles was what she wanted, anyway. If he moved into her house, he would *be there*. All the time. There would be no buffer zone between them on the occasions when he showed his ass, like he did yesterday. The way he had reacted pissed her off. Instead of voicing his concerns like a man, he reverted into his passive-aggressive "I'm upset so I want you to be upset, too" childish mode, and disappeared for fifteen hours.

So when he had walked in last night, she was prepared to curse him out in two languages. That was until she saw that idiotic, self-serving look on his face. She then decided that he wasn't worth it. No, that was too harsh. What she really decided was that she didn't want to give him the satisfaction of dictating her behavior. She knew what he wanted was an argument, and she wasn't going to play into his toddler-like antics. So, screw you, *pendejo,* you just sit there and stew, this lady is going to bed. A sly smile tugged at the corners of her mouth as she remembered the look of frustration and bewilderment on his face.

After picking up Winston from Amir's, Myles and Marisa went to his apartment. Upon playing the phone messages, they found out that Jackie's grandmother had died the previous night. She and Carlos had left for Puerto Rico early that morning and would not be back until next weekend.

"Did you ever meet her?" Myles asked Marisa.

"Yes, one summer I went to P.R. with Jackie. I used to talk to her often on the phone when Jackie and I were roommates in college," she replied wistfully. "She was a sweet lady."

Myles looked over at her. She looked mournful and pensive, like she needed a hug. However, he wasn't of the mind to provide any sort of comfort.

Besides, she would probably just brush him off with a shrug lest she ruin her longstanding role as the non-needy Cuban Superwoman. He went into the bedroom to lie down, while Marisa went to lie down on the couch.

Winston walked back and forth between the bedroom and the living room, trying to figure out what the hell was going on. He finally settled next to the couch and lay down.

That traitorous mutt. Myles hoped he remembered where he chose to make his bed the next time he got on Marisa's nerves and she challenged him to a brawl. He'd better not come scurrying to him.

The next morning at school Myles wasn't himself. Marisa had gone out yesterday, and when she got back in—late, he might add—she had spent the night in her apartment. He tried to never bring any moodiness to school with him, but the kids sensed that he wasn't with them. The death of Jackie's grandmother had done little to ease his self-pitying. Anybody with a grain of sense would have realized that in the grand scheme of life, his problems were trivial, right? Or at the very least, he could have the common sense to try to reach an understanding with Marisa. But any chance of that happening ended for Myles at approximately a quarter after twelve that afternoon.

While his kids were at lunch, Myles walked into the teachers' lounge. Brian, Ron, Mike, and Tim were all hunkered over a magazine, giggling. When they saw him, he could tell by the looks on their faces that he was the butt of the joke.

"What gives?" he asked.

For some reason they found that question funny. They all looked at each other and started laughing. Brian, the self-appointed group spokesperson, decided to hold court.

"That's what we were gonna ask you, son. What, or better yet, *who* gives, and who may she be giving it to?" Whatever he was talking about, he was cracking himself up, more so than the others. He slid the magazine across the table to Myles.

It was the new copy of *Philadelphia Magazine*, and it was turned to an article on Marisa. It showed a nice picture of her sitting in Fairmont Park under the heading "Philly's Hottest Import." Myles then remembered that a while back Marisa had mentioned in passing that they were doing an article on her.

"So?" he said, figuring it was your basic puff piece.

"Read on. The material becomes more interesting. I took the liberty of highlighting some of the passages," Brian said.

Uh-oh, he wasn't stuttering. This did not bode well.

Myles flipped the page to where the simpleton had used a Hi-liter and continued reading:

> . . . *Amazingly, Ms. Marrero, who receives almost as much attention for her stunning looks as she does for her powers of persuasion and gift of gab, does not have a significant other in her life at the present time, but is looking.* "Emphasize that 'Ms.' please," *she told this reporter. So, hombres of the Delaware Valley, you can be buoyed that there is still hope* . . .

Myles's jaw dropped like a cartoon character's.

"Excuse me, I hate to interrupt, but did you get to

the part about the 'significant other,' or lack thereof, yet?" Brian asked.

Myles ignored him and kept reading the article to the end.

"Because if you had, let's just say that this opens up certain avenues that a brother thought were previously closed. And to think, I've been asking you did she have a sister. Hell, I was setting my sights too low. I think I'm going to ask her out instead."

Myles grabbed Brian's neck with his left hand and yoked him up.

"Yo—" Brian gurgled.

Myles backed him into the soda machine and slammed him against it. He threw an overhand right that landed squarely on Brian's chin. As he started to crumple to the ground, Myles released him and drew his fist back to hit him again.

He looked around and saw the looks of horror on the faces around the room. He looked down at Brian, who was bleeding from his lip. Myles picked up the magazine and stormed from the room.

He went back to his empty classroom and tried to get hold of himself. Had he lost his mind? Fighting on the job? He knew one thing, he'd better get himself together. So many times he had lectured the children on being too quick to fight, and here he was acting a fool. He glanced at the clock. He had twenty minutes before he picked up his class from recess. That is, if Mrs. Still didn't find out about his act in the teachers' lounge and send him home. He took a deep breath and read the article again.

This was some shit that no man should have to be subjected to.

Myles somehow made it through the rest of the day and left work at exactly three. Some of his kids were used to him staying after school with them to help them with their homework and let them play on the computers, but they didn't want to be around his preoccupied, forlorn ass anyway. Myles didn't know what his hurry was to get home. Marisa wouldn't get off work until late. He was probably hoping to get home before she left for her shift.

When he pulled up in front of the apartment building, Myles noticed Marisa's car was gone. Bernard was out front trimming some bushes. His son, who was nearly a year old, was in a walker nearby.

"Yo, Bern, Marisa left already?"

"Yeah, about twenty minutes ago," he said. He then broke into a wide smile. "When she was coming back from walking your dog around noon, she started playing with my son. He started grinning like a fool when she held him . . ."

Typical. Despite being the source of endless self-doubt and consternation in his life, little fuckin' Ms. (emphasize the *Ms.*) Sunshine is constantly spreading her rays of mirth and merriment wherever she goes, Myles thought. It was a thought that only served to piss him off more.

". . . So I asked her when she was going to have one—"

"Bern, she'll have to find a 'significant other' before that can occur."

Myles went through the door and bounded up the steps, leaving Bernard to wonder what the hell his problem was. Damn, Myles thought, he hated when he got like this. He hated that a woman could have so much control over him that when she upset him, he was unable to hide it from the rest of the world. Like his students, Bernard, or anybody else Myles encountered wanted to deal with his dumbass wearing his heart on his sleeve. That was another violation of a sacred Amir edict: the rest of the world should never be able to gauge how things are going between a man and his woman by his behavior.

But not me, Myles thought. He was as easy to read as a second-grade primer.

See Myles sad,
See Myles blue.
If your girl hurt your feelings,
You'd be, too.

He walked into the apartment and sat on the couch, putting the magazine (turned to the highlighted page, of course) in a position of prominence on the coffee table. Winston came sauntering over. Myles picked him up, put him on his lap, and turned him around to face him.

"You know, Winston, you dogs got it easy. You see a lil' bitch walking that catches your eye. You go up to her, sniff her hindquarters a little as way of foreplay, and boom! You're riding that doggie ass. You pull out, and that's it. No cards, no gifts, no follow-up calls, no further correspondence, and no heartache. Hope you enjoyed it, biiii-iiitch."

Hell, dogs of the two-legged variety didn't have to deal with bullshit, either. Because they knew what "good guys" like him always seemed to forget. That women are like sunsets. No matter how breathtaking one is, just wait a day or two and you'll see one more spectacular.

Even in his present state, Myles wasn't delusional enough to believe that nonsense. Marisa is the total package, he thought. She's the smartest woman I know, she's the funniest woman I know, she's the prettiest woman I know, she's the sexiest woman I know, she's the . . .

Goddammit! Why was he singing her praises? A female he adores lets the entire metropolitan Philadelphia area know that he is not the one she intends on building a future with and he's sitting here nominating her for woman of the year? If one woman encompassed all these different things to him, then maybe he needed to get out more. "For if she truly is so fucking great as all that, then what would she want with me?"

Riding this emotional roller coaster exhausted him, and soon he fell into a doze. He woke up at quarter past six. He still had four hours to wait until he saw Marisa, who was at the station working her normal shift, despite the fact that she was supposed to still be on vacation. Yesterday the station had called saying that her replacement host's wife had just gone into labor and asked Marisa could she fill in. If the phone rang, Myles decided not to answer it. It might be her, and she would be able to hear in his voice that he was pissed and thereby steel herself for the verbal fury that she had awaiting her tonight. The way he saw it, he had nothing to lose, since she evidently wasn't his anyway. She was going to tell him *something* tonight. No more hand wringing and no more marches, it's nation time!

Myles decided to do something constructive and write down all the things that he was going to hit Marisa with tonight. He listed eight cogent points of contention he had with her and committed them to memory. He didn't want to be outgunned by Ms. Marrero's (emphasize *Ms.*) "powers of persuasion" and "gift of gab." Myles turned on the radio to her talk show and heard her giggling about something with Cassandra. She made him sick. When he was at work, he had damn near committed manslaughter in the teachers' lounge, and here she was just humming her carefree ass right along like she didn't have a care in the world, which in the stark reality of it all was probably an accurate summation of how she felt. If, Myles told himself, she is capable of feeling anything.

ℜ Twenty-six

When Marisa turned the key and entered Myles's apartment, he was sitting in a chair in near darkness awaiting her. No TV or radio was playing, he was just sitting in silence, trying in his melodramatic way to appear contemplative. She sighed. Before she met him, she never thought a straight man could be a drama queen. Her prayers for serenity would go unanswered tonight because it looked like he wanted to clown.

She had tried to call Myles during two of the commercial breaks, but there had been no response. She wondered if he was teaching her a lesson in his juvenile way by being unavailable to her. He could still be pissed from down at the shore, which would be the height of gall considering he was the one who had disappeared for an entire day. She could just imagine what kind of fool he would cut if she pulled a stunt like that. Or, he might be mad that she didn't get in until late last night, or . . . who knows? Truth be known, she didn't feel like enduring his bullshit last night or too much of it tonight. But she might put up with a little just to broker a peace between them. She felt like a massage.

"Hi," she said softly.

"Good evening," he said.

"What are you doing?"

"Just catching up on some reading."

"In the dark?"

"Yeah. Have you ever read something that really moves you? Maybe it's the way the author turns a phrase or an especially thought-provoking passage, but it's such that you just have to sit and let the magnitude of the words weigh on your mind for a little while?"

"Wow, sounds deep."

She put down her purse and went into the kitchen and turned on the light. Myles heard her going into the refrigerator. Oh, so she wasn't going to ask what he was reading? No problem, he'd just sit here and wait. He had all night.

Myles heard her pour herself a glass. Her voice emanated from the kitchen, "Hey, Winston, *que pasa, perro*?"

After a couple of minutes she came back into the living room with a glass of cranberry juice.

Oh yeah, Myles thought, he forgot it was about that time. He wondered if she was having cramps or if she needed a massage—stop it, you pussy-whipped sonofabitch! He'd always been so attentive to her and where had it gotten him? Tonight was going to be about what he wanted.

She sat down on the couch and took a sip while eyeing Myles suspiciously. She set her glass down on a coaster right next to the magazine. It looked to him like she was deciding her next course of action.

Maybe she was contemplating simply picking up her purse and heading to her apartment and whether that would thwart any unpleasantness she might have to endure this evening. Not really, because his ass would be right behind her waving the magazine in the air like it was incriminating hair she had cut from Samson. She must have decided to make a stand because she didn't attempt to leave.

"So, where is the book you were reading?"

He thought she'd never ask.

"Actually, it's not a book but a very revealing magazine article."

Myles picked the magazine off the table and handed it to her, studying her face. He could tell that she hadn't read the article yet.

She flipped to the cover to see the name of the magazine.

"I haven't seen this yet."

She then began to read the article on her. She stopped when she got to the highlighted section and looked at him.

"Are the highlights yours?"

"No, Brian Boyd's."

"Oh."

She finished reading the article. Then she had the nerve to start *laughing*. Once again Myles wondered, What manner of creature is this?

"Are you sure you're reading the right article? Because I didn't find it humorous."

"Oh, come on, Myles," she said. "Aren't you being a bit melodramatic?"

"Melodramatic?" he said, his voice rising. "My girl has just told me that I don't hold a position of significance in her life. No, I stand corrected, told *everybody* that I don't hold a position of significance in her life and that she is still in the market for a man, but I am being melodramatic. I go to work and am ridiculed as a cuckold and *cabron,* and I'm being melodramatic."

"Exactly. In order for you to be a cuckold and *cabron* we'd have to be married," she said, attempting to be funny.

"It's nice that you can proffer a witticism, Marisa. Believe me, you don't have to remind me that I am no closer to marrying you than I am to being crowned the prince of Wales. If that was your intention."

"Myles, I never told the writer that I didn't have a man. I did tell her I was single. I'm guessing my publicity people at the station probably fed the rest to her to make me look more appealing and accessible. 'Emphasize that *Ms.,* please.'" She started laughing again. "Can you honestly say that sounds like me?"

She had a point there.

"All right. The problem is easily remedied. Let's just pen a letter to the editor in which you fix the omission by stating who your man is."

She looked at Myles like his mental faculties had taken leave of him. "I hope you aren't serious."

"What, you think demanding a retraction would be easier?"

"Do you know how ridiculous that would make me look?"

"No, Marisa. I have no fucking idea what it would be like to be made to look ridiculous in a magazine, this magazine in particular. Hell, I don't have any

ideas, thoughts, or feelings at all, for that matter, because I'm a non-entity, remember?"

"All right, let me clarify it for you. Do you know
how insecure *you* would look? That I have to write
a letter to boost your self-confidence?"

"Ohh, so you have my best interest at heart? Don't
worry about that. As you know, I fancy myself some-
what of a penman, so I have taken the liberty of
starting is for you."

Myles took out the pad that he had been using to
put his points of contention down.

"Dear Editor,
   There was a glaring omission in the article in last
month's issue. I am happily involved with someone,
and am not *on the market. Though my man has as-*
sured me that this missive was unnecessary, I felt
inclined to let the people of the Delaware Valley
know—"

"How would Brian, and everyone else you seemed
to be so concerned about, know who 'my man' is?"
Marisa interrupted.

"—about the wonders of one Myles Moore. For he is
truly a great man . . . my man."

"Oh, puh-lease," she said, snarling.

Even though Myles was kidding about the last
part, he didn't like the sarcastic bent of her "Oh
please."

"You don't have to give my name. Let me worry
about whether they know that your man is me."

"Myles, you're a bright guy. I know you know that Brian has wanted to screw me since he's first laid eyes on me. He's jealous of you, surely you must know that."

"I'm not so obtuse as not to recognize that. Nor are you not to know that this is larger than Brian Boyd."

"I must be. Why don't you explain it to me?"

"I want to know where I stand."

"Why are you so consumed by identification and labels? What, we have to get T-shirts made up that say 'I'm with her/him' when we go out in public?"

"Are you gonna send the letter or not?"

"As I said before, you're a bright guy. What do you think?"

"I knew you wouldn't," he said, rising and balling up the paper.

"It would look unprofessional and might have a deleterious effect on your career, and we simply can't have that."

"Exactly," she said.

"Because nothing or no one takes precedence over your almighty career," Myles said sarcastically.

"*Correcto*," she said coldly. "Whatever gave you the false impression that something or someone did?"

That hurt, and she knew it. Myles sat back down.

"Myles," she said softly, "I crawl into your bed every night. Do you know what that means to a woman like me?"

"I'm not sure if it means anything to a *woman like you*," he said harshly.

That drew blood. He regretted it as soon as he said it. She turned away to hide her face and got up to take her glass to the kitchen. She spent a minute in there to gather herself before she came back out.

"You sure are expending a great deal of energy on someone you think is a whore."

"Marisa, you know I don't think of you that way."

"No, I believe subconsciously you do. Hey, look how fast I gave myself to you. Surely you must of wondered how many others fucked me so easily."

"You? I was worried about you thinking I was easy."

She didn't find his attempt at humor the least bit amusing.

"Well then, I'm in love with one," he said.

"Maybe you have a predilection for whores."

"Marisa, I would marry you right now if you would do me the honor."

"Honor? What would a *woman like me* know about honor?" she scoffed. "I think maybe you think that a whore is all you deserve."

What the hell did she mean by that? Myles wondered. No matter, this whore motif was getting him sidetracked.

"Please, Marisa, spare me the theatrics. I was speaking more of your secrecy than your sexual past. You know I worship the ground you walk on, so please, would you spare me the wounded bird act?"

"Oh, I see, you're the only one allowed to have feelings."

"What, Marisa! You have feelings? Alert the town crier! Send forth the heralds! Sound the trumpets! Who knew? And to think, all this time I thought I was saying 'I love you' to the fucking walls."

"So since you can't inspire love, you're going for hate?"

"Any emotion is a step in the right direction, I figure."

"You figure wrong."

They sat there quietly for a couple of beats. Myles started to get scared.

"Marisa, you're my life."

She paused.

"Myles, I don't want the responsibility of being anybody's life."

"What do you want me to do? Wait and hope you'll love me back one day? You're impossible to read."

"First of all, you can start by stop trying to analyze me all the time. I am not some book whose plot is guaranteed to reveal itself to you as you flip the pages or some puzzle that can be pieced together. I'm a work in progress, I don't know why you can't just enjoy me as such. Furthermore, why is it incumbent on me to tell you what to do? I asked you to be patient before, but you take every step I make toward you and dismiss it as trivial. You make me feel like shit for not feeling for you in the manner that you feel for me, as if I'm trying to hurt you."

"Marisa, please understand that you are far and away the best thing to ever enter my life and that I am ridiculously in love with you."

"It's not enough that you love me, Myles," she said wearily. "I'm scared . . . that—"

"You won't love me back with the same devotion or intensity, right? Let me worry about that."

"How big of you," she said, and then hesitated. "But . . . a leap of faith."

She was fumbling for words, which she rarely did. It was like she was trying to spare him something.

"What is it, Marisa? I'm a big boy."

She muttered something to herself—Myles thought it was "Exactly." She turned those big, beautiful eyes of hers to the ceiling momentarily and took a deep breath like whatever she was about to say would take her down a path whence there would be no return.

"Myles, the way you act, I find it hard to take you seriously. Sometimes, too often, you're not a man to me."

Myles' cheeks flushed with anger. Did he hear that right? In the world according to Marisa, her fear of not being able to love him back was not due to some failing on *her* part but because he lacked the attributes to warrant her respect as a man? This smug, condescending shit was way over the line.

"You know, Marisa, I thought you were better than that, the stereotypical Latina need for machismo bullshit. Maybe you don't think someone's a man unless he's bossing you around or kicking your ass, or cheating on you or hiding his feelings from you so you're always in a state of doubt. Is that the definition of manhood you speak of?"

"Maybe I want a man who doesn't sulk and pout when he doesn't get his way. Maybe I want a man who sees things beyond the limited scope of Lawndale. Who recognizes that he is in a great many aspects ignorant and make adjustments. That knows when to be still and listen. Maybe I want a man who knows that there is a time to be accommodating and pliable and a time to be inflexible and strong, and a man that can tell the difference. A man that trusts in his own gifts. A man who has the strength and self-confidence to be patient and bet that he has so much to offer that a sane woman couldn't possibly walk away from him."

"Marisa, this urgency was brought about when you dropped the bombshell about moving back home, without giving one hint as to where I fit in the equation."

Myles paused. His thoughts went back to when as a child, he would sit and listen to the conversations of the old ladies in his mother's beauty shop. They often said that a woman, no matter how headstrong and independent she was, still had a natural inclination to want to believe in and follow a man. "Just as long as you don't ask her to follow behind no fool," one would add, making the others laugh.

While Myles was still reeling from the notion that he was apparently that "fool" in Marisa's eyes, she spoke.

"I don't know what to say," she finally offered, giving him a look like he was the most pathetic thing on two feet.

That did it, he was through.

"Why don't you show some character for once and say what you really want to say?"

His "character" implication vexed her greatly.

"A man that can tell the difference. A man that knows what to do, which evidently you don't," she said scornfully.

"Oh, now I'm supposed to be a mind reader. What, I'm supposed to demand that you don't take the job in D.C. so you can resent me and take it anyway? I'm supposed to insist I move in with you in D.C. so you can accuse me of crowding you and being too clingy? Please, Marisa, you're really killing me. Why don't you do me and you a favor and be honest with yourself? The cold, hard truth is that no matter what I do, it would be the wrong decision. No matter how I act, you'd find something wrong. Why? Because you fear commitment and are looking for an out, which this job relocation provides you with. You are too scared to give yourself the chance to love me, which you could if you weren't so pitifully jaded. I find it ironic that you seem to know so much about manhood when you haven't even got womanhood down yet."

"Yeah?"

"Oh, yeah. Whoever heard of a female who is too emotionally stunted to tell the man that she's sleeping with that she loves him? Whoever heard of a female who is unable to express her love for a man excepting when her legs are spread?"

That hurt her deeply. He just kept right on going, too angry to know when to stop.

"Whoever heard of a woman who didn't want to get married? Whoever heard of a woman who didn't want to have children? Whoever heard of a woman who has a great, wide, gaping chasm where her fucking heart is supposed to be?"

"Are you done?"

"Let's see . . . I think that about covers it."

She got right in his face, like she did on their first date when he made that curried shrimp dish.

"I mean, are you truly done, Myles Moore?"

Fuck it, she was looking for an out anyway. He was just helping her find it.

"Yeah, I'm done, Marisa."

Her gaze lingered on him for a couple of seconds.

Though she was staring right into Myles's eyes, her face was emotionless. She stood up, picked up her purse and her jacket, and opened the door. Before she stepped out into the hallway, she turned back to look at him.

"Just a point of order, Myles. I never said I didn't want to get married and have children."

What was this? Myles perked up. Was she getting cold feet? Was there about to be a reconciliation, thus ending the shortest breakup in the history of mankind?

"I just never wanted to get married to *you* or have *your* children."

She then stepped out, and closed the door behind her.

Oomph. Shit. His eyes widened and moistened. He was barely able to hold back the tears long enough for her to get out the door.

❧ Twenty-seven

The next couple of days, Marisa was as hard to find as she had been that hectic first week she moved into the building. Myles knew she had another week of vacation coming to her, so he assumed that she was spending it at her house in Silver Spring. He couldn't be certain, though, because he refused to call her. If she wanted to apologize to him, she could do so to his face. Though he knew he had gone over the line as well.

Myles was surprised that on Wednesday, while he was at school, she came into his apartment and picked up various clothes and items she had in there, but he figured she must have driven up for the day. She had left his spare key on the coffee table, a gesture of finality that jolted him when he saw it lying there.

Myles woke up Saturday morning with some hope. Jackie and Carlos were due back today. He sure was going to be glad to see them. He didn't know how they were going to react when they found out about his blowout with Marisa.

Myles was hoping that Jackie would speak on his behalf to Marisa. He missed her already; any anger he'd had about her comments had faded. Well, not really. It wasn't easy to forget a woman telling you she doesn't want to have your kids . . . and that you're not a man. Damn, that shit was way out of bounds. If she really did feel that way, there was nothing to salvage. Not a man? If that wasn't cause for a brother to take a stand, then he didn't know what was. He had to draw the line somewhere, right? Plus, she didn't love him anyway, so fuck it, they had a nice run. He wasn't the one who liked spinning his wheels, wasting his time, when he knew he was in a relationship that wasn't going anywhere. Myles knew nine months wasn't a tremendous amount of time, and he had never got the impression that his footing was secure. To him, it was almost as if she was cooling her heels with him while she was waiting for a better offer to come along. Maybe he was just the interim brother.

The way Myles saw it, whether or not it was difficult for Marisa to truly commit to a man, it wasn't going to be him because she didn't believe in him. Nine months, nine years, what's the difference?

The longer he spent with her, the less time he was going to have finding someone who was ready to settle down. Hell, he was ready for kids. Besides, her moving back to D.C. was her way of signaling the beginning of the end anyway. It just would have been a slower, more pain-inducing death. Their airing out had helped to expedite matters. Still, he didn't expect her to be as MIA as she had become.

Carlos had called him yesterday when he was out.

Their flight wasn't due back until ten p.m. Myles decided to go over to Amir's shop to see what he was up to. Myles hadn't seen him all week, partly due to the fact that he didn't feel like fielding questions from Kenya concerning Marisa's whereabouts. And never mind the twins. For as far as Deja and Jade were concerned, he'd better not make too much of a habit of coming around without Marisa in tow, lest he wanted to start ducking flying "Keesha" dolls.

But he figured the barbershop was safe. The only thing airborne there would be the bullshit spewing forth from the brothers' mouths.

When Myles walked in, his brother was, as usual, pontificating. From what Myles could gather, one of the customers, named Will, had been caught trying to run two women and had not handled the situation well, because now neither woman wanted anything to do with him. Amir listened with amusement before speaking with his usual aplomb:

"Will, Will, Will . . . have you learned nothing in all these years? 'Will' you ever learn? It's too late for you this time but, please, listen for future reference. Now, let me see if I got this straight. When those two sisters rolled up on you in that parking lot to confront you, all you did was stand there befuddled, hemming and hawing."

"Yo, Amir, they caught me off guard."

"I understand that, but that's no excuse. Son, if you can't run with the big dogs, then stay on the porch. If you're going to attempt to be a player, then be a clutch player. One that thinks fast on his feet. If not, then keep your ass on the bench before somebody, namely you, gets hurt. You can still be a mop-up guy. You know, the one that comes in for garbage time and gets the discarded girls and leftover skanks of the true players."

The people in the shop started snickering.

"I was in a no-win situation," Will protested. "What would you have done?"

"You should have immediately made a tactical maneuver called the 'parry and carry.' You see, they were united in a bond of sisterhood against you, a no-good cheating nigga, but that is a shaky, bond at best, because they both have feelings for you and are, I'm sure, a little mistrustful of each other. You should have exploited this by immediately deciding which one you liked the best and cursed out the other one in front of her. And when I say 'curse out,' I mean a vicious all-out assault on any kind of sensibilities, with no regard for common decency. Man, you can't pull any punches. And lie if you have to. An example could be: 'What, bitch? You been trying to suck my dick for the past six months, and because I keep turning you down, now you trying to turn my girl against me? Damn, ho, what's next? You gonna go spread your lies to my mother, too?' "

The shop erupted in laughter. Amir continued.

"The 'parry' is that you deflected the initial thrust of their united venom by dividing them. The 'carry' is that you then shift all the emphasis and blame on the woman you didn't choose and away from you. She then becomes the asshole, not you. She looks like she's trying to come in between you and the 'winner,' i.e., the girl you chose."

"Ahhh, so me trying to reason with both of them . . ."

"Was a waste of time. There was no way you were

going to keep both of them, so you should have cut your losses," Amir said.

"But damn, do you really have to be so vicious to the other woman? I mean, to curse her out like that?" Will asked.

Amir was made so incredulous by that question that he stopped cutting his customer's hair.

"What? Fellas, do you hear this? This cat's worried about ethics. Will, if you think it's beneath you, if you don't have the stomach for it, then stop trying to be a player. Find yourself a good girl and sit your ass down somewhere. Hell, I sure won't think any less of you. That's what I did."

That's true, Myles thought. The threat of losing Kenya had made Amir stop his womanizing. In fact, Amir's story was similar to Will's except that he had to parry, carry, and *marry* to keep Kenya.

The conversation of the shop then shifted to basketball, so Myles walked over to talk to Amir.

"What's up, man?" Amir said, shaking his hand. "What you been up to all week?"

"Been keeping myself busy in school."

He eyed Myles suspiciously. "So how's Marisa?"

Myles decided not to tell him anything. All throughout the past week he had given himself pep talks trying to convince himself that logically it made sense that they parted because she didn't want the things that he wanted, nor did she love him as he loved her. Not only that, she evidently didn't hold him in the same regard that he held her.

"She's fine. Kenya and the girls home?"

"No. They're going with Mom to Baltimore today. You and Marisa coming over for dinner tomorrow?"

Even in the best possible scenario, including Jackie's intervening on his behalf, Myles couldn't envision Marisa and him attending Sunday dinner at his parents' house. Hell, Jackie was just coming back from burying her grandmother. The last thing she probably felt like doing was getting involved in his and Marisa's nonsense.

"Maybe."

"Carlos and Jackie back yet?"

"No, they come back tonight."

"You and Marisa picking them up from the airport?"

"Unhh-unhh. I don't think they need a ride." This was like the third time in the conversation that Amir had brought up Marisa's name. It seemed like he knew something, but Myles wasn't sure.

Amir finished with the customer and walked him over to the register. After they were done with the transaction, he came back over to Myles.

"Let's go in the back so we can talk," he said.

He followed Amir into his makeshift office. Myles sat down in a chair, and Amir sat on the edge of his desk.

"Brian came in yesterday."

Now Myles knew he knew that something was up. He was probably wondering about the state of the relationship and his mental state as well. Hell, by the time Brian got done telling him of their episode in the teachers' lounge, who knew what he thought? With the way he was fishing about Marisa, Myles was sure his reluctance to take the bait was making him even more concerned.

"Don't worry, I didn't kill her. It's not like her corpse is rotting in my apartment or anything."

Amir chuckled slightly. "You may have not physically harmed her. I'm just wondering how much blood you spilled with your tongue."

"You mean, did I perform a 'vicious all-out assault with no regard for common decency'?" Myles asked sarcastically.

"Shii-it. You'd better learn the difference between a man talking shit to skanks and how he talks to his lady. You best believe I know the difference."

"Yeah, well, she had plenty to say, too." Myles really didn't want to go into details right now. Not until he knew for sure the final outcome.

Amir could tell that he didn't want to because he didn't press him for specifics. "Well, you okay?" he asked.

"Yeah. I'm not the lovestruck simpleton you think I am," Myles said, knowing full well that was exactly what he was.

"Maybe. Either that or you still have hopes of getting her back."

"Getting who back? I never said she was gone."

"You don't have to, Myles."

"And if she is gone, I never said I wanted her back."

"You don't have to."

❧ Twenty-eight

Myles decided to wait until school Monday to talk to Carlos instead of bothering him and Jackie on Sunday. He figured that Marisa would have to come back for work so he would see her then anyway.

Myles went to see one of the kids in his class, Nichelle, sing at a church in Philadelphia. She was singing a solo that day and had invited him to come hear her. She did a very good job, as he knew she would because she had a voice far beyond her tender years. During the announcements when the lady asked if there were any visitors in attendance, Myles stood up and introduced himself to the congregation.

After the service, several of the women invited him to their Wednesday night ministry, which was for singles. A couple of them seemed to be subtly offering him more than spiritual fellowship. Not because he was such a be-it-all stud, he figured, but because of the dearth of black men in the church, he probably seemed like one to them. All it did for him was reinforce how reluctant he would be to reenter the dating scene.

At school the next day, Myles had to attend a math workshop in Cherry Hill and was out of the building until two-thirty. He came back just in time to ask his substitute which of the kids had acted like fools, and to keep those wayward souls after school. Around three-thirty Carlos came into the room. Myles decided to dismiss the children from detention so that he could talk to him freely.

"Hey, man," Myles said, shaking his hand warmly. "I'm sorry about your loss. How's Jackie taking it?"

"She's cool. It wasn't totally unexpected. She'll be fine," he said as he sat down. "So, I heard you had a loss as well."

"How'd you hear that?" Myles asked, assuming that Brian Boyd had been running his mouth.

"Marisa called Jackie last night."

"Yeah?" he asked, wishing it was him that she had talked to instead of Jackie. Myles sure was glad that today was Monday. He couldn't go much longer without seeing Marisa. Though she had given him back his key, she was still accessible, living right down the hall. "What did she have to say for herself?"

"Nothing for herself, but plenty against you. Mainly, that you were a piece of shit who showed your ass while me and Jackie were gone. Man, by the time she got done listing your offenses, when Jackie finally hung up . . . the look she gave me . . . damn if *I* wasn't walking on eggshells."

Myles laughed. At least Marisa wasn't indifferent about him. Then he'd really be worried.

"Carlos, you only got one side of the story."

"True," he said, laughing as well. "But right about

now, as far as you're concerned, isn't that the only side that matters?"

Myles had to cut his conversation with Carlos short because he had promised Marquis that he would go see his baseball game. That past week Myles had attended every extracurricular function that any child in his class was involved in. The kids and their parents appreciated his supporting their different activities, but he was doing it as much for himself as he was for them. It kept his mind off Marisa.

Myles enjoyed the game. Marquis played a flawless first base and got a big hit to help propel his team to victory. Despite his best attempts to focus strictly on the game, though, all throughout Myles found himself glancing at his watch. As if mandated by divine intervention, at exactly six p.m. the game ended. Myles congratulated Marquis, said his goodbyes to his parents, and beat a hasty retreat to the car. When he got in, he turned on the radio and pressed the preset button for WLAT. Myles heard Marisa's sweet voice, which he hadn't heard in a week. As she spoke *Español* in her lyrical way, he felt his heart soften. All of a sudden the beefs that he had with her seemed inconsequential. Maybe in time she could learn to love him. Perhaps one day she'd even be able to tell him so. Then, was it too far-fetched to think that he could be her husband? Then, dare he dream of the possibility of children? A little adorable baby girl that looked like Marisa? Jesus, he couldn't imagine being that blessed. *Beep!* "*Watch where you're going, you asshole!*"

He was going to be able to ask Jesus face to face if he didn't keep his mind on the road.

As far as he was concerned, he could chalk up the hurtful things that Marisa had said to him last week as "shit every man has to eat" from his lady. Myles wasn't sure when Marisa was transferring, but figured it was a while yet, since she had just told him about it last week. It would be probably sometime in June. Hell, next month school would be out. He could spend the entire break with her in D.C.

Myles listened to her voice. He just hoped she let him keep a modicum of self-respect when he spoke to her tonight. Though to be honest, he'd be willing to do a "buckdance" in the town square if he had to. He went back to giving the radio his undivided attention.

". . . Marisa, desde Washington, D.C. Llame al 1-800-877-2244 con una pregunta o un comentario sobre nuestro topico: La imagen de los Latinos en la Television y el Cine. Nuestro invitado es el Dr. Jorge Casiano, autor de . . ."

Myles felt like he was going to be sick. He pulled the car over, turned the engine off, and concentrated on the radio. Though he was a novice as far as speaking and understanding Spanish, he knew what he had just heard.

The show went to a commercial. Myles turned the car back on and sped home.

When he got in, he picked up the phone and called WLAT with the number Marisa had given him to call. The lady that answered the phone told him what he had suspected, confirming his fear. Marisa's show was now being syndicated from Washington.

Myles put the phone down and bounded down the stairs. He knocked on Bernard's apartment door. When he answered, Myles could tell that he had interrupted his dinner.

"Hey, Myles, what's up."

"Hey, Bernard, did Marisa move out?"

Bernard must have seen the wild look on his face. He stepped out into the hall with Myles and closed the door behind him.

"Yeah. On Wednesday she paid the remaining rent on her lease and turned in her key. She said she would send for her things. I thought you knew."

"No, man, I didn't." Myles's head was spinning. He knew he must look pathetic, but he didn't care. "Did she say anything else?"

Bernard studied him for a second, like he was deciding whether he should tell Myles or spare his feelings. He gave a slight shrug as if to say, "All right, the brother asked . . . "

"When I asked her why she was turning in her key when the apartment was paid up through September, she said because she had no intention of ever coming back."

Jesus. Myles knew better than to ask him, "Did she say anything about me." There was no telling what he might've said. "Yeah, she said to tell you that she's moving on to bigger and better things, thumbdick."

Myles walked back up to the apartment, dizzy as all hell. He sat on the couch and looked at Winston.

"Damn, why didn't you stop her Wednesday when she came in to drop off the key?"

The dog looked at Myles as if to say, "Stop her? You know can't nobody tell that headstrong girl what to do. You're the dumbass that pissed her off."

Myles picked up the phone and called Carlos.

"Hello?"

"Yo, 'Los, Marisa moved back home."

There was silence at the other end.

"Did you hear me?"

"Yeah, I heard you. I thought you knew."

Why did people keep saying that to him?

"You knew?"

"Yeah, she told Jackie she was going to if the station told her it was feasible now, and apparently it was. And as far as the TV show is concerned, she's done taping them for the year. When it resumes, from what she says, the facilities in D.C. are better . . . Yo, man, I was wondering why you were taking it so well. I should've suspected you didn't know."

"Will you watch Winston for me?"

"Why?"

"What do you mean, why? Because I'm out, that's why."

"You going to D.C.?"

"You're damn right I'm going to D.C."

"I don't think that's a good idea, Myles."

Myles had no patience to listen to his attempts to dissuade him.

"I gotta go, 'Los." He hung up the phone and called Amir.

"Hello?"

"Hey, Kenya. I gotta go out of town for a day or two. Can you watch Winston for me?"

"Sure, bring his ugly ass over."

"Thanks."

Myles hastily packed enough clothes for a couple of days and put them in his big duffel bag and threw it over his shoulder. He then called the school's voice mail and left a message that he wouldn't be in tomorrow. He scooped Winston up under his arm and closed the door behind him.

When Myles pulled up in front of Amir's house, he noticed Carlos's Camry was there. He got out of his car, leaving it running. Fuck him, he was dropping Winston off and getting on the highway.

Amir and Carlos came out of the house.

"Myles, turn off the car," Amir said.

"Boys, you don't understand. Whatever I gotta say to her, I'm going to say. Whatever I gotta do for her, I'm going to do. Whatever I gotta change about myself to please her, I'll change. For her, I'll do anything."

Amir appeared unimpressed. "That's a noble sentiment, Myles. I'm touched, I truly am. Now, please turn off the car."

"I gotta go, 'Mir." Myles said, placing Winston inside the fence.

"You don't gotta do anything. Now turn off the fucking car."

Myles looked at him. He looked fully prepared to whip his little brother's ass. He then looked at Carlos. He was giving him the look like "You my boy and all, but if an ass whipping is what it's gonna take to make you see reason . . ."

Myles reached in the window, turned off the ignition, took the key out, and leaned against the car. He stretched out his palms as if to say, "So speak."

Amir spoke first. "Do you think you are in the right frame of mind to do anything? I want to know exactly what it is you are trying to accomplish."

"I want my girl back."

"Assuming she was ever yours."

What was he trying to do, insult him?

"Yeah, Amir, whatever. May I go now?"

"Myles, if a woman can walk away from you after one fight without looking back, can you honestly say she was yours to begin with? Can you honestly say she cares enough about you for you to be pursuing?"

He was making sense, which pissed Myles off.

"She's not the type of person who lets her emotions out readily. It's easy for her to shut down—"

"And you think you being in her face is going to help, right?" Carlos said, interrupting him. "What are you going to tell her that she doesn't know? That you love her? She knows. That you regret what you said to her? I'm sure she knows. That you want her in your life? She knows that, too. That you're a great guy, a good-hearted person, and all of the other many positive attributes of one Myles Moore?"

"Who's better equipped than me to tell her?" Myles sputtered.

Amir looked at him like he was an idiot.

"Myles, you would never force yourself on a woman, would you?"

"What?"

"You heard me. You would never try to strong-arm pussy, would you?"

"What's wrong with you? Of course not."

"Then what makes you think you can force a woman to love you? If you wouldn't think of asking a woman to surrender her body, then why would you ask her to do so of her mind? Hell, women will tell you, you got a better shot asking them to give up temporary custody of their body. And as far as the mind is concerned, how can you honestly say you love a woman when you don't respect her right to decide her own fate?"

"Amir, I do love her."

"But you don't respect her?"

"I love and respect her," Myles said wearily. "I just think she may be a little scared or confused or feeling vulnerable—"

"And you might be right," Carlos interjected. "I think she definitely has feelings for you. Feelings that may be foreign to her or that she has spent years fighting down. Hell, you've lasted longer than any of the other men that Jackie and I have known her to date. We can tell she really likes you."

"Thank you. Now, as the man in Indianapolis says, 'Gentlemen, start your engines.' " Myles opened the door, slid in, and put the key back in the ignition.

"Your goal is to get her back, right?"

"Yes," Myles said. "Which I can't do sitting here, so if you two will excuse me . . ."

"But is that your ultimate goal?"

"Huh?"

"Myles, to use a baseball analogy, do you know

how teams are always saying they want to compete with the Yankees."

"Yeah, so?"

"Well, that is a loser's mentality. Every year they try Band-Aids and quick fixes for immediate gratification instead of patiently building for the long haul and taking their lumps in the interim. They're not successful because their goal shouldn't be just to compete with the Yankees; rather, they should want to *be* the Yankees, and take the necessary steps to do so."

"Your point being?"

"Right now you should be in it to win it. You've invested too much of your feelings already to be happy with just contending, being an also-ran who valiantly tried for Marisa but ultimately fell by the wayside due to lack of foresight. You should want to give yourself the best opportunity to achieve your long-term goals, which is Marisa's devotion . . . and respect."

"Which I can do from a hundred fifty miles away?"

"Listen, you can't sacrifice every principle you believe in just so you can have Marisa on your arm. You'll lose 'you' if you do that. You shouldn't want Marisa to take you back simply because you supplicate yourself, and are remorseful, or because you're handy; you'll always be a junior partner in the relationship. Rather, you should want her to accept you because she misses you and she *loves* you. Otherwise, how are you gonna stop this situation from repeating itself over and over again?"

"What if she—" Myles stopped short.

"If she doesn't, then she was never yours in the first place," Amir said, knowing what he was thinking.

"You have to let her go, Myles."

"Fellas, I'm as familiar with the expression, 'If you love somebody, then set them free,' but I just feel that I would have a better chance if I was close to her. You know, around her."

"No, you don't. That's a cop-out and you know it," Carlos said. "You've just gotten used to having a pair of titties in your back every night."

"Not that there is anything wrong with that," Amir said, trying to be funny and partially succeeding. Carlos laughed before he continued. "And if that is all you ever want from Marisa, then go with my blessing. If you beg her the right way, and make enough concessions, she'll accommodate you, I'm sure. Just be prepared to remain in that devalued, reduced role forever because there is no upward mobility, not with her."

"It'd be analogous to a woman who initially accepts the role of mistress who then decides she wants to become the wife," Myles said, admitting defeat.

"Exactly. And apparently that isn't enough for you, because that is what you had already," Amir said. "Now, me on the other hand, back in my day, that would have been enough for me. But then again, I had no character, or shame, I might add."

No matter what Myles was feeling, Amir could always make him smile. If their mom knew half of what he had done, she would disown him—after whipping his ass first, of course.

"Remember when I asked you a long time ago,

'Are you prepared to do whatever it takes to get the girl?' You said you were. Now then, prove it."

"But damn, 'Los, I miss her already."

"But your feelings aren't in question. Give her a chance to miss you."

He was right. It was a chance Myles had to take. He knew that if he went down there begging her to let him back in her life, he wouldn't have her respect. Not Marisa's. Perhaps other women would think a man chasing after them was gallant and romantic, but Marisa might rebuff him just because she resented that he was in her face telling her what was best for her. Or, if she did take him back, she would take his neediness as carte blanche to run roughshod over him whenever the situation suited her. What's worse was that Myles didn't even think that she would realize that she was doing it. It wasn't easy for her to allow herself to be compromising in a relationship, to participate in the give and take that all couples must do if they are to last.

"You're right," Myles said, getting out of the car, "both of you are. I should give her some space. Besides, I'm the one who is always saying women choose men, not vice versa."

"Look at it this way, Myles. When you really think about it, you have nothing to lose. If she comes back to you of your own volition, then you can be sure of what she feels for you," Carlos said.

"True that. And if she doesn't?"

"Then you'll know where you truly stand, and can decide your next course of action armed with that knowledge."

"And ain't it better to know?" Amir asked.

"Knowing is half the battle."

"Yeah, then I would know what I was up against and be able to move on with no lingering questions."

"Yeah. Though after a reasonable amount of time has passed, if she still decides that she doesn't want to get serious, if I were you, I would still go down there and barge up her occasionally, just as a matter of g.p."

"Amir, please."

"What? Cut your losses, I say. Salvage something. If you can't have your cake and eat it too, then dammit, just eat it."

"You truly are an asshole," Carlos said, laughing.

"Hey, I never tried to deny that."

🦎 Twenty-nine

Carlos and Myles were in his Camry traveling north on the New Jersey Turnpike. It was a Saturday morning, and they were going up to see the Yankees play an afternoon game against the Mariners. It had been almost a month since that night Carlos and Amir had stopped Myles from driving to see Marisa.

To keep himself from going crazy thinking about her, he filled every waking minute of his life with activity. He went to see his students in their various baseball games, dance recitals, fashion shows, and gymnastics meets. If none of them had anything going on, then Myles would catch the twilight show at the movies, even reducing himself to seeing mind-numbing action films. He also went back to writing that novel he had been working on for the longest. Every night he would go to the gym and work out like a madman until it closed. That way, when he got home, he would be so tired that he'd quickly fall asleep instead of lying there staring at the ceiling, wishing you-know-who was lying next to him. Hey, he might be lonely, but his body had never looked better.

He worked every Saturday (excepting this one) in his father's barbershop and was in church every Sunday—for both morning and afternoon services.

He thought it was nice to be hanging out with Carlos today. Ever since Marisa left, he hadn't seen too much of him outside of work. Jackie was into her fifth month of pregnancy, and Carlos was Mr. Attentive to her every whim and so-called need.

Damn, that was uncalled for. He didn't even know why he was spewing forth the sarcasm. Truth be known, he envied him.

Besides, watching Carlos's Gunga Din–like slavishness wasn't the real reason he didn't go to his house much anymore. Rather, it was his discomfort with being around Jackie. It's not that she said or did anything wrong. It's just that, well, they definitely were not as tight as they used to be. Maybe it was just his imagination, but a part of him felt like she harbored some ill will toward him over Marisa, which he supposed was understandable, being that was her girl and all. Maybe she felt that Marisa would still live five minutes away if he hadn't been such a moron. Last week Myles had asked her if she had heard from her, and she offered no information other than that Marisa was doing fine.

Myles was a little surprised that she hadn't tried to insinuate herself into his situation. She seemed to be pretty much staying out of it, which bothered him because he took it to mean that she had lost faith in his ability to make her girl happy. A vote of no confidence.

Myles already had signed up to teach summer school and take the last two courses he needed to get his master's degree from Cheyney. So he had the summer covered as far as keeping busy. Damn, if it wasn't for that fateful conversation with Marisa that night, he would have been making plans to spend the summer with her.

He tried not to dwell on that because there was nothing he could do about it now. He was also starting to get a little scared that the plan of "giving Marisa enough space to miss him" was rapidly turning into "giving Marisa enough space to forget him." But if she did forget him, then she lacked the devotion he would've required to make him happy anyway.

"I hope Torre plays Ledee today," Carlos said, stirring Myles out of his thoughts.

"Yeah, me too." Myles looked over at him so he could gauge his reaction to his forthcoming query. "Has Jackie heard from Marisa?"

"What do you think, Myles? They're best friends. Of course they talk."

"Well, what? Let a brother know something."

"As far as Jackie tells me, she's zooming along on the career track. She likes doing her show from D.C., is busy making preparations with her TV show, and has started practicing law again, doing mostly pro bono work."

"Damn."

"Yeah, so don't sweat it. That leaves little time for romance. I don't think she has the time to be seeing anybody."

"Does she ask about me?"

"If she did, Jackie probably wouldn't tell me.

Myles, don't start stressing over her. She's too eccentric to waste your time trying to figure her out."

"That's easy for you to say."

"True that, but it's the truth and you know it. When she left, you knew there was a chance that it might be over. You have to come to grips with that possibility."

"I just want one more go-around with her."

"That possibility exists as well."

Myles laughed at him. "What's with the cryptic noncommittals? You bucking for a career in politics?"

"No, I just don't know what's going to happen. Trying to get inside Marisa's head is a job for Frasier Crane."

"And even he might have to bring Dr. Katz along as reinforcement," Myles added.

They chuckled like two kids talking about someone behind their back.

"She's not as crazy as you think," Myles said, feeling obligated to defend her.

"The hell she ain't."

Marisa swung and popped a ball straight up into the air.

"Just under that one," she said to herself as she dug in to take another swing. Her mind traveled back to that cold night when she had nearly taken Myles's head off with that line drive. She laughed at the memory. That had been funny, the look of discombobulation on his face. She then remembered the way the rest of that night had unfolded, and how he had started professing undying love for her and had gotten upset when she didn't do likewise. That was so typical of him, putting her in a tight spot and making her squirm. Who needed that? She took another hack. Why did he have to mess things up by getting so crazy serious on her? Why couldn't he have just relaxed and let things come instead of pressing?

She had been spending a lot of time at the batting cage. Some of her more bourgeois colleagues who preferred tennis and golf were always asking her to play, but she didn't take to those sports as she did to baseball.

The only person who could match her love of the game was Myles. She remembered a time when they had been driving home from seeing the Phillies play an interleague game against the Yankees. He had this silly thing he did whenever they came to a stop sign. He would look both ways, turning his head rapidly, twenty times like he was trying to cross a Los Angeles freeway on foot and not some quiet, residential road that didn't have another car in sight. Not only that, he would then reach over to move her head like it was some massive object that was impeding his view.

"My head is not that big," she would protest.

"Not that big? On a woman your size? Hell, I'm still trying to figure out how you keep your equilibrium."

He always made her laugh when he poked fun at her. She knew it was because she was assured of the fact that in reality, he truly loved her. So much so that she was more than a little shocked that in the time that they had been apart, which was about six weeks, he had not tried to contact her. She had expected him to be right on her heels as soon as he found out she was gone, and for him to set up camp on her front lawn if she spurned him.

But he hadn't, and it was probably for the best. She did miss him, but it was a selfish type of feeling. She missed the way he made her laugh, the way he would make her feel. She missed his silliness, like the way he would reach for a fictional oxygen mask (because she was so "breathtaking") whenever she wore something the least bit revealing. She missed how, if she so much as winked at him from across a room, he would slide his hand in between his shirt buttons over his heart and move it in and out to simulate his heart pounding against his chest. She missed how he always noticed if she wore something new.

But what she especially missed was the look on his face when she walked through the door after she got off work. His eyes would open wide, and his face would be filled with such joy that it was like he hadn't seen her in years instead of since that morning. Of course, it was the exact opposite whenever she was leaving, with him playing "Ain't No Sunshine" on his stereo. She laughed as she took a hack at a pitch.

Nor had she ever thought that with the passage of time, his love for her would fade. She could still imagine him doing the same things, and feeling the same way, twenty years down the line.

There had never been a moment when she was in his presence, save for the night of the argument, when she ever felt like she wasn't the most precious commodity on this earth. Which she felt was a double-edged sword.

For if a man is offering all of this to a woman, doesn't it stand to reason that he deserves a woman who is going to reciprocate? Myles deserves that, she thought as she swung and sent a ground ball up the middle.

She thought of the night of their fight and the hurtful words that had passed. No doubt about it, he had crossed the line. From those same lips that had passed some of the sweetest sentiments that she had ever heard had spewed some of the most hateful indictments that had ever blistered her ears. Nothing she had ever heard in court had ever gotten to her as Myles's barbs had that night, and she knew why. Because she had never allowed herself to be as susceptible to anyone else.

And as far as "anyone else" was concerned, she wasn't even remotely thinking of it. Reentering the dating scene was not something that she was looking forward to. Hell, Myles had ruined her. He had spoiled her to the point that any other man who didn't do for her in the same fashion wouldn't stand a chance. He took pride in tending to her pleasure and comfort, before she asked.

But damn, what could she offer him? What did he get out of it?

ℜ Thirty

The doorbell interrupted some research Marisa was doing for a case. She walked from her study to the front door and looked through the peephole. She squealed with delight.

"Hey, what are you doing here?" she said as she opened the door.

"I spent the weekend at my parents' house in Baltimore," Jackie said as she stepped in. "I thought I'd take a chance on you being home before I went back to Jersey."

Marisa hugged her happily. "I guess I'd better be careful," she said, loosening her grip. "Right, Mommy?"

"Oh, stop, I get enough of the delicate treatment from Carlos. He treats me like I'm a china cabinet and he's the bull. And this beeper has become a pain in the butt. He doesn't give me a moment's peace, calling me every hour on the hour." She walked into the living room and sat down.

"He's excited, Jackie. I think it's cute that he's so concerned."

"For about five minutes it is. Then it gets on your nerves."

"Can I get you anything?"

"No, I'm fine."

"You don't look very big for five and a half months."

"Really? I think I'm huge."

"Nonsense, you look radiant. Besides being over-protective, how is Carlos?"

"He's fine. He's working with his uncle this summer at his auto body shop."

"How's Amir and Kenya?"

"They're okay. Kenya asked about you."

"I should call her. And the twins?"

"Excited about starting school next month. Of course, their uncle and grandparents are already trying to decide what college they will attend."

"So, how is he doing?"

"Who?"

"Myles."

"Oh, so you are able to say his name. I thought you were like the villain from *Superman*, Mytzlpk or whatever, where if you said his name, you would disappear."

"That only happens if he says his name backward, Jackie."

"Oh yeah, that's right."

"So, how is he?"

"He's walking on sunshine, Marisa. How do you think he is?"

"How am I supposed to know?"

"I find it a little hard to believe you could be so close to him for the time you were and not know how crazy he is about you. Do you think it would lessen just because you put some miles between you and him?''

"Well, if that's the case, he should've watched his mouth, then."

"Yeah, because there are so many perfect men out there who never say anything ridiculous out of their mouths. For example, there's Jesus of Nazareth. Another one would be . . . hmm, help me out . . .''

"What's your point?"

"My point is, you're not being honest with yourself. I'm your *hermana*, I love you. So, I'm not going to sugar-coat it."

"Sugar-coat it? I didn't know you felt this way. I thought you were on my side," Marisa said, sounding betrayed.

"I'm always on your side, Marisa."

"When we talk on the phone, you never let on that you have a problem with my decision.''

"I figured you just needed some time to sort things out. Besides, I wanted to see you face to face when I say what I want to say."

"Well then, you're here. By all means, proceed," Marisa said, a little more crossly than she meant to.

"I don't think you're being fair to him or to yourself. I think you are running from a great opportunity because of your fear of intimacy and commitment, which insulates you from hurt but also keeps people from loving you and you from loving them. Myles has such a heart that even all of your barriers could not block it. You were beginning to reciprocate, which scared you to death and you split rather than see it through. The tragedy is this, Marisa; he is the perfect man for you. When I say perfect, I mean a truly complementary fit. His weaknesses are your strengths and vice versa."

Marisa noticed that Jackie was saying some of the same things that Myles had sent bristling at her. She knew there was truth in it. Still . . .

"Jackie, he wants things that I don't. That I can't give him."

"Such as?"

"You know, marriage, two-point-three kids, membership in the PTA, family outings."

"How horrible. I see why you left."

"Jackie, that's not me. I love working, being out, being active, being vibrant, and contributing to society, not domesticity."

"And Myles told you he didn't want you to work?"

Marisa thought for a moment. "No, he never actually said that."

"Oh, I see, then it's the role of motherhood that is diminished in your view. You don't feel raising decent, moral children is contributing to society?"

"It's not that. Of course I see the value in it. It's just not a role for everybody."

"And it definitely isn't for you?"

"I'm not saying that either . . . not definitely, but . . . "

"Well, hell, Marisa, I'm listening. Why don't you tell me exactly what it is that you want?" Jackie said, her voice rising.

Marisa hoped Jackie didn't think she was putting her down, being an expectant mother and all. "Jackie, why are you getting upset? I wasn't taking a swipe at motherhood."

"Please, Marisa. What, you think I'm offended? I know you well enough to see beneath your bullshit. You don't even believe half the claptrap you say. Now once again, I ask you, what is it exactly that you want?"

"For success in my career."

"You already have that."

"For *continuing* success in my career."

"And I have no doubt that you will have that as well. You're a very talented person, and I am very proud of you. What else?"

"That's priority number one. As far as the rest, I am keeping my options open."

"As far as 'the rest'? You mean to tell me that the only way you define yourself is through your work? That other than your career, the rest of your life is arbitrary, that you are going to leave what happens with it to chance?"

"By 'the rest of my life' you mean what exactly?"

"Who you choose to be with, for one."

"I'm not looking for that right now."

"Um-hm. Sooner or later you are going to require more than what that vibrator in your bedroom drawer is giving you."

"True that. When that occurs, I'll just move up to the next larger model. From the eight-inch Mr. Wonderful Twat Tamer to the twelve-inch Richard Ebony Coochie Controller."

"Be serious, Marisa. A vibrator can't take care of you when you're sick. It can't hold you when you're down. It can't"—*beep beep*—"Jesus Christ! Beep you incessantly when you're away from him."

"It also can't make you sick. It doesn't demand

anything in return. It doesn't have an ego or feelings that you have to worry about . . . and it can't hurt you."

"Who told you that people who are in love don't occasionally hurt each other? Human beings are fallible. What, you think Carlos hasn't said things that made me want to wring his neck? You think I haven't said things that have hurt him? But you know what, it's worth the tradeoff, because my head hits the pillow every night knowing that man is *down* for me regardless. And I'll crawl butt naked over broken glass for him, and he knows that as well. Now, I'll wager that's a comfort that your 'Richard Ebony' can't provide you. His devotion lasts only as long as his batteries have juice. Excuse me."

Jackie went into the kitchen to call Carlos. While she was talking to him, Marisa heard her going into the cookie jar, and she allowed herself a smile. Jackie wasn't showing much yet, but she knew Jackie was a girl who had to work hard to stay in shape even when she wasn't pregnant. The way Carlos was always pawing her, he might howl if she didn't retain her curvaceous figure after the baby was born.

Jackie came back out of the kitchen with a glass of milk, a muffin, and a couple of cookies on a napkin. "So, where were we?"

"You were slamming my vibrator."

"Oh, yeah," she said, drinking the milk.

"I never said that my only companionship would be battery-powered forever, Jackie."

"Which brings me to another point. You were sleeping with Myles for all that time. So what, that doesn't mean anything to you? You'll just move on and start sleeping with another guy? How many more men are you gonna add to your list before it's complete?"

Marisa got up and walked over to the window. Jackie had never been that scathing in her criticism of her before.

Jackie walked over and put her arm around her. "Marisa, it's time for you to make a stand. You can be so impetuous and bold with your career. Look what a chance you took last year entering a whole new field. Yet when it comes to your personal life, you act like a scared little girl whenever things get a little tight. What I'm saying is, you've gotten away with it so far because, let's be honest, you haven't been with much of anybody that was worth writing home about."

"That's true. I sure can pick 'em."

"However, this might be the man that you should take the chance on. The rewards may be such that you don't want to let this opportunity pass. There's nothing wrong with a little balance, Marisa. Who says you can't have it all?"

Marisa smiled at her. "I'll really think about it, Jackie, I promise."

"*Bueno*. Besides, you can sit your ass on that four-thousand-dollar couch and stare at these hardwood floors for only so long, right? You can't tell me you don't miss him."

"I never said I didn't."

"So why are you denying yourself? What exactly are you accomplishing?"

"Damn, Jackie, you should've been the lawyer. I said I'll think about it."

"Although," Jackie said, sitting back down to finish her feed, "knowing you, you've probably spent enough money on Duracells and Energizers for that vibrator to cause fluctuation in the stock market. If you ever got back with Myles, it may spell a downturn for the economy. Hell, maybe even a recession."

"Why don't you just shut up and tend to your food, fatgirl?"

That night Marisa purposely went to bed late, hoping the fatigue would induce sleep, but to no avail. She just lay in the bed rehashing her conversation with Jackie. She stared at the ceiling. It was as though the words hovered over her, impeding her view. She tried closing her eyes, and the words sprang to life behind her eyelids.

She threw the covers off and got out of the bed. She went over to her desk and sat down.

Of course she missed him, she told herself. But she had honestly thought it was for the best that they weren't together. She wasn't being heroic or self-aggrandizing, she really believed that. Until Jackie's impromptu, unsolicited advice had caused her to do some soul searching.

She had to admit, Jackie had touched a nerve.

But whether her reasoning was flawed or not, it was ultimately her decision on what path her life took. And she didn't have to justify her decisions to anyone else, because she was the one who would have to live with the pros and cons of her judgments.

She traced her fingers along the antique desk. It had belonged to her Aunt Esther, and was the one thing she had taken from her house after she had died.

That's what she would do, approach it logically. That's what Aunt Esther would tell her to do, lest she become too reliant on emotional impulses and make a rash judgment. Logic and reason had always served her well in her career decisions, such as this move back to D.C. She would write down the pros and cons of trying to build something permanent with Myles. A real, honest to God, lasting, committed relationship. One in which she gave her all. She turned on her desk lamp and opened the drawer. She pulled out a pen, and a legal pad and opened it. On the top page, she saw handwriting that she immediately recognized as Myles's.

Marisa

Sweet Marisa, have you ever been in dismay?
Disillusioned, discouraged or in such a way,
That you resolve yourself to silently suffer
With low expectations as your built-in buffer

Shattered ego, 'cause this wasn't how you planned it
That so-called men would take your heart for granted,
Coldly thinking it's their God-given right
To have a sister love them with all her might

Spurned and burned, but nevermore, nevermore
Got nothing in return so what was it for?
Brothers weren't appreciative, of what you had to give
So as for your heart, nevermore

*Will you surrender it easily, in fact it's gonna come
    quite hard
Caution will be your new calling card
The next man that steps, better face the fact
That when it comes to you, he's gonna pay back tax*

*On a debt he never owed, reaping what he never
    sowed
He's gonna pay for every last, ugly past episode,
So be it. Bring your tests of faith and frustrations to
    the table
And I'll ease your apprehension, with a love that's
    stable*

*and binding, 'cause the more I live I'm finding
the true attainment of manhood is nothing new
it's achieved with a total commitment to you.
If my wish is granted, and if it would please you
I'll make an ideal world for you, Marisa.*

*I love you,
Myles*

By the time that she had reached the last stanza,
tears were flowing down her face. She put the pad
down and went over to the bed and lay down. She
wanted to read the poem again, so she got the pad
and went back to the bed. After reading it a second
time, she rolled over on her stomach and flipped to
the next sheet of paper and divided it in half under
two headings, *Pro* and *Con*.

Under the *Pro* side she wrote:

1. Because he loves me.
2. Because I love him.

With that she ended the list. She went to the *Con* side and wrote:

1. For any problems, refer to the other list (Sorry, Aunt Esther).

She reached over to pick up the phone. She knew he would be alone, because his heart belonged to her and only her, which was the sweetest and most comforting feeling in the world.

"Hello?" the familiar but groggy voice said.

"Hi," she said, "you sleeping?"

"No, no, I'm awake," the suddenly aware voice answered.

Liar, she thought. It's three a.m. and he's *not* sleeping?

"I just read the poem you wrote me."

He didn't say anything for a couple of seconds, like he was trying to recall what she was talking about.

"Oh. The one titled 'Marisa.' "

"Yeah." She rolled over and closed her eyes. It felt good to hear him say her name. She liked the way he said it.

"Do you still feel that way?" she asked.

He hesitated before answering. "Let me tell you about this Cuban girl I had the good fortune of meeting last summer. She was my every prayer answered and my every wish granted. My every dream realized and my every longing fulfilled. She was the pay-off and the justification for every principled, right, decent thing I have ever done on this earth."

Whoa, he definitely was awake now.

"I know that my life with you would be happier than any one man has a right to deserve, and I think that maybe you were right, that I couldn't possibly return it in kind."

She cringed when she heard him say that. She could be so cruel. Tears returned to her eyes.

"So, Marisa, while I do pray for the opportunity to be with you, I also ask God to grant me the ability to make you as happy as you would make me."

She was on the verge of crying, which she didn't want to do with him on the phone, knowing that he would really lose it if he heard her.

"Myles, I gotta go," she said.

"Marisa, don't . . . Marisa, I—"

When she heard the sudden panic in his voice, she could think of nothing except soothing him. "No, babe, listen, just for now. I'll call you tomorrow night. You hear me, sweetheart? I'm not saying good-bye, just good night for now, okay?"

He seemed placated by that.

"Myles, before I go, I have to ask you one more thing. Why do you love me so much?"

After a short pause he answered. "Marisa, you've always worried that I love you too much. But the truth is, I can't love you *enough*."

After Marisa hung up the phone and wiped her face, she was no longer restless. For her, the tears had been cathartic, Myles's voice had been a panacea, and his words a lullaby. She quickly drifted off into a peaceful sleep.

*   *   *

When she woke up it was nearly nine o'clock. As she lay in bed, the life that stretched in front of her no longer seemed a series of debatable propositions. Instead she was granted such stark clarity that she immediately knew what she was supposed to do. She got out of bed and headed for the shower.

By ten o'clock, she was on I-95 in her Benz convertible with her goggles on and a cream scarf wrapped around her neck, flapping in the breeze behind her. The salsa version of the Billy Ocean song "Suddenly" was pulsating from her speakers. She smiled whenever she thought about what awaited her when she reached her destination. She was going to claim what was hers.

ℜ Thirty-one

Myles had finished teaching his summer school class and was deciding whether to stay to study for his evening methodology class or go to the library and do some research. After finally convincing himself that he had not dreamt his conversation with Marisa last night, he had somehow been able to focus himself enough to go about his daily activities.

Needless to say, he was definitely looking forward to her call tonight. He was going to let her talk, and he was going to listen, really listen. He was excited and hopeful, however, because of last night's conversation. Myles couldn't remember the poem that she had stumbled upon verbatim, but he knew it spoke of his desire to build a future with her. For her to call and ask if he still felt the same was indeed promising. He hoped it just wasn't the effusiveness caused by the poem speaking. He hoped that the morning didn't bring with it any second guessing on her part. He could see Marisa waking suddenly, her first thought being "What the hell did I just do?" regarding their conversation last night.

Myles got up to erase the board. While he was doing

so, he heard someone enter the room. He turned around and saw Marisa standing there, looking like a 1950s movie star in her scarf and sunglasses. His heart started to palpitate so rapidly, it was scary.

"Hi, Myles," she said.

"Hi, Dorothy Dandridge." He tried to appear cool by turning around and continuing to erase the board, but she knew he was really trying to gather himself because he kept erasing the same spot over and over.

She walked to a student's desk in the front row and sat down to wait for him to finish. She looked him over. He was thinner than she liked. She hoped it wasn't from stressing over her.

Finally he gathered himself enough to stop the pretense of being so interested in the meticulous scouring of the board. He put down the cloth he was using and turned around to face her. He walked in front of his desk and leaned against it.

"Did I catch you at a bad time?" she asked.

"No, not at all."

"So how have you been?"

"Fine. I'm taking the last two courses to get my master's. How about you? You haven't been having any nightmares, have you?"

"No, I haven't," she said quietly. "I tend to get them only when I'm in emotional turmoil or if I'm in a state of confusion regarding what direction I want my life to take." She then looked him straight in the eye. "I don't anticipate I'll be getting them anymore."

"No?"

She shook her head seductively and smiled at him. He averted his eyes and blushed.

"So, you're going to become a principal?" she asked with a slight inflection in her voice. She remembered him telling her once that he had no desire to go into school administration.

"Yeah," he said, correctly interpreting the bent of her question. "Lately, I've been thinking that life isn't always going to go the way I envision. I have to let reality intrude sooner or later. I think it's best that I start letting logic dictate the decisions I make. Becoming a principal makes career and economic sense whether it's something I particularly want to do or not."

"Oh," she said. "Though a little romantic idealism, you know, striving for the idyllic, isn't such an awful thing, is it?" she asked.

Dimples formed on his face as he looked down at the floor. She found him so adorable. He bit his bottom lip before raising his head to look back at her.

"No, it isn't, I suppose. As long as it's tempered."

"Exactly," she said, managing to contain the smile that wanted to spread across her face. "So how's my *perro?*" she asked. "You've been taking care of him?"

"He misses you."

She got out of her seat and started to walk toward him. He shifted nervously when he saw her approaching.

"Is he the only one?"

"Of course not. The twins miss you, too."

She was right on top of him by this point. She wrapped her arms around him and felt a familiar poking against her.

"It seems someone else misses me as well."

"He's a loose cannon. He doesn't speak for me."

"Myles Moore, if you don't put your arms around me, I'm going to scream bloody murder."

He wrapped his arms loosely around her. "Geesh, Marisa, you would act up in my place of employment? How *unprofessional* of you."

"Kiss me, you fool."

He met her lips with his. He pulled away before she wanted him to.

"Pick me up. I want to talk to you."

He scooped her up in his arms as she wrapped her arms around his neck. She moved her mouth close to his ear.

"Myles," she whispered, "don't be afraid to hold me as tight as you can. Don't be afraid to kiss me as long and as deep as you want to, and don't be afraid to tell me anything that comes to your heart. And do you know why?"

She felt his breathing stop as he shook his head.

"Because I love you back, Myles Moore, that's why. Did you hear me? I'm in love with you, and I'm not going anywhere."

His grip tightened around her, and he started kissing her with the soft passion that she remembered. He then gazed at her like she was the single most extraordinary thing on God's green earth.

"Well, did you hear me? I said I'm not going anywhere. Can you handle that?"

"I don't know, I'll have to think about it. You do have your ways about you . . ."

"What?"

"Hey, how do I know the real reason you came

back isn't because your braids are starting to get raggedy?"

"Ouch. I've been rebuffed. I guess I'd better head home," she said, attempting to pull away from him while knowing there was no way in hell he was going to let her go.

"But I may be willing to give it a chance, since you are good peoples," he said.

She looked up wide-eyed. "Yeah?" she asked.

"Yeah. But I suggest that we don't talk in such grandiose terms, Marisa. I don't need to have you forever."

She gave him a look that reminded him of Gary Coleman right before he used to say, "What you talking 'bout, Willis?"

"You don't?"

"No. I just want the next fifty years or so. Then you can do what you want, skank it up, whatever. You can be the eighty-year-old girl shaking her ass at the club."

They both laughed.

"I'm glad to hear that you have been sleeping okay. When you called me so late last night, that's the first thing I thought of."

"Like I said, I only get them if I'm in a state of turmoil. I'll be okay as long as you never stop loving me."

"Then you're gonna be fine."

"Yeah?" She grinned.

"Most definitely. I'm no fool. Marisa Marreros don't grow on trees."

As they walked out of the school, their arms around each other, Myles whispered a silent prayer to God thanking Him for bringing her back to him.

"So, a principal, huh?"

He shrugged his shoulders. "Well, it's a way to stay in education. You know I love kids."

"This is true. Hmm, then may I offer a suggestion?"

"By all means."

"If you love children so much, what do you think about becoming a father?"

Myles stopped walking so he could look at her. Yep, she was serious.

"I think I would like it very much."

"Good, then it's settled. Congratulations, Mr. Stay-at-Home Dad."

"Whoa, I didn't say all that, now."

"Myles, while education is a most noble profession, it simply doesn't pay well enough to keep Princesa Marisa living in the fashion that she's grown accustomed to."

"This is true," he said, laughing.

"Therefore, I suggest you take a hiatus from education to become a writer. I figure by the time the first young'un comes along, that novel you're writing will be a best-seller. Then you can concentrate on writing children's stories as well, for *our* children."

Myles was excited that she was talking about "our children," but not so much so that he hadn't noticed what else she had said.

"Marisa, how do you know about the novel?"

"Oh please, Myles. I found your hidden cache way back in January. So tell me, does the protagonist get the girl or not? I'm dying to know."

"What do you think?"

"I think everybody loves a happy ending."

"But won't that be too sappy? Too unrealistic? Too fairy-tale?"

"Myles, don't be so cynical. There's nothing wrong with loving blindly, wearing your heart on your sleeve. It's like I always say, 'If more people followed their hearts, the world would be a better place.' "

He leaned over and gently kissed her on the forehead.

"So, Cuban girl, where have you been all my days?"

"Waiting on you, of course."

"You're a true marvel."

"Uh-uhn. I'm just Marisa."

Didn't she know that they were one in the same as far as he was concerned?

Here's a special preview of

FOUR GUYS AND TROUBLE

The boldly hilarious and sexy new novel of loyalty, love, and friendship from

Marcus Major

A Dutton hardcover on sale in April 2001

"I'm so proud of you, baby," Mrs. Truitt said as she hugged Bunches tightly. With both her hands occupied, she was unable to dab her eyes, and the tears that had been present all afternoon flowed unchecked down her face. Grandmother and granddaughter finally separated and smiled at each other.

Dexter and Mike, who had been watching from a distance to give them some privacy, came over to where they were standing. Dexter reached into the breast pocket of his gray blazer, handed Mrs. Truitt his handkerchief, then reached for Bunches.

Bunches, mindful of her perfectly coifed hair, flawless makeup, brand-new pumps and immaculate off-white Donna Karan outfit under her graduation gown, reached to give him a safe, ladylike pat-on-the-back hug. Dexter instead snatched her off her feet and twirled her around, sending her cap flying. Mike picked it up and handed it to Mrs. Truitt.

"Now, there's my girl! Ms. Phi Beta Kappa, I'm so proud of you!"

She giggled at Dexter's exuberance and forgot about her state of high fashion, wrapping her arms snugly around his neck. "Thanks, Dex."

"Yo, man, you're too big to be that rough. You're gonna break the poor girl's back," Mike said. "She wants to go to medical school—not the medical center."

When Dexter finally put her down, she and Mike embraced tenderly. Bunches rested her head on Mike's shoulder, while he rubbed her back. "You don't think you're better than us, now that you're an Ivy League graduate, do you?" Mike asked as they let each other go.

"No," Bunches replied. "I *always* thought I was better than y'all." She gave him a kiss on the cheek, leaving a raisin-colored reminder.

"Bunches, you need to stop," her grandmother half scolded, half laughed.

Ibn and Tiffany walked over. They looked dapper as always—Ibn made sure of that. He was wearing a beige linen suit with a powder blue shirt, and Tiffany had on a beautiful dress patterned with earthen hues. Ibn planted a kiss on Bunches's cheek.

"Phi Beta Kappa, huh?" he mocked. "What, you couldn't make valedictorian? Or at least salutatorian?"

Bunches playfully rolled her eyes.

"Mind you," Tiffany said as she handed the video camera to Ibn, "this is coming from a man who couldn't be bothered with graduating himself." Tiffany and Bunches hugged. "Congratulations, girl."

"Hey, hey. We're not talking about my academic achievements," Ibn said.

"Achievements?" Mike asked, surprised. "What achievements? Most parties attended in a semester?"

Everybody laughed.

"Ib, you have to admit your scholastic record is a bit spotty," Dexter added.

"What is this?" Ibn complained. "National-Pick-on-Ibn Day?"

"Don't pay any attention to them," Mrs. Truitt said. "College isn't for everybody."

"Exactly," he said. "You don't need a piece of paper when you make as much cheddar as I do." Ibn gave Mike and Dexter a playful sneer.

Seeing Ibn reminded Bunches of who was still missing. "Where's Colin and Stacy?" she asked.

"Stacy was a little under the weather and couldn't make it," Tiffany said. "She told me to tell you congratulations."

The three men groaned.

"Be nice, boys," Mrs. Truitt said. "It's not fair to deny someone the benefit of the doubt."

Ibn gave Bunches a wink. "Colin drove to get your graduation gift."

"You guys didn't have to do that," Mrs. Truitt protested. "Believe me, you boys have already done enough for Bunches."

"You sure didn't," Bunches added, not near as sincere as her grandmother.

"Oh, please," Ibn said. "You know that if we didn't get you something, we never would have heard the end of it. You just playing that humble role 'cause your grandmother is standing next to you."

They all chuckled.

"Let's head on over to parking lot eight," Dexter said. "We told Colin we'd meet him there."

Bunches slid one arm inside Dexter's and the other inside Mike's and looked up at both of them. "My, my, I have two handsome escorts."

Dexter cut his eyes at Mike over Bunches's head. "*One* handsome escort, Bunch. Maybe one and a half."

"C'mon, Dex, why do you wanna sell yourself short like that?" Mike responded. "You're not that ugly."

Bunches smiled. She loved all the guys, but she was closest to these two. They had been the ones able to devote the most time to her the last couple of years because they hadn't had full-time girlfriends.

The group forged their way through the sea of graduates and their families. It was a long hike to the parking lot, made a little longer by Bunches's stopping to hug and congratulate fellow classmates that she recognized.

"Yo, Bunch," Dexter said after yet another one of her

stops, "you might want to keep the well-wishing to a minimum. I'm ready to go eat."

"When aren't you ready to go eat?" she replied.

"What, do you think this studly body comes about without proper nourishment?"

Dexter flexed his massive right bicep, making the fabric of his jacket stretch tightly.

"He isn't the only one," Mike chimed in. 'Save some of this bliss for y'all's class reunion."

Mike took off his jacket and loosened his tie. He glanced at Ibn, who was a couple of steps ahead of him, looking like something fresh off the pages of *Ebony Man* and walking with his usual aristocratic stride. Without even trying, Ibn had a manner and presence that subtly said, "I'm better than you."

Mike couldn't resist. He ran by him, smacking him roughly across the top of his head as he passed. "Take that, Pretty Ricky!"

Ibn started after Mike but stopped after a couple of steps. One, it was too hot to be running around. Two, he needed to check on the state of his hair. "Peasant!" he yelled at Mike.

When Bunches saw the sign for parking lot eight, she was relieved. These pumps were for aesthetic purposes only, not for hiking. As the group stopped, she scanned the half-full lot. She saw Ibn's black Benz and Dexter's forest green Saab parked side by side, but there was no sign of Colin.

Right when Bunches was about to ask what was up, a cherry red Celica came to a stop in front of them. Tiffany turned the video camera back on.

"Did I say Colin drove to get your gift?" Ibn asked. "What I meant to say was that Colin was *driving* your gift."

Bunches gasped in disbelief.

Colin got out of the car, came around front, and dangled the keys. His green suit was too big, as were most things he wore. Because of his skinny build, Colin didn't wear clothes—clothes wore him.

"Lord have mercy!" Mrs. Truitt said in amazement.

Bunches yelped at the top of her lungs and jumped into

Colin's arms, very nearly toppling him onto the hood. "I don't believe this!" she said.

"We can't have you going back and forth to Thomas Jefferson University in that putt-putt Escort of yours," Ibn said.

"Omigod, omigod," Bunches said, still clinging to Colin.

"Get in, girl," said Tiffany, who was videotaping the entire scene. "Let's see how you look in it."

"First, peep the license plate," Dexter said.

She looked down at the front plate: BBYGRL-MD

"We should of got one that said, 'Beneatha,'" Mike said, laughing.

Everybody looked at him puzzled except Bunches, who laughed as she walked to the driver's side door.

"Y'all know," Mike said, looking around hopefully. "Beneatha is the little sister—"

"—from *A Raisin in the Sun* who wanted to be a doctor. I got it, Michael." Bunches said.

"Oh," Ibn said, rolling his eyes at Mike's attempt at humor. "C'mon, Bunches, we want to see how you look in it."

Bunches slid behind the steering wheel. She peered at the group through the windshield with the world's widest grin.

"We got it loaded," Ibn said, walking around to the passenger side and getting in. "Let me show you some of the features."

Mrs. Truitt looked at Colin. "How much did you guys pay for this? This is too expensive to be giving her—she can't accept this."

Bunches got out of the car and looked at her grandmother as if she was concerned that Alzheimer's was setting in.

"Mrs. Truitt, it didn't feel like we took a hit at all," Colin said. "We've been planning this for two years."

"Yeah, pooling our money, putting aside some each month," Dexter explained. "The same way we did to buy those rental units we own."

"And the way we did back when we were still in college to get Ibn the start-up money for his business," Mike added. "As a matter of fact, it was originally Trevor's idea for us to combine our resources to give ourselves greater purchasing power."

Mrs. Truitt smiled sadly at the mention of her grandson's name. "I wish he and her mother were here to see this."

"They are, Mrs. Truitt," Mike said, pointing at his chest. "They're with all of us."

Bunches and Mike embraced.

She focused on Mike. When he smiled, his dimple was too cute. As he returned her gaze and leaned over to kiss her on the forehead, Bunches had to quell her impulse to tilt her head—so his lips met a more agreeable target.

Three years later . . .

"Are you decent?" a voice called out.

"Come in, Bunches," Dexter said.

She walked in and, seeing Ibn, scrunched her nose. "Uh-oh, wrong question. Decency is probably the last thing that's going on if you're here."

"Did I miss a memo or something? Is this National-Fuck-with-Ibn Day?" he asked.

Bunches laughed and walked over to him. She'd had the day off and taken full advantage of it. She had gotten her hair and nails done and was wearing a brand-new outfit: black Guess jeans and a purple acrylic-cotton blend fitted shirt with a square neckline, Enzo boots, and a black belt. She wrapped her arms around his neck and gave him a kiss on the cheek. "Are they picking on you again?"

"You know that, Bunch. These cats don't appreciate me," Ibn said. "How you been, cutie?"

Bunches sat on the arm of the chair and started playing with his hair. "Fine."

"You look good, Bunches. Those jeans almost make your skinny self look like you got a butt," Colin said.

"Yo, sport, you talking? You'd have to eat every wing on that tray just to be called malnourished."

"She smells good, too," Ibn added.

"Oh, Ib, you're such a charmer, you are." She pinched his cheek.

"You going out tonight, Erika?" Mike asked.

"Uh-hm," she answered without bothering to look at him.

"On a date?" he asked.

"Something like that. I just came down to borrow some eyedrops for my contacts." She looked at Dexter. "Do you have any?"

Dexter had a mouthful of food, and he had to swallow before answering. "Look on the dresser in my bedroom," he replied.

Ibn looked at Colin, and they both nodded knowingly. Colin had been stirring ever since he heard the word "date."

"Bunches, can I borrow that movie you showed us a while back?" he asked innocently.

"Which one? *Sankofa?*"

"Yeah, that's it."

She had no idea what he was up to, and she pointed toward the door. "It's upstairs in the living room. I'll bring it down when I go get my coat."

"Don't bother. I'll get it." He jetted out of the room and they heard him bound up the stairs.

Bunches went down the hall.

"Yeah, Colin has been dying to see that movie again, Bunch," Ibn said loud enough for her to hear.

The Jaguars kicked off, and the Titans ran the ball back to the thirty-two yard line. Bunches came back into the room. She looked into a wall mirror and started putting in the eyedrops. While she was making sure her eyeliner was still okay, she and Mike made eye contact in the mirror.

"So where are you going?" he asked.

"Just out," she replied casually.

Colin came back into the house and waved the tape at Bunches. "Thanks."

"No problem. Just don't let Stacy break it," she said, and winked at him. She sauntered over to where they all were sitting and started massaging Dexter's shoulders, lightly scratching with her fingernails. "Who's playing?"

"The Titans and the Jaguars. Air McNair is about to open up on these boys," Dexter answered.

"See, that's why I'm Mr. Football and you're not," Ibn snorted. "If you had half a brain you would know that—"

He was interrupted by the faint sound of a doorbell. Someone was ringing the bell at Bunches's place.

Bunches abruptly took her hands off Dexter's shaved bald head and stepped back in horror. She had been so preoccupied that she had failed to see how the situation foretold disaster. All four of the guys were together, and she had a man coming over. She attempted to make a dash for the door but was beaten to it by Ibn.

"My man," Ibn called out the door, cordially flashing a wide grin. "Bunches—I mean, Erika—is over here. Come meet the family." All the while he used his body to shield Bunches away from the door.

A tall, light-skinned man with horn-rimmed glasses stepped into the apartment. He smiled when he saw Bunches. "Hi, Erika."

"Hi, Quincy." Her face was uneasy. She was anxious to get going. "Why don't we head on upstairs? I'll get my coat and we'll go." She made a move in that direction, but Quincy was forestalled by Ibn, who put an arm around his shoulder and began to lead him over to the couch.

"Bunches, it's not like you to be so rude. Why don't you go upstairs and get your coat while I introduce Quincy around?" He pretended not to see her fuming. "Come meet the boys, Q. This here is Dexter Holmes."

"Pleasure to meet you, Dexter." He extended his hand. Dexter ignored it and gave him a quick, suspicious nod.

"This here is Colin Rogers,"

"How ya doing, Colin?" Colin shook his hand but didn't say anything. He just stared intently at Quincy, as if he was trying to read his mind. Quincy looked away, clearly uncomfortable.

"And the gentleman over there is Mike Lovett."

Mike waved at him. "Nice meeting you, Quincy."

"The pleasure's mine." Quincy waved back and relaxed a little. At least one of them was normal.

"And I'm Ibn Barrington. Have a seat, Q. You like football, don't you?"

"We don't have time for that," Bunches said.

"Are you still here?" Ibn asked. "You could have been

upstairs and back by now. I was about to get the brother something to drink."

Bunches weighed her options. Suddenly, asking Quincy to come to her house wasn't such a good idea. She rarely had dates pick her up at the house because of Dexter's hassling them. He alone was bad enough, but with Ibn's fool self here too, who knew what they were capable of?

But if she acted too much of a fool and started cursing the guys out, Quincy would think she was nuts, and she wouldn't blame him. Who needed that kind of drama on a first date? Besides, the fellas weren't crazy enough to really do anything to him, and they wouldn't have the chance anyway. She would grab her keys and they'd be gone.

She walked over to where Quincy was sitting. "I'll be *right* back."

"Take your time. Q's in good hands," Ibn called out from the kitchen.

Bunches left, and they heard her running up the stairs. Colin went to the door and locked it behind her. He strolled over and looked out the window. "Is that your car out there, Quincy?"

"The black one? Yeah, it's a Mazda 626."

"With the Pennsylvania plates, number JHY 219?"

"Um, yeah," he said warily.

"JHY 219," Colin said as he made his way to the couch and sat down next to Quincy. "JHY 219," he repeated softly. He fixed Quincy with an engrossed stare.

"So, Q, are you in a fraternity?" Ibn asked from the kitchen.

"Yes, I am," he said proudly. "I'm an Alpha."

A sound of disgust came from Dexter. "That figures," he muttered.

Quincy was still wondering what to make of Dexter's reaction when Ibn walked out of the kitchen, carrying two beers. "What's your last name, Q? Where you from?" Ibn gave one to Dexter, who opened it and began drinking. He then sat on the other side of Quincy.

"Carson," Quincy replied. He shifted his body away from Colin, who was making him uncomfortable with his staring. "I'm from Malvern."

"Carson from Malvern? Do you have a brother, Q?" Ibn asked.

"Well, uh, yes."

"What's his name?" Ibn asked.

"Samuel."

"Sammy Carson from Malvern, Pa." Ibn thoughtfully rubbed his chin. Then a look of recognition lit up his face. "I know that nigga!" he said, happily slapping Quincy on the knee.

"Um, I don't think so," Quincy replied. "He's only twelve years old."

"Trust me, I *know* that nigga," Ibn said. Mike muffled a laugh. He was the only one out of Quincy's line of sight, and he had been amusing himself, listening to Bunches frantically walk around upstairs trying to find her keys. She was doing so in vain, because Colin had taken them when he went upstairs to get the movie.

"What do you do, Q?" Ibn asked.

"I'm a law student at the U of Penn."

That drew another sound of disgust from Dexter. "Just what the world needs, another goddamned ambulance chaser."

Ibn pushed the other beer in front of Quincy. "Have a drink, Q."

Mike knew the brother was done for now. If he took the drink, all hell would break loose with his first sip. ("What, nigga! You drinking and driving! With *our* Bunches! Get the fuck out of here!") And if he said no, then he'd just better be careful how he said it.

"No, thank you, Ibn . . ." Quincy said.

Leave it at that, kid. Leave it at that, Mike thought.

". . . I don't drink," Quincy added smugly.

Dexter scowled at him. "He didn't *ax* you if ya drank, muthafucka."

Quincy looked at him, bewildered. "Excuse me?"

"I'se said," Dexter stood up menacingly, "he didn't *ax* you if ya drank, mutha-*fucka*," he repeated, tilting his head from side to side to emphasize each syllable. Quincy looked at Colin for help, but he was still staring at him like a mental patient. He then turned to Ibn, who all of a sudden was very interested in the football game.

"I just meant—"

"I'se knows what ya meant, *nigga*. Jus 'cause I didn't get book learnin' at some Ivy League school don't mean I'm stupid, muthafucka!" Dexter took a step toward him with his fists clenched by his sides. Ibn sprang to life, standing between Dexter and Quincy, who was scared as hell sitting on the couch.

"Take it easy, Dex. Q didn't mean anything by it," Ibn said.

"Naw, fuck that! This boozhee Negro tryin' to play me. What, jus' cuz I'se like an occasional *dra-ank*, it makes me sum kinda aka-holic?"

Mike almost lost it at this point. Normally he would have come to the poor brother's defense by now, but he was enjoying Dexter's performance too much tonight.

"Naw, that's not what you meant, is it, Q?" Ibn looked at Quincy pleadingly, as if to say, "You best save yourself."

"No, brother. I—I meant no offense."

"See, Dex. It was just a misunderstanding," Ibn said.

Hardly placated, Dexter mumbled something and sat back down. The sound of Bunches coming down the steps meant it was time to put this to an end.

Ibn sat down next to Quincy, whose forehead was glistening with sweat. "Please understand, Q, that you are looking at four men to whom the single most precious thing in the world to them is Bunches—Erika, as you call her."

They heard the doorknob jiggle. "Unlock the door," Bunches cried, exasperated.

"So I'm not gonna apologize if we get worked up, because no matter what happens between you two, you'll never love her like we do."

"Oh, this is just our first date," Quincy said nervously.

"Open the door!" Bunches shouted.

"Understood. I'm just saying that if your intentions aren't to come correct, I would hope you would have the intelligence to make this y'all's *last* date." Ibn, Dexter, and Colin stared at Quincy until he nodded.

"I understand," he said quietly.

"Good," Ibn said, slapping Quincy's knee again.

"Michael! Open this goddamned door!" Bunches yelled at the top of her lungs.

Ibn walked over and opened the door. "Oh, Bunch, were you out there long? I guess we couldn't hear you over the game."

She pushed him out of the way and saw Quincy had become a sweating, disheveled mess. She looked at Ibn, Colin, and Dexter disgustedly, then searched the room until she found Mike, upon whom she fixed her most pissed-off glare.

"You'll have to excuse these fools, Quincy. I assure you they're harmless."

Ibn gave Quincy a look of caution over Bunches's shoulder, as if to say, "You can believe that if you want to, son."

"Some people are caught in a state of perpetual arrested adolescence," she added, continuing to glower at Mike. He averted his eyes to the TV. Bunches grabbed Quincy's hand. "Let's go."

Ibn, Dexter, and Colin followed them to the door. "Have a good time," Ibn said and slapped Quincy so hard on the shoulder his knees buckled. Then he leaned in close to Quincy's ear. "Just remember what we talked about," he whispered.

"You say something?" Bunches snapped at Ibn.

Ibn held his hands up. "I just said have a good time."

Bunches stormed out the door, dragging Quincy in tow. Ibn, Dexter, and Colin came out on the lawn to see them off.

"When will you be back?" Dexter asked.

"When I get back!" Bunches answered angrily. She and Quincy got into his car.

"JHY 219, JHY 219," Colin intoned like it was a mantra. Bunches looked at him like he was a fucking weirdo.

Quincy and Bunches took off. Once the car was around the corner, the three of them nearly fell down on the lawn laughing. They made their way back into the house.

"Did you guys like my use of broken English and the way I slurred my words?" Dexter asked. "It's a new wrinkle I've been working on."

"I noticed that," Colin answered. "Kudos are in order,

Dex. A brilliant piece of improvisation." He and Ibn applauded. Mike joined them.

"Thank you, thank you," Dexter said, bowing.

Ibn looked at Mike suspiciously. "How come you stayed so quiet when we were messing with that dude? Usually you try to rein us in."

Dexter and Colin looked at Mike. Like Ibn, they were waiting for an explanation.

Mike shrugged his shoulders. "To hell wit' that cat. I'se didn't like the looks of that boozhee Negro nohow."

They laughed. Mike joined them in front of the TV and grabbed a buffalo wing.

"Colin, when you put Erika's keys back, don't put them in such an obvious place this time. We don't want her to think she's going crazy," Mike said.

"Put them in my bedroom on my dresser. She went in there," Dexter added.

As they turned their attention back to the game, Ibn spotted a look of discomfort on Mike's face. "What's with you?"

"These wings are too spicy," Mike answered, wrapping his bones into a napkin.

"Man, you're soft," Ibn sneered. "I'm about to put some hot sauce on mine."

Mike stared at the carpet. Ibn was right about him being too soft, but the queasiness he was currently feeling had nothing to do with the wings—and everything to do with a feeling he felt guilty for even having.